Steel Kisses

by

Laura Strickland

A Buffalo Steampunk Adventure

Steel Kisses

COPYRIGHT © 2017 by Laura Strickland

Cover Art by *Diana Carlile*

The Wild Rose Press, Inc.
PO Box 708
Adams Basin, NY 14410-0708
Visit us at www.thewildrosepress.com

Publishing History
First Fantasy Rose Edition, 2017
Print ISBN 978-1-5092-1399-3
Digital ISBN 978-1-5092-1400-6

A Buffalo Steampunk Adventure
Published in the United States of America

Dedication

For Mike Reynolds and his Lily

She smiled at him. "How would you like to begin?"

"I don't rightly know."

She reached for the buttons on the front of her dress, sewn of pearl-colored silk. "Most of my clients like to see what they have paid for. Would you like me to strip?"

He swallowed convulsively. A dull flush rose to his cheeks.

"Have you ever visited with one of Landry's Ladies before?" Maybe he did not know what to expect, thought she would not look or feel like a human woman. Unless he touched her in certain places, he should not be able to tell the difference.

"No. No, I haven't."

She wondered how to put him at ease. She abandoned the buttons and reached for her hairpins instead. "Would you like me to take my hair down?"

"I would. I'd like that very much."

A scratch came at the door, and then it opened to admit the little mechanical maid with a tray holding whiskey and one glass.

The client leaped away, but as soon as the maid left, he filled the glass with whiskey and gulped half of it down.

"Oh, I'm sorry." He extended the glass to Lily. "Will you take some?"

"I cannot drink."

"No?"

She shook her head. Her loosened hair fell down around her shoulders in separate tendrils, and he took a step closer.

"My God, you're beautiful."

Praise for Laura Strickland

Laura Strickland's novella *FORGED BY LOVE* won first place in the short historical category of the International Digital Awards.

~*~

"The world building is phenomenal."

~Daysie W. at My Book Addiction and More

~*~

"Laura Strickland creates a world that not only draws you in, but she incorporates it…seamlessly.…the kind of book that keeps you awake well into the wee hours, and sighing with satisfaction when you've finished the very last page."

~Nicole McCaffrey, author

~*~

"As I read I became so involved with the story, I found it difficult to put down the book. …Definitely …an author to watch."

~Dandelion at Long & Short Reviews

Chapter One

Buffalo, the Niagara Frontier, July, 1884

"There he goes again, the fool," mocked Sasha Belsky in his gruff, thickly accented English. "Once more on the run. It must be eight-fifteen."

Belsky's voice chased Reynold Michaels out the rear door of McMahon's coffin shop and into the alley that led to Niagara Street, closely followed by that of Reynold's boss, Liam.

"Ah, leave the lad alone, will ya? There's no harm in it."

"But what a simpleton he must be! He thinks—"

Reynold lost track of their conversation then. The alley cut between two buildings and ended in an iron gate that faced the busy street beyond, one of the main thoroughfares of the city. He had no key for the gate, so he wrapped both hands around the metal bars and pressed his face against them like a man in a prison cell.

Here came the tram—slowly, slowly, stopping along the way as it did every morning and puffing steam. It eased to a halt across from Reynold's gate, and a number of people streamed off—men, women, a child or two. Reynold watched for only one, the others all but invisible to him.

And there she was. All in blue today, dressed in a stylish outfit with a short, fitted jacket that hugged the

1

contours of her perfect figure. Slender waist; high, pointed breasts. Legs that moved gracefully under the tapered skirt. She wore a matching hat, also— Reynold's mind, which worked at its own particular speed, groped for the name of the color: peacock. Peacock blue. It contrasted with hair the color of spun gold, and the angle at which it sat on her head suited her delicately featured face.

She did not look in his direction; she seldom did. He doubted she even saw him there, gaping like a gargoyle, and he didn't care. He needed but to see her, to watch as in the company of several other young ladies from the tram she walked off up the street in the bright morning sunshine, until the brick corner of the building next door cut off his view.

Not a lot. Not much to live on for a day and a night—or longer on Saturday—but enough. He released the breath pent up in his lungs on a wave of bliss.

"Is that her? The one with the blonde hair—the little dove?"

Reynold started and swung around as Sasha spoke in his ear. The man could move as silently as a ghost when he chose; Reynold never guessed Sasha had trailed him down the alley, though he should have smelled him. From the reek, the fellow must eat garlic at every meal.

And now he'd gone and ruined the moment, spoiled the picture Reynold meant to carry through the long day.

But no—nothing could spoil it.

"Leave me alone," he said even though he knew Sasha wouldn't relent. Sasha never did. For some reason he reveled in tormenting Reynold every chance he got.

True to form, a big grin split Sasha's face. It showed off his stubby little teeth and squinted-up eyes like those of a devil. Reynold longed to punch him in the face just to make that look disappear, though he never had in the past and doubted he ever would.

Sasha, built thin like a string bean, must figure that, or he wouldn't keep prodding the way he did. Reynold had several inches on him in height and probably fifty pounds in muscle. Toting corpses around the city tended to build a fellow up.

"Hey!" Pete appeared at the other end of the alley, calling to them. "Liam says get back to work."

Liam McMahon, who had pretty good instincts about trouble, would have sent the fourth member of the crew to avert any discord. Pete, a mere stripling and still in training, had been half raised by Liam's wife, Clara—one of the many waifs she'd taken in off the street.

"Tell the big boss to hold his horses," Sasha called back. "We are coming." He laid a hand on Reynold's shoulder. "Our friend here has had his little glimpse of heaven."

"Get off me." Reynold shrugged the hand away before pushing past Sasha and hurrying back down the alley in Pete's wake.

Liam gave him a measuring look when he came back in through the rear door. The big Irishman had bought the coffin shop from his former employer, Franz Hengerer, two years ago—just before Reynold came to work for him. They'd relocated and expanded to include a showroom and now offered services other than the mere manufacture of coffins. For a small fee, they'd willingly collect the deceased from hospitals or scenes of the crime and deliver them on to wherever the bereaved wished, decently enclosed, of course, in new coffins.

That was Reynold's job—the collecting and delivering. He had a special cart he used for the task, and he did it well, not minding the company of the dead. They never badgered him the way Sasha did and for the most part provided peaceful company.

He had a sudden, sharp vision of Sasha Belsky lying in one of Liam's coffins, his hands folded neatly on his chest, silent at last.

"All right, lad?" Liam had a rich brogue, straight from the old sod.

Sasha, entering on Reynold's heels, answered for him. "Oh, yes, he has seen his—what do you call it?— so virtuous maiden. He is set for the day." Mockery still filled Belsky's voice. Reynold couldn't understand why. What was it to Sasha if Reynold watched a beautiful girl pass by?

"Leave it," Liam told Sasha in a sharp tone. As a boss, the Irishman was usually pretty easygoing. He asked their best of them and that they work as hard as he did—pretty hard. But he was fair and had a streak of kindness under it all.

Sasha walked to the coffin on which he'd been working before he dashed out in Reynold's wake. He picked up his sanding block. "But can you believe how stupid the lummox? He does not even know what she is."

Liam and Pete both shot Reynold sharp looks. Reynold didn't understand what Sasha meant, and he hated when Sasha called him stupid, which seemed to happen on a daily basis, couched in a variety of ways. His thoughts might move differently than other people's, as his ma used to say, but he wasn't stupid and resented the label.

Anyway, what could Sasha Belsky possibly know about the woman in the blue dress that he, Reynold, didn't? She was just a beautiful girl who passed by each morning.

The first time he'd seen her—oh, that remained burned into his brain. He'd been bringing back a corpse on his cart, an early pickup all decently covered, for as Liam said, the good citizens of the city didn't need to see a stiff trundled past. He'd picked the fellow up at one of the taverns following a night brawl and had waited for the tram to pass before crossing the street. But the tram stopped right in front of him to disgorge a bunch of passengers. The beautiful woman—*his* woman, as he now thought of her—had been among them.

He'd been closer to her that day than ever since. And that time she'd looked right at him, her heavenly eyes—blue but far paler than the dress she wore today—meeting his for an instant before sliding away. Something in the stillness of her face, its quiet perfection, captured him then and had not let go.

Now he rounded on Sasha, facing the sullen man down. "Right, then—what is she? Best tell me, since you want to so bad, and know so much."

A series of expressions chased their way across Sasha's face—glee foremost among them.

"Sasha," Liam began.

But Belsky ignored him. He leaned closer to Reynold and in a false, confiding manner said, "She's a prostitute."

"She is not." Reynold had no hesitation in denying it. In all his twenty-four years he'd never beheld a woman so perfect, so pure and unsullied. "You're lying."

Derisively, Sasha asked, "Are you sure? Do you even know what it is, a prostitute?"

"Well, sure. What do you take me for?" He'd been drunk enough a few times to visit the girls down on the waterfront. They held no more resemblance to his goddess than a candle flame to the sun. And because he always wound up feeling so sorry for them, he had stopped going.

"I know what I take you for," Sasha retorted. "A babe in the woods. An innocent." He raked Reynold up and down with his gaze. "Your little dove is just a high-priced whore. She and her sisters get off that tram and march right down to the Crystal Palace up the street. Haven't you ever seen?"

Reynold hadn't. It seemed tawdry to follow her, even for another glimpse.

"Isn't that the place run by Dr. Landry?" Pete piped up. "The one Clara says is an abomination?"

"The very same," Liam agreed unhappily. "Now, Sasha, button it. Do I pay you to stand around jawing?"

Ignoring him, Sasha said, "I know what we should do. Take up a collection among us, and send him down to the Palace, where he can pay for her favors—scratch his itch, as they say. Maybe then he will be able to tell what she is."

"Drop it," Liam snapped, sounding angry now. Easygoing he might be, but when he lost his temper he went all Irish.

"What?" Sasha spread his hands. "That is charity, *nyet*? And, boss, you are always preaching charity."

"I'm also after preachin' getting orders out on time. There's someone waiting for that coffin you're supposed to finish."

"Let them wait. The dead have no feelings, after all. Just like prostitutes—and automatons."

Chapter Two

"She can't be a prostitute," Reynold whispered to Mr. Kowal, whom he'd just loaded onto his cart quite tenderly. The old man had died at the home of his daughter, who'd been caring for him in his last days, Mr. Kowal's wife being too aged for the task. But now the deceased's wife wanted him home for the viewing.

Reynold would cart him back to McMahon's, where he'd be fitted for his coffin, washed down, and dressed. The deceased's daughter had placed all that in Reynold's hands along with a set of clothes, probably the best Mr. Kowal owned, declaring herself and her mother unfit for the task.

"Don't you worry," he assured her earnestly. "We'll take good care of him."

More and more families had begun to avail themselves of the service, though most still preferred to tend the departed on their own. When called on to do so, Reynold sponged them down in the room at the back of the shop. He didn't mind any more than he minded their company.

He didn't talk a lot to living folks. The dead were different.

He considered the frail Mr. Kowal, now lying in the cart with his neatly-folded clothing on his chest. White hair, wasted limbs—the fellow had been easy to load. Hard to believe Mr. Kowal had ever been a robust man earning a living and fathering at least one child.

Liam always said Reynold's size and strength made a great advantage. He rarely had trouble shifting the corpses he was sent out to fetch. He'd had to move them from some challenging spots, such as tiny garret bedrooms accessed only by narrow staircases. And the bereaved did not like seeing their dear departed manhandled roughly, no matter the situation.

Reynold always employed the greatest respect, as now, when he spread the leather cover over the top of the open cart, saying as he did, "Just a little ride and then I'll take care of a few things before you go home to your wife."

For the last time.

Reynold didn't add that part. He couldn't say but the dead heard the words he spoke to them. From time to time he almost believed so. And there'd been that one...

He'd been called to a charity home where an old woman lay dying. When he arrived, she hadn't yet passed, and he waited outside the dormitory while a nurse tended the patient, him looking in through the door. He'd seen a curious thing—at one moment a hazy mist like white film had trailed up from the body. Only then had the nurse come and told him he could take the corpse.

Either way, Mr. Kowal might be listening, and he had no one else to tell. He got the cart moving with a mighty push and trundled off down the street.

"She sure doesn't look like a prostitute. I've never seen a woman so pure and lovely. And anyway, it makes no sense. If she were a prostitute, why wouldn't she live there—at the Crystal Palace? Why would she come every morning on the tram?"

In the company of her sisters, as Sasha had said. Reynold could not but notice she always disembarked with a number of other women, often the same ones, though they never chattered or gossiped together like other girls walking along.

"Sasha's just picking on me," he told the silent Mr. Kowal. "Since he knows I fancy her, he'll never leave it alone."

Did he fancy her? No point in admitting it—prostitute or not, she was worlds above him. What woman would ever look at a man who toted corpses for a living? Might as well drive one of the wagons that hauled out shit from the public toilets of the city.

"Not," he told Mr. Kowal apologetically, "that I'm comparing you to a load of shit. Not at all. It's just that I never expect to win a woman's affection the way you did. I like women—I like them a lot. But I don't suppose I'll ever have a wife."

Mr. Kowal's only response was a flop to the right as the cart rounded a corner. Reynold paused and straightened him surreptitiously. An idea occurred to him.

He might adjust his route a bit while taking Mr. Kowal for this ride—go the long way, which would take them down Niagara Street.

Past the Crystal Palace.

Should he? As Liam always said, business must be kept to business; they had a certain sacred duty to their clients. But Mr. Kowal, who seemed quite sympathetic, might not mind.

Muscles bulging, he pushed on to Niagara Street and took a right. He usually used the back streets; this thoroughfare, busy with steamcabs and pedestrians, would be more difficult to negotiate. But the Crystal Palace lay just ahead on the left, its doors open to the warm morning.

Had he ever guessed what the place truly was? Not really. It looked like one of the fancy clubs that dotted the city, and he would have bet his life Buffalo wouldn't permit a whorehouse to operate in this neighborhood.

If asked, he supposed he'd have declared it a theater, albeit a private and very high-class one. Now, from the opposite side of the street, he and Mr. Kowal paused while he peered in.

An automaton swept the front hall, which might explain why the doors stood open. One of the basic models, it had a shiny silver face with molded features, and it worked steadily, moving invisible dust.

Even as Reynold watched, it progressed outside to sweep the broad stoop and stone steps, arms continuing their monotonous motion. Nothing else—absolutely nothing—could be seen inside.

Reynold wondered whether automatons thought, and if so, what they thought about. Did they mind their endless tasks? Did they mind that they must always obey?

****

Lily Landry sat perfectly motionless, her hands folded in the lap of her blue skirt, and listened as Dr. Landry spoke. Around her in careful rows sat her sisters, also listening quietly. Not one so much as twitched, and the only sound in the chamber was that of Dr. Landry's voice.

Landry's Ladies they were called, named after

Candace Landry because she had created them. Lily didn't know a lot, but she knew that much. Knowing seemed like a magical ability; she had acquired certain knowledge since being activated, but not enough. She'd been created to learn easily, to adapt readily, and had a thirst for information.

Now she discerned Dr. Landry felt angry. Dr. Landry—being human—had feelings. It had been borne in upon Lily that she and her sisters had no feelings and were, in fact, unworthy of them.

Lily couldn't be sure how she felt about having no feelings or the fact that Dr. Landry had been hollering at them for fifteen minutes, according to the big case clock in the corner. They met every morning before the start of the work day for instructions and what Dr. Landry called reinforcement of their training, but today was different.

Dr. Landry had spent most of the time so far telling them what they were—and what they were not. As if Lily didn't know. Every morning at the dormitory she reported to Kristoff, who stoked her internal furnace and made sure her boiler was full and operating properly. This before she even put on any clothes.

Dr. Landry went on, "And you should perform your duties without dissent. You were created—constructed—to do nothing but that. It is the whole point of your existence. You are meant to relieve the human population of a tawdry and burdensome duty. The very idea that one of you should balk at providing any service is an abomination."

Lily raised her gaze to Dr. Landry's face. In her late forties, Mrs. Landry could not be considered a beauty—not that Lily was intended to make those kinds of assessments. Tall and thin as a plank, Dr. Landry wore her brown hair in a severe bun that accentuated her sharp features: nose and chin like twin axes, merciless eyes. Lily had looked into many eyes since she'd been put into operation, mostly those of clients. She'd been trained to do so in order to gauge whether or not her actions pleased them, whether she fulfilled her purpose. Created to read signs, she excelled at it.

Which told her Dr. Landry now held her temper by a thread.

People, being superior to automatons, were allowed to lose their tempers. Automatons must simply endure.

"Under no circumstances," Dr. Landry stressed, "are you to refuse to fulfill a client's wishes. These men—and occasional women—pay large sums of money to visit you. You will accommodate whatever they ask."

Money, as Lily knew, was a kind of god, a powerful one. It bestowed value—the more money something cost, the higher its worth.

Odd they should cost so much to visit, then, when worth so little—not enough even to make their own choices.

"Yesterday one of you attempted to refuse a service to a client. I am ashamed to say that client later came and complained to me. I wish never to feel ashamed of any of you. Discipline is required. Constance, step forward."

Lily jerked her gaze around. Constance had been built at the same time as she and operated out of the room at the end of her corridor. She now got to her feet, her face expressionless—or nearly expressionless. Did

Lily see something in her eyes?

Constance, as beautiful as all Dr. Landry's ladies, had wide, hazel eyes and perfectly molded features. Today she wore a burnt amber gown, and her auburn hair had been piled atop her head.

Like the rest of them, she had little resemblance to an ordinary automaton. That, as Dr. Landry also stressed, was the point. Constructed on the model of the hybrids that made up the Buffalo Police Force's Irish Squad, Landry's Ladies had steel frames fitted with real skin, hair, and eyes—all obtained from cadavers. Certain pertinent internal structures had also been implemented. Clients being serviced were not supposed to be able to tell these Ladies from human women. A miracle of engineering, Dr. Landry always declared them. But they remained her creations, and that gave her the power of life and death over them.

Lily wondered what the discipline would entail and whether Candace wondered. Lily thought so. Candace walked to Dr. Landry's side, where she stood, not quite still—trembling.

"Candace," Dr. Landry said with severity, "have you anything to say for yourself?"

Candace parted her lips. Her fingers twisted together. Lily could almost hear her searching through her artificial intelligence for the right words to say.

"Do you admit you refused the request of a client?"

"I…" Candace's gaze flitted over the listening automatons as if seeking help. It touched Lily and moved on. "I did not refuse, ma'am."

"That is not what he says. Do you accuse a patron of lying?"

The tone of Dr. Landry's voice implied that doing

so would be considered far worse than disobedience, and Constance shook her head.

"Then explain yourself."

"He—he wanted to perform an act I had undertaken with a previous client, one that hurt me. I merely protested…I did not refuse."

Dr. Landry's eyes fairly spat flame. "You are not permitted to protest. You are to be compliant—always. You are to display pleasure at whatever act is performed. Moreover"—Dr. Landry's voice gathered steam, so to speak—"you could not have been *hurt*. You are not capable of feeling *pain*."

Constance stood for a moment, face expressionless, eyes full of anguish. "It hurt," she whispered.

"There is no hurt. It is not part of your experience. Do all of you understand this?"

The seated automatons, Lily among them, nodded. She hoped Dr. Landry would let Constance sit down; Lily could see her legs shuddering.

Instead, Dr. Landry turned to Constance and said, "You must learn this lesson. Discipline is clearly required. Your sentence is to be switched off for the period of two weeks."

Switched off. Though all the automatons remained silent, Lily felt horror sweep through their ranks. Terrifying. Unimaginable. When switched off, one ended. "Switched off" equated death.

"No, ma'am, please," Constance pleaded. "Not that. Anything else, I beg. I will obey—com-comply. I will do whatever he asks next time."

"Still attempting to defy me? To argue? Come here."

When Constance failed to move, appearing

incapable, Dr. Landry stepped to her side and roughly fumbled with the back of her dress. "There is a secret switch," she informed her listeners, though they all knew it already. "One only I can find." She did something inside Constance's clothes and the automaton sagged where she stood, the life draining out of her and the light leaving her eyes. Two wisps of steam came out of her nostrils.

Dead.

"Just remember, all the rest of you," Dr. Landry said viciously, "as far as you're concerned, I am not only your owner. I am God."

Chapter Three

"Here you go, *zadrota*. You would not believe the great chances I had to take to get that."

Sasha slapped a thick wad of money down on the counter where Reynold worked. No craftsman, Reynold, but Liam sometimes assigned him the job of polishing the coffins or the brasswork. He labored at that now, buffing handles for their latest customer's coffin.

Kindly Mr. Kowal had long since been delivered to his wife and, presumably, planted in the ground. Reynold didn't get to see that part. He sometimes thought what a shame it was, all the time and skill that went into making a coffin just for it to go into the ground. Liam said that wasn't the point—the picture the bereaved carried away, in his or her mind, of their loved one resting in comfort was the point.

Now the shop went silent as Liam, Pete, and Reynold all stared at the wad of bills.

"What the hell?" Liam exclaimed.

"What's that for?" asked Pete.

"For the *zadrota* to go see his expensive whore. The fool does not learn. He's still running down the alley just to stare at her."

"By God!" Liam sounded angry. "Not that again. Will you not leave the lad alone?"

"Leave him alone? Only look how generous I am

with him. I won that at the pit last night. I might spend it on my own whore, *da*? Instead I give it to him so he can satisfy his yen."

"You're talking about the dog pit, aye?" Liam snapped. "An abomination. I thought Jamie Kilter and the anti-cruelty league shut them all down."

"They are shut down." Sasha waved a hand. "They open again in the back of another alley. So when I win all that, I think to help our friend, here."

"You don't want to help him," Pete put in. "You just want to spoil the illusions he's carrying around in his head."

"You use big words, for a pipsqueak. If you mean I want to set the fool straight, then *da*, I do."

"Stop calling me a fool." Reynold hated it when people questioned his intelligence. He touched the wad of money with one finger. Sasha was the fool, giving away so much dosh. Reynold should take it, just to show him.

Liam said, "What Rey thinks is nothing to you. And you needn't be surprised over Pete, either—my Clara teaches her bairns all sorts of words."

His Clara, as he called her, was due to deliver their first child any day, a child they'd been convinced would never come. Oh, they'd raised a household of waifs, Pete included, but had none of their own till now.

Reynold liked the way Liam spoke of Clara, with love and respect. If he ever had a wife...

He eyed the money again.

"Take it," said Pete who sometimes thought like Reynold. "Serves him right."

"Go ahead—take it." Sasha grinned, displaying those ugly, stubby little teeth. "Go visit your pure flower. I ask around, and the way it works, you choose the lady you want to poke from a bunch of pictures they show you. Of course, you might have to wait, her being busy getting poked by some other man when you get there."

"You're an arsehole, do you know it, Sasha Belsky?" Liam pronounced. "Don't know why I keep you on."

"Because I am the best joiner in the city," Sasha declared. "You know it. Old world craftsmanship, that is what you get from me."

Liam muttered something under his breath—it might have been *fecker*—and fixed Reynold with an intense blue stare. "Take the bastard's money, Rey," he advised.

Reynold's fingers moved of their own accord and snatched the wad.

Sasha laughed out loud. "If only I might see his face when he learns the truth about his little dove!"

****

Reynold straightened the front of his shirt for the fifth time and wondered if he looked good enough—respectable enough—for a trip to the Crystal Palace. He had a nagging fear they might toss him out on his ear, never so much as allowing him the chance to see the girl from the tram. Even given all Sasha had said, he didn't feel convinced he needed only money to visit the place.

He squinted at his reflection in the scrap of mirror that hung on the wall of his room. A wild crop of brown hair, thick and in need of a decent cut; he couldn't remember the last time he'd visited a barber. A broad face with heavy cheekbones inherited from distant

Welsh ancestors, or so his ma always said. Shoulders like a bull and a strongly-made body that could work all day without tiring. Mild brown eyes that even to him seemed to regard the world with a child's confusion.

What would the little dove, as Sasha called her, think of him?

He scowled into the mirror. He didn't know if he believed what Sasha said about the Crystal Palace—it wasn't always wise to trust what Belsky said. He'd learned that much.

But Liam McMahon wouldn't lie to him, and Liam had implied if he took Sasha's money up there he'd have a chance to see this woman, be in the same room with her.

Touch her?

He shivered where he stood. He still couldn't accept it. He'd watched her through the bars every morning—this very morning. Her cool, poised perfection made a lie of Sasha's assertion.

The whores and doxies he'd seen stood on street corners and shouted at passersby and each other. They wore soiled dresses, had tangled hair and desperate eyes. They called up Reynold's pity, not... Well, he couldn't even say what he felt toward his dove. Admiration. Respect, maybe.

Awe.

He stepped away from the mirror and checked again to make sure the money remained in his pocket.

Be a man, he chastened himself. You're just going up there to see what's what. Get a glimpse of her if you can. That's all.

****

An automaton met him at the door, not the one

he'd seen sweeping the steps before. This one had painted features and wore a maid's uniform. It regarded him with a blank stare and inquired politely, "May I help you, sir?"

"I…wanted to come in."

The steamie opened the door more widely and bowed. Reynold stepped onto a floor so highly polished he could have shaved in it. The foyer was large, with a ceiling that went way up and a staircase that swept aloft in two great wings. The steamie waved Reynold to a seat on a sofa—red and plush—before ringing a bell and subsiding into motionlessness.

A woman appeared from a room on the left. Tiny yet aristocratic, she had snowy white hair arranged in curls atop her head and wore an elaborate, dark blue gown. She also wore a pendant and chain attached to a pair of pince-nez through which she scrutinized Reynold, up and down.

"Yes, sir, may I help you?"

Reynold had this part memorized. He'd practiced the words all the way up the street so he'd get them right and not make a fool of himself. He began, "I'd like—" before all words deserted him and his throat closed.

The woman cocked her head at him. He tried again. "I understand you have girls here."

"Girls?"

Reynold, suddenly convinced this must be some elaborate joke on Sasha's part—that Liam had somehow been persuaded to join in—wanted to fall through the floor.

The woman took a step closer, lowered her voice and said very politely, "I am afraid the company of our ladies—Landry's Ladies, as they are called—is quite expensive."

"I have money."

Her eyes sharpened. "A visit costs a minimum of fifty dollars."

Holy shit. "How long?"

"I beg your pardon?"

"For how long would I get to…visit, for fifty dollars?"

"Two hours. Longer visits are available at proportionate cost. That includes all services."

"All?"

"Whatever you want the girl to do for you. They are trained to provide any comfort you desire."

Reynold's face burned—not because he found himself discussing such a thing with a woman but because it seemed Sasha had not lied after all. Of course he hadn't seen her yet—his dove. That might still be a lie on Sasha's part. Sure, this could be a high-priced whore house, but…

He whispered, "I would like two hours. I was given to understand I'd get to choose…"

"The lady with whom you'd like to spend time? Yes." She seemed to reach a decision. "Please come in."

She escorted him into the room from which she'd emerged, empty except for two gentlemen who sat on a sofa over against the far wall, conversing. That they were gentlemen Reynold could not doubt. Their manner, even more than their expensive clothing, declared it.

They looked at Reynold; one of them raised his eyebrows before they resumed their conversation and ignored him.

Reynold said to the woman—was she Dr. Landry?—"I was given to understand there are pictures."

"Of course. Please sit down." She indicated an elaborate chair situated beside what must be her desk. He sat on the edge of the seat, and she pulled forward a large album, the cover of which she flipped open.

Pictures, they'd said, but these were drawings—portraits, some of the most exquisitely delicate things Reynold had ever seen. The woman flipped the pages before handing it to him. "See if there's anything you like, and choose whichever catches your fancy. Oh, and the fee…"

Reynold began to sweat. What if she wasn't in the book? He would lose all that money for nothing. "Do I have to pay you now?"

"I'm afraid so."

"What if none of them…catches my fancy?"

"They are all quite beautiful. I'm sure something will."

He gnawed the inside of his cheek. An enormous sum. But two hours made a generous allowance. The whores he'd tumbled in the past had given him barely time to get his trousers undone.

He still couldn't believe she—his dove—might be a prostitute, even in a place like this.

The book had fallen open to a picture of a young girl with brown eyes, flawless skin, and butterscotch-colored hair. Not his dove, but Reynold felt sure he'd seen her before in his dove's company, exiting the tram.

He dug the money from his pocket and counted it out carefully. Not his money anyway.

The woman took the bills and used a key on a chain dangling from her wrist to open a small drawer in the desk, where she put the money away.

Then she rose.

"Take your time making your selection. Let me know when you decide."

Heart pounding, hands shaking, Reynold flipped to the front of the book. Each drawing had its own page. All beautiful. None his.

A woman appeared at the door, snagging his attention. Young and immensely beautiful, with red hair and a serene face, she posed, and the woman fetched one of the men from the sofa on the far wall. They went out together.

Maybe he should leave now. Sure, he'd lose the money, but—

He turned to the next page and found himself gazing at his dove. Smooth brow, finely boned features set in a perfect oval of a face. A rose of a little mouth, golden ringlets, and eyes that stared directly into his from the page.

Ice blue eyes.

Each page had a name inscribed across the bottom. Hers said *Lily.*

Reynold got to his feet, the book clutched in his hands.

Chapter Four

"This is our Lily. Lily, you will entertain this gentleman for the next two hours."

Lily nodded. She had come at once when summoned. Dr. Landry did not like it when they dallied once the receptionist called them; she would hear about it later if Miss Crump complained. Dr. Landry usually stopped in at least once a day to oversee operations.

She focused on the gentleman in question, the only one in the room at the moment. They were not supposed to care what the client looked like. Clients came in all shapes and sizes—had all kinds of tastes— and Dr. Landry stressed they were all to be accommodated in every way possible.

Automatons—even highly sophisticated hybrid specimens like Lily—had no preferences and were not permitted to *mind.*

Only, inexplicably, she found she did mind. Some of the clients were rough. Some left marks on the delicate surface of her skin, which could bruise and tear. Some grunted and farted and swore at her and asked for impossibly degrading acts.

That, as Dr. Landry explained, was why Lily and her sisters existed—so real flesh and blood women would not have to do those disgusting things. If Dr. Landry earned a good amount of money in the process, enough to build more units, so much the better.

Lily wondered what this man would want. At first glance, he did not look demented. But she had learned that at first glance few of them did.

This one—tall and broad—at least had a healthy look about him. Though she was not expected to have opinions or tastes, she liked his hair, which tumbled over his forehead in a rich, brown mop. He looked tentative and uncertain, but his brown gaze fastened on her when she came in, to the exclusion of all else.

Maybe this one would not be too awful.

"Run along then," Miss Crump told her. "Up to your room. He has until five o'clock."

Lily bowed her head, turned, and went out, leaving the client to follow. At the foot of the stairs, she paused and looked into his face. "Would you like whiskey sent up? It is included in the price."

"That would be nice." He had a husky voice, deep.

Lily nodded again and called to the receptionist. "Have them send up whiskey, room eight."

They climbed the stairs, Lily just ahead of her guest, so all she could see of him was one hand on the banister. Big hands. She wondered if he were as large everywhere else. Honoria once had a client so big he tore her up inside. She had to be shut down almost a week for the repairs.

"In here." She pulled open the door to her room and invited him with a sweep of the arm as she had been taught. Always be welcoming. Smile no matter what they ask. Seem eager.

Her chamber, decorated in lavender, contained the bed—of course—one chair, and ample floor space. Some clients liked to use the floor. In the corner stood a screen behind which Lily took care of necessary maintenance—cleaning between clients, occasional light repair, and refreshing.

Her client shut the door behind him and stood looking at her. He appeared nervous. But he would complain later if he thought she had wasted time.

She smiled at him. "How would you like to begin?"

"I don't rightly know."

She reached for the buttons on the front of her dress, sewn of pearl-colored silk. "Most of my clients like to see what they have paid for. Would you like me to strip?"

He swallowed convulsively. A dull flush rose to his cheeks.

"Have you ever visited with one of Landry's Ladies before?" Maybe he did not know what to expect, thought she would not look or feel like a human woman. Unless he touched her in certain places, he should not be able to tell the difference.

"No. No, I haven't."

She wondered how to put him at ease. She abandoned the buttons and reached for her hairpins instead. "Would you like me to take my hair down?"

"I would. I'd like that very much."

A scratch came at the door, and then it opened to admit the little mechanical maid with a tray holding whiskey and one glass.

The client leaped away, but as soon as the maid left, he filled the glass with whiskey and gulped half of it down.

"Oh, I'm sorry." He extended the glass to Lily. "Will you take some?"

"I cannot drink."

"No?"

She shook her head. Her loosened hair fell down around her shoulders in separate tendrils, and he took a step closer.

"My God, you're beautiful."

"Would you like to tell me your name?" Some clients did; others liked to remain anonymous. Many expected her to call it out at the moment of climax.

Not that she ever climaxed, but they did.

"Reynold. You can call me Rey."

"Thank you, Rey. I hope you enjoy your afternoon. I am instructed to provide any pleasure you require. Would you prefer the bed or the floor?"

He took another big swig from his glass. "Neither."

That did not make sense. Lily put her head to one side, searching her intelligence.

"I've seen you before, you know." His voice, low and gravelly, sounded breathless. "You get off the tram up the street every morning. I can see you from the alley that leads from the place I work."

"Where do you work?"

"McMahon's. I… But it doesn't really matter what I do, does it? I couldn't believe you worked here. I mean, you look so untouchable and perfect. Yet here you are, after all."

"Everyone must be somewhere, Rey." Most humans could not comprehend her sense of humor—only the other girls understood.

But he smiled. "I guess that's so."

"If you would like to remove your clothes, we will get started. Or would you prefer me to remove them? Some clients do."

"Clients."

"Or you can perform with your pants open. In this room, your word is law."

"Don't you mind?"

"I beg your pardon?"

He lifted both hands, one still holding his glass. "I still can't believe it. I'm standing here looking at you—hearing you offer to take your clothes off for me—yet I can't get hold of it. How can this be the only way for you to make a living? Why would you let men, strangers, put their grubby hands all over you? And worse."

Did she mind? That question again. She had been created for the purpose he described and no other. Yet lately, just lately…she had noticed some things displeased her.

Carefully she answered, "I am not allowed to mind."

She reached for her buttons again and continued to unfasten them. For some reason, men liked that and, indeed, his eyes followed her movements avidly. Her breasts had been formed of human skin over molded gelatin. Her clients tended to focus a lot of attention on them.

But he reached out and caught her wrist. "Don't." His fingers felt warm to her sensors, and his brown eyes met hers earnestly. "I didn't come here for—for that. I just wanted to see you up close, to meet you."

She recoiled. This had never happened before. Men wanted what they wanted, with considerable variations. Never just to meet her.

She stood with his hand still clutching her wrist, staring blankly. She admitted, "I do not know what to do."

"Sit down. We'll—we'll just talk. Talk to me."

He released her wrist, and she backed up a step and lowered herself onto the edge of the bed. Dr. Landry had said to accommodate their clients' every request, and this definitely was one.

He perched in the single chair with the whiskey in his hand, never taking his eyes off her. "Tell me about yourself."

"There is not much to tell."

"There must be. How did you come to be working here? What happened to your family? Was it poverty that drove you to this? Some other misfortune?"

Lily tipped her head and consulted her artificial intelligence once more. Did he not comprehend the truth about Dr. Landry's creations? Did he even understand what she was—a manufactured, third-generation, high-quality steam unit?

He believed her a human woman. A human prostitute. One of the very women she had been created to relieve from lives of danger and degradation.

Provided a client had sufficient money.

Her intelligence contained no information about this. Those who had designed her had assumed all clients would already know what she was.

She wished she could go downstairs for instruction, but she was never to leave the room—ever—before the end of the session.

When this client's allotted time was up, a chime over her door would sound. If the client refused to leave then, two steamies would come to escort him out.

Should she tell this man the truth? He seemed so earnest and so…so kind.

Lilly knew how to deal with impatience, cruelty,

and brutality.

Kindness, for her, made a new proposition.

Chapter Five

"I've made you uncomfortable," Reynold observed, marking Lily's hesitation and her apparent bafflement. She didn't know how to respond to a man who wished to treat her like something more than a piece of meat. That made him angry, and he was not a man who resorted to anger easily, as Sasha Belsky could attest.

But the implication that this exquisite woman wouldn't so much as consider her own feelings—more, wasn't allowed to consider them—argued such abuse he wanted to tear this awful place apart with his bare hands, find whoever was responsible, and obliterate him.

He couldn't imagine adding to her misery. Not that he didn't want to see her unclothed—the glimpse he'd had of her breasts through the unbuttoned front of her gown made his mouth go dry. And not that he didn't want to touch her, and more. His member had responded as soon as they came into the room and he saw the bed, and it hadn't settled down yet. But the last thing he would do was disrespect her.

"I am unprepared for this," she admitted, her ice-blue eyes meeting his. "My story is a very simple one. I was always destined for this life, nothing else."

He frowned. "How is that possible? No one is destined for…"

"Please Rey, could we speak of you? I find it much more interesting."

"Do you?"

She nodded. "Yes. Tell me about your work. What do you do for a living?"

Well, here it comes, Reynold thought—the moment when he destroyed any chance of a future relationship with her. Did he want a future relationship with a prostitute, however beautiful? One who'd been pawed, and worse, by God alone knew how many men?

His head said probably not. His heart shouted *yes*.

He drew a breath. "I collect corpses for a living."

She tipped her head again, those amazing eyes still fixed on him. Not so much as a flicker there to betray dismay or repugnance. One golden curl slid along the white column of her neck when she moved, and it fell inside the open front of her dress. Reynold's fingers twitched.

"That is an interesting profession."

"I work for a fellow who makes coffins. He sends me all over the city at the request of our clients. Not the dead clients, you understand, but the bereaved."

"The dead do not speak to you then?" She half smiled, letting Reynold know this for a kind of joke.

"Once or twice," he admitted. "They do make little sounds when I move them. And I tend to talk to them— I'm in their company so much, you see, and they're good listeners." Now she'd think him mad. He'd made a terrible impression—but why should he be surprised? Sasha never left off reminding him he was dull and thick, a fool in the body of a bear, with nothing to recommend him.

Yet she said, "A worthy and honorable line of

work, performing a vital service."

"You think so?"

"I do. I have been informed that what I do is vital, also."

"Well, I suppose so." Reynold tried to think about that and failed, his mind more or less blanking at the point where she and some other man walked into this room and…

"Speak about your family, Rey. Do you have a wife?"

"Me? No. I wouldn't be here if I did."

"Many married men come. They request acts their wives refuse to perform."

"And you…you perform those acts?"

"Yes. I am trained to fulfill every request."

And how could she be so matter-of-fact about it, so accepting? How did her expression remain so serene? Had she been drugged?

"I can't understand how you can do that," he burst out. "I mean, a stranger walks in here, someone you've never seen before, and you just let him…" A sudden cascade of images tumbled through his mind: Lily naked, her skin glowing white. Lily with her legs spread on the bed, in invitation. Lily on her knees, offering her mouth not to some stranger but to him, Reynold. His member leaped in agony.

He could not ask for that. Not now.

No, no, no.

But other men did.

He wasn't other men. As his ma had always said, he was like nobody else.

"Do you have other family?" she asked, ignoring his passionate comment. "Parents? Siblings?"

"I never knew my pa. He was killed when I was only two."

"Killed?"

"He worked the docks and was crushed when a stack of cargo slipped. My ma said he lived four days in terrible pain. She died of a fever a few years ago. At first it seemed like the winter ague—she kept going out and working. Worked as a laundress. I tried to persuade her to call a doctor, but she said she'd get better on her own. We didn't have the money, see, to pay a doctor's fee." And here he'd spent a fortune to sit talking to a prostitute. "By the time she was down in bed and I insisted on calling the doc, it was too late."

"I sympathize with your loss. Any brothers or sisters?"

"One of each. My brother—he's the oldest—moved away years ago. My sister's married and living on the other side of the city. I'm the youngest. You? Tell me about your family." He still couldn't accept they'd leave her to this life if they knew.

But she shook her head. "Dr. Landry says the other girls here are my sisters. It does seem that way. There is a bond. Tell me about your childhood—your life."

And so he did, sitting there in the comfortable chair and talking more than he ever had in his life, while she perched on the edge of the bed and listened, apparently rapt. He'd never known anyone to listen to him that way, and it drew things from him he'd never confided to anyone.

At last, though, a chime sounded, reverberating through the room. He stopped in mid-spate; her gaze left his face for the first time and moved to the door.

"What's that?" he asked.

"The signal. Your time is up."

"It can't be. That can't have been two hours."

"Please finish what you were telling me."

Instead he stumbled to his feet. He didn't want to leave her company. He didn't want to abandon her here. But now, suddenly, the words all clogged up in his throat.

She rose also, slid from the edge of the bed, and came to stand before him. The top of her shining head barely reached his nose.

What to say to her? What, in parting? He didn't know.

She smiled at him. "I have enjoyed this encounter very much, Rey."

"As...as have I." Except he didn't want to leave. Doubtless none of her clients wanted to leave.

"Would you like anything else before you go?"

He couldn't keep his gaze from moving to the half-open front of her gown. He denied himself manfully. "No."

"Perhaps a kiss...in parting? It seems you have had so little for your money."

"I've had a lot. More than you can know. But yes—I'd like a kiss."

She closed her eyes and lifted her face, precisely like a child. Reynold drew her into his arms, close against him, and lowered his lips to hers.

Just one kiss as she'd said—in parting. But sensation arose and battered him. She felt warm—so warm—there against his chest. She smelled of flowers and tasted sweet. He wrapped his arms tight, and her mouth opened to him, allowing his tongue inside.

He didn't care then that other men's tongues—and

worse—had been there before him. In a curious way, for those few seconds, she belonged to him.

He released her, and she opened her eyes. What did he see there? More emotion than during the whole two hours before.

"You must go," she whispered.

"I don't want to. I hate leaving you here."

She tipped her head again. "I would prefer you did not leave. But they will come soon and escort you away."

He cupped her cheek in one hand. Her skin felt like velvet.

"Lily—will you be all right if I go?"

"I have always been all right."

"Maybe I can find a way…"

A knock sounded on the door. "Go," she urged, "or they will not permit you to visit again."

He nodded, turned—stiff as an automaton—and fumbled the door open. Speaking of automatons, two steamies stood there—big ones—in silent demand.

He stepped out. He ached to turn back and reassure Lily, but the door closed very, very softly behind him.

He followed the steamies down the hallway, down the stairs, and through the big foyer. They ushered him out, and he found himself standing on the steps, his mind astir and his entire life changed.

Go, or they will not permit you to visit again.

Did that mean she wanted him to return?

Oh, God, yes.

Chapter Six

"Liam, you have to give me more work. I need to earn some extra dosh, and there are no side jobs hanging about."

Liam raised his eyes from the accounts spread on the counter and regarded Reynold with an intense blue stare. Reynold had intended to wait as long as necessary till they were alone before approaching his boss—he didn't need Sasha for an audience. But Sasha had been sent early this morning to oversee a delivery of lumber, and Pete had gone off with Liam's wife, Clara, to have his hand—injured late yesterday when an adze slipped—seen by the quack.

"Side jobs?" Liam repeated. "Do I not pay you a fair wage?"

"Sure." Ordinarily, when he didn't need to raise a huge sum quickly.

Discernment kindled in Liam's eyes—he was a quick one, was Liam McMahon. "Don't tell me you've been to see your little dove and want to go back?"

Reynold nodded, refusing to be sheepish about it. It was all he wanted—to see Lily again. He thought about it morning, noon, and night. Two days, and he worried for her, wondered if she watched for him.

He'd seen her both those days through the bars in the gate. He'd even called to her once, but noise in the street kept her from hearing him.

"Lily." He pronounced the name with reverence. "She's like no one I've ever known."

"Well, I should think so."

"So pure, so beautiful."

The expression in Liam's eyes changed. "Pure? She's a…"

"I know, but there's just something about her. I have to see her again."

Liam drew a breath. "Rey, lad, how is it you do not know—"

He broke off when Pete entered the shop, his hand swathed in white bandaging. Clara McMahon followed him, and for that moment, Reynold knew, Liam saw nothing else.

Something special happened when Liam beheld his wife—Reynold couldn't put a name to it, but he recognized it. Akin to magic, it must be. Folks whispered Clara McMahon had some magical abilities. Reynold didn't know about that but suspected she'd long ago enchanted Liam.

Now she entered briskly on Pete's heels, stripping off her gloves, dressed all fine in a green walking suit. The great bulk of Liam's child preceded her, but she moved lightly in spite of it.

"Doctor says his hand's broken," she announced. "Won't be able to use it for three weeks."

"Well, and that's ill news, indeed." Liam scowled at Pete. "What have I told you, lad, about haste?"

Pete hung his head. "I'll still be able to work with the other hand."

"And do what, sand on a board or two? No lifting, no carrying—you're as good as useless to me." Liam sounded rueful rather than angry. "And so what am I to do? Folk will not stop dying because you've hurt your hand."

Clara leaned on the counter close beside Liam. "You've needed to hire more help for a long while. This just precipitates things."

"I suppose so."

"When the baby comes, you'll be wanting to spend more time at home."

"So I will. But I've no time to train up anyone now."

"Couldn't you put Sasha in charge, have him train someone?"

Liam's gaze flicked to Reynold. "I do not think that would be a good idea."

Pete grunted his assent. "I can still be here, deal with the customers." He nodded at the papers on the counter. "I could do the accounts for you. You know I'm good with numbers."

"And I," Reynold put in hastily, "am willing to work double shifts."

"Double?" Clara looked at him. She had curious, gray-green eyes that sometimes seemed to look through him. "I should say you work hard enough already."

"He was just after telling me he wants more work." Liam and Clara exchanged a look, one of those so private it almost made Reynold feel embarrassed.

Liam went on, "What worries me, among other things, is leaving the two of them without proper supervision—Rey and Sasha, I mean."

Reynold stiffened in indignation. "I don't need supervision. I'm not a child."

Clara laid a cool hand on his arm. "Liam did not mean that." He felt a tingle where she touched.

"I did not." Liam shook his head. To Clara he added, "'Tis just that Sasha rides the lad unmercifully."

Clara wrinkled her nose. "If that's the case, why not let Sasha go?"

"I've thought about it. But where am I to find another man with his skills? And now that we're to be short-handed…"

She sighed. "At least ask around." She placed both hands in the small of her back. "I'm going home."

Liam instantly looked concerned. "I will take you."

"No need, my love." She leaned up and kissed him with inexpressible tenderness. Reynold looked away.

"Nay," Liam said as soon as the kiss ended. "Just let me finish up a few things. Pete, you come and look at this."

The two hurried off to the back of the shop, and Clara shrugged at Reynold apologetically.

"He's concerned for me. I believed I'd never bear a child, you see. The women of my family have considerable trouble with it." She grinned suddenly and looked like an imp. "Certainly no lack on Liam's part. But he's worried himself sick over it because my mother—well, when I was born I didn't survive. She brought me back to life."

Clara spoke it so matter-of-factly, Reynold could do nothing but believe.

"I wish you every ease and happiness," he whispered.

"Sweet boy." She reached up and patted his cheek, even though he made two—or more—of her in size. "It will be a lucky woman snags your heart. Which reminds me—" The look in her eyes changed, became bright with golden light. "This girl you've been

41

watching, the one from the Golden Palace…"

"You know about that?" His face flamed with heat.

"Liam mentioned it. My darling, take a better look at her. She is not what she seems, and not what you think."

"How could that be?" He'd sat talking with her for two hours, gazing nowhere but into her crystal blue eyes. "I mean, I already know she's a prostitute."

"Rey, sweetheart, not only is she a prostitute; she's an automaton."

"What?" Reynold barked the word. The heat that drenched him was followed by a flood of cold. "Impossible. She isn't."

"You truly didn't know? I suppose it must be very hard to tell. I've met members of the Irish Squad, of similar construction, and they're terribly convincing. Word says the models at Dr. Landry's are even more sophisticated."

"Models? No! She's a woman. I went to see her, sat and spoke with her. I…I kissed her."

Clara's expression turned pitying. "That's the whole point, isn't it? In theory, Candace Landry created those automatons to alleviate the plight of women in this city who risk their safety and their lives on the streets."

Reynold made a strangled sound.

"But Dr. Landry got carried away with her skill— or perhaps her investors insisted on a return for their money. I honestly don't know. But she set up her prototypes in that place on Niagara and charges a fortune for their favors. And common women still risk their lives at the hands of brutes, with no relief."

"Lily…" Reynold choked.

"Is that her name? I'm sorry, Rey, so sorry to burst your pretty bubble."

She paused as Liam came up beside her, looking rueful.

"You've told him, then?"

"Someone had to. It's cruel to let him go on believing what's not true."

"Sorry, lad," Liam said. "I was going to clue you in—"

"Did everyone know? Everyone but me?" Reynold's face burned. "Sasha? He gave me that money as a joke, right? He was laughing the whole time."

Clara said briskly, "I thought everyone in the city knew the truth. Dr. Landry is infamous. Some think she's doing wonderful work and some abhor her. Topaz Gideon, who possesses considerable wealth, was one of her original backers, I believe. Mrs. Gideon is quite concerned with the plight of streetwalkers."

Reynold didn't give a fig about any Mrs. Gideon. His heart still protested what he'd been told.

"But," he said helplessly, "we spent two hours together and had a real conversation. You mean to tell me she runs on steam? I would have been able to tell."

"Maybe not," Liam rumbled. "Have you met Patrick Kelly?"

Reynold shook his head.

"He's a hybrid steam unit, and a Buffalo police officer. He got married early this year to a human woman called Rose. He's living an ordinary life."

"That might be possible for Lily, then."

"Nay, lad," Liam said quickly. "Best not to go there even in your mind. Kelly is a special case, a free

43

hybrid automaton. Those units—the prostitutes—are property of this Dr. Landry. I don't see her letting go of them. Do you, my love?"

Clara also shook her head, regretfully. "I'm afraid not. I'm terribly sorry, Rey."

She touched his wrist again before she and Liam departed the shop together, leaving Reynold wrapped in dismay.

Lily was not property—he refused to think of her that way.

And the next time he saw Belsky, he meant to smash him right in his big, ugly mouth.

Chapter Seven

"Come here. I want to see the damages."

Roughly, Dr. Landry hauled Lily closer so she might inspect the bruises on her arms and the bite marks on her breast.

Lily stood naked in her own chamber. She had reported the mistreatment to one of the steamies as soon as the client left and then waited for Dr. Landry or someone else to come. When Dr. Landry was at the house, she always handled these kinds of things herself.

"Hmm," she said, rubbing one thumb across a bruise. "Quite extensive. What did you do to provoke him?"

"Nothing, Dr. Landry. I was obedient. Just as you always say we should, I acquiesced to his every demand. But he hurt me."

Candace Landry fixed Lily with a mud-colored stare. "He did not hurt you. You cannot feel pain."

"I did feel, Dr. Landry." Lily glanced down at her breast. "I felt that."

"You experience sensation. The sensors embedded in your skin and exterior organs allow you to translate that sensation into the appropriate response. You have no brain and therefore cannot feel pain as such." Dr. Landry glared harder. "Do not get notions above yourself."

"No, Dr. Landry."

"That being said, why did you not signal for help when he began damaging you?"

"You always say never to interrupt the session, Dr. Landry. Not for any reason. He had not finished."

Miss Crump, who stood by during this encounter, gave a ladylike grunt. "At least this one is obedient."

"Yes." Dr. Landry spoke to Miss Crump and not to Lily. "I hope I did not go too far with this model. I built them to be adaptable and to learn from their environment. The information bank is capable of virtually infinite expansion. I never intended for them to become autonomous."

"Nothing worse than an autonomous automaton," Miss Crump said dryly.

"Precisely."

"What about the next batch?"

Lily and all her sisters had heard for weeks that Dr. Landry meant to bring in a new set of Ladies—that was what she called them, a set.

"I may need to fine tune them, delay their release." She returned her attention to Lily. "Get on the bed, and spread your legs."

Lily obeyed.

"Did he damage your vagina?"

"He—bit me there also."

Mrs. Landry performed a thorough examination, during which Lily fixed her gaze on the bed canopy and thought of something else. She thought of Rey, as she seemed to do so often since his visit.

She had hoped he would return to see her. Each time she was called to fetch a client, she held an expectation it might be him. Why did he not come? Had he figured out what she was? Had he lost interest because she was not a real woman?

"Nasty," Mrs. Landry said. "Miss Crump, this unit has sustained considerable damage and will have to be pulled out of service temporarily."

"Can she be repaired?" Miss Crump asked.

"Yes, but it will take me some time. Advise the clients accordingly."

"Yes, Dr. Landry. Speaking of which, if the client who damaged the Lily unit returns, should I refuse him?"

Dr. Landry stepped back from the bed. "Of course not."

"But…"

"That particular client is quite wealthy and patronizes us often. We are not in business to turn clients away."

"I see. But if he should ask for Lily again—"

"Then she will entertain him, once she's back in service. Will you not, Lily?" Dr. Landry fixed Lily with a stern eye. "And be even more accommodating."

"Yes, Dr. Landry."

But Lily wished that client would never return. She wanted Rey instead.

****

"It's a little girl!" Pete, his face wreathed in smiles, delivered the news as soon as Reynold stepped into the shop. "Born last night—what a night it was! I didn't get any sleep. Liam's well pleased."

Reynold nodded. "Everyone all right?"

Pete's smile faded. "There was a bad moment. Baby came out not breathing. Mrs. Collwys was there—you know Mrs. Collwys?"

Reynold nodded.

"She held the baby up to Clara's face—Clara puffed at it, so I heard, and it started wailing."

"Well, isn't that a wonder?"

"It is. They've decided to name her Grainne, after Liam's mother. Liam sent me down to open the shop, and he says no trouble between you and Sasha."

"Where is Sasha?" Reynold hadn't seen him since he'd learned the truth about Lily, but he wanted to, very badly.

"Not come in yet."

The clock high up on the wall ticked, and Reynold looked up. "He—hang on," he told Pete, and ran.

This time he didn't go out the back. Instead he dashed around and pelted up the street that ran parallel to the alley, as fast as he could go. He'd been built for strength, not speed, and was breathing hard when he reached Niagara and saw the tram coming down the street.

He parked himself on the curb and waited. Every day he'd watched through the bars, seen Lily and her "sisters" arrive at the stop, watched the steamies who he now could tell accompanied them as guards. Today he wanted her to see him too. He didn't know what impulse moved him, why it felt so important that Lily should see him. It just did.

The tram stopped, and the beauties began to disembark. Reynold counted them under his breath...six, seven, eight, nine. And that was all. No Lily. She wasn't there.

He stiffened. In all the weeks he'd been watching her, this had never happened. Where was she? He stepped out from the curb, half intending to ask one of the other girls, and the nearest steamie guard turned its blank face toward him. The guard held a very small steam cannon close against its side; even a small steam cannon could kill.

Rey backed off a bit, worry gnawing at him with sharp teeth.

He wanted to follow them, wanted to march into the Crystal Palace and inquire for Lily—more, demand to know where she was.

Instead, he watched the little party move down the street and saw them turn in at the appropriate door.

He didn't know what to do. His thoughts didn't always move as quickly as those of other men, though sometimes they moved very swiftly indeed. Now fear made it worse. He felt as if a blanket of fog possessed his mind.

He walked back around and into the shop to find that Sasha had arrived in his absence.

The tall, thin man grinned at him in the derisive way he had. "Well, did you see her?" he jibed.

"No."

"Not in time? No matter—there is always tomorrow, *nyet*? And, Rey, you never did tell me— what does it feel like when you hump into one of them? Could you tell it from a real woman, then?"

Pete came out from the back room. "Sasha—"

He got no further. Reynold had Sasha up against the wall before either of them could blink, one arm across his scrawny throat and toes off the floor. Energy—that of rage—fired his muscles and lifted him beyond himself.

"Don't talk about her that way."

"Her?" Sasha still sneered, though it appeared more a rictus. "Not a *her*, but an *it*. Admit the truth

49

Rey; you went and poked a machine. Ha—joke is on you."

Reynold eased his grip on Sasha but only so he could slam him against the wall again, still harder. The boards shuddered, and tools fell to the floor. Pete swore in alarm.

"Rey! Let go of him."

"*Da*, Rey," Sasha mocked. "Better let go of me, if you know what is good for you."

"Give me more money," Reynold growled. "Give me money, and I'll let you live. Otherwise I'll kill you, I swear."

"Jesus!" Pete leaped on Reynold from behind, only partially hampered by his broken hand. Reynold barely felt the impact.

"What?" Belsky could barely speak now, most of his air cut off, yet he ground the words out. "You want to go see her again, even though she is nothing but fancy steel that other men have used over and over again?"

He wanted to go see her again—doubly so now that fear for her safety rode him. "Give me thirty dollars." With what he had left from before and his stash back home, that would be enough.

Sasha coughed. His face had begun to turn purple. "You *zadrota*. I will have the law on you."

Now Reynold sneered. "What, not man enough to fight your own battles?"

"Rey—" Pete attempted once more.

"You stay out of it. He's got this coming."

"Maybe. But you'll get in trouble if you kill him."

In trouble. Jail. Then how would he find out what had happened to Lily?

He pressed Sasha into the wall still harder.

"I don't have thirty dollars," Sasha croaked.

"You can get it."

"Why should I? Visit the whores on the waterfront if you want it so bad. At least they are flesh and blood."

"You played me for a fool. Set me up and laughed at me behind my back."

"Not behind your back—I laugh in your face." Sasha had started to sweat but remained defiant. "Only an idiot or a little child could not tell what she—it—is."

"I might be an idiot," Rey said bitterly, fearing it true, "but what does that make you? What kind of bastard prods at a man twice his size?"

"I am not afraid of you."

"You should be."

"You do not have what it takes to beat me up. You do not have the balls."

"You sure?"

"*Da.* You are like a child."

"Sasha." Reynold didn't know what Pete saw in his eyes but the younger man leaped forward and insinuated himself between them. "Sasha, just shut up, will you? Rey," Pete pleaded, "no trouble. Don't make me fetch Liam down here."

Reynold stepped away, though still flaming with anger. "Keep away from me, Belsky, unless you're giving me that money."

Sasha spat and straightened the front of his jacket. "You ever manhandle me again, you will wake up dead."

"Leave it," Pete begged. "We have work to do. Three new orders and, Rey, there's a body for you to pick up on Bidwell Parkway."

"Go get your cart," Sasha jabbed. "It is all you are fit for. Big as a cart horse and twice as dumb."

Chapter Eight

"Hold still. I will not tell you again." Dr. Landry snapped the words as she leaned over Lily with her instruments. They were in the basement of the Crystal Palace where Dr. Landry kept what she referred to as her auxiliary workshop.

Dr. Landry had held Lily here rather than permitting her to go home to the dormitory—for repairs, she said. Repairs, not treatment or care. Workshop, though anyone else would have gone to the hospital.

As if Lily were a thing, not a person. Which she was—a thing. She must keep that always in mind.

Dr. Landry had already put compresses on her bruises and repaired her breast. That had hurt—or rather had not hurt, as Dr. Landry insisted. Now Lily, still naked, lay on the steel table face up with each leg suspended from a separate winch—to give Mrs. Landry better access to her damaged vagina, she supposed.

Whatever Dr. Landry did to repair the tear there *did not* hurt most of all.

"I said stop squirming." The woman paused with grisly instruments in her hands and glared. "Every time you move, it makes the procedure more difficult."

"But it stings."

"I have told you—you are incapable of feeling pain as such. I need to clean the damaged material away before laying in the graft." Dr. Landry fixed Lily with a fierce eye. "Would you prefer I shut you off?"

"No, Dr. Landry. Please."

"Perhaps I should."

"I will be still. And silent." No matter how much it hurt.

She wondered just where her shutoff switch was located—amazingly, she did not know. It could not be anywhere it might be triggered accidentally by a client, and that ruled out most everywhere. Lilly remembered Dr. Landry shutting Constance off—she had reached through the back of her dress and fumbled inside. It must be somewhere in back.

Where?

Constance had not yet made a reappearance, still under disciplinary shutdown. Lily wondered what happened to her intelligence—her *beingness*—when she was shut off.

Dr. Landry applied her instruments and pain flared between Lily's legs. She fell back on what had become her mainstay distraction and wondered about Rey. Where was he now, what might he be doing? Collecting a body? It seemed a noble profession.

He seemed a noble man, withal.

"There. The graft is laid in. I need only let it take hold to effect the repair."

"How long before I may work?"

"Ready to get back to it, are you? About time you showed a proper sense of industry. I should say two or three days before you are suitably presentable."

"And healed?"

"The units of your line heal very quickly. Make sure you use the enzyme wash every morning and evening. It is that which nourishes your organic parts."

Lily understood that. She neither ate nor drank, and her tissues had to be kept alive on the steel frame. Twice a day she put drops in her eyes, which had been harvested from a cadaver, and flushed her skin, mouth, and vagina with nourishing enzymes formulated by Dr. Landry herself.

"In three days I will be back to work?" Maybe then Rey would come.

"Yes. Until then you will remain here at the Crystal Palace. Now go to your room."

Dr. Landry released Lily's heels from the clamps. She righted herself with difficulty and slid from the table.

Obedient, she crept away.

****

"She will be safe with me, sir. I assure you."

Reynold spoke to the top of the man's head—all he could see. The man knelt in the street over the body of his dead wife, who'd been knocked down by a cart horse. The ensuing melee had lasted more than an hour. In all that time, the woman had lain sprawled in the street till a police officer ran and fetched Reynold.

"You pick up dead bodies, right? Well, come and get the one blocking the street."

By the time Reynold got there, the cart horse—trapped in the heat by traffic—had also gone down. Reynold couldn't immediately tell if it was dead or alive. It made a gruesome scene.

"Fellow won't let anybody pick up his wife," the police officer said. "Immigrant. I'm not sure he understands she's dead."

Reynold went and knelt on the bricks at the man's

side. Not only was the woman dead, most of her blood had leaked into the street through her cracked skull.

"Sir, sir, you don't want to let your wife lie here. It's not right—not respectful."

That snagged the man's attention. He looked up, and Reynold saw he was young—not above Reynold's age—and quite obviously in shock, eyes red from weeping and face wet with tears.

"Let's get her out of the street," Reynold urged. "I'll help you."

"Na, na!" The fellow's accent sounded a little like Sasha's, if much thicker. Sasha, as Reynold knew, had lived here in the city since quite young. "You will not take her from me."

The man stooped protectively over his wife's body. Reynold didn't know what to do, beyond attempting to pull him off.

He looked around desperately. People—including the police—eyed them but didn't approach. Loud rattling heralded the arrival of a large wagon that had "City of Buffalo Anti-Cruelty League" painted on its side. It couldn't get very close either, but a man emerged from it, moving purposefully.

Reynold couldn't help but stare. Tall and powerfully built, he wore rough trousers and a white shirt open at the neck. His face, though, might as well be a mask—half of it ordinary, topped by a fall of auburn hair, the other half of his head hairless, the face marred by scar tissue that disfigured the cheek, jaw, and neck.

The man took in the scene, his gaze connecting with Reynold's for an instant, and went directly to the downed horse.

"Well, now, old fellow," Reynold heard him say, "let's get you up."

Reynold found a sweating police officer at his elbow. "Will he let us move her?"

"I don't know. Who's that?" He indicated the scarred man.

"Him? Don't you know Jamie Kilter?"

So that was Jamie Kilter—Liam had mentioned him. Or had it been Clara? Reynold watched as the big man ran infinitely gentle hands over the horse, murmuring to it persuasively all the while.

Touch—perhaps that was the answer. Reynold turned back to his own charge, laid a hand on the fellow's shoulder. "Here, now. What's her name?"

"Anya. She is my Anya."

"And your name, friend?"

"Tomas Bylacek."

"Have you been married long?"

Tomas blinked rapidly, seeking coherence from the depth of his misery. "A year. Just a year."

"How did you meet?"

"In old country. Her family come here, and mine. We move near each other, marry. Today she—she tell me…she will have our first child."

Oh, hell. Reynold's heart overflowed with sympathy. He said, "Then you definitely don't want her lying here in the street, right? I promise I'll lift her ever so gently. You can come along."

Tomas visibly struggled with it. To their left, the scarred man had got the cart horse up with efficiency and embarked on an argument with its owner.

"No one's going to take her away from you," Reynold went on softly, and the cart driver charged up to their side.

The man, flushed with anger and the heat, already belligerent from his conversation with Jamie Kilter, glared down at Tomas. "I'll have you know I accept no blame in this. The two of you stepped out directly in front of my horse. It's not my fault your wife is dead."

Tomas tipped his face up. "Dead? My Anya?"

"Jesus," Jamie Kilter said. He asked Reynold, "Will he let you move her? I'm taking the horse into care for the time being. They're going to want to clear the street."

Reynold nodded, touched Tomas's arm again, and looked into the man's shattered face. "Will you trust me to pick your wife up?"

"You will not hurt her?"

"I promise."

Tomas nodded brokenly. Reynold leaned down and, with tender care, gathered the corpse into his arms. She weighed almost nothing, and he lifted her with ease.

Almost nothing, to make up someone's world.

Jamie Kilter gave him a smile and clasped his arm briefly. The sweaty police officer nodded in relief. With Tomas at his side, Reynold walked to his cart.

"We'll just put her in here, all right? Very carefully. You can walk along with her if you like."

"Where you take?"

A good question. "Back to our shop. It's cool and quiet there, and we can send a message to your people, tell them what's happened. All right?"

Tomas looked at him blankly. "You are kind. I hold her hand."

They must have made a strange sight trundling

through the streets—Reynold perspiring as he pushed the cart, Tomas walking gravely, his clothing splashed with blood, and the dead woman staring at the sky. Fortunately, the crowd thinned rapidly as they moved away from the accident site. Reynold found himself wondering: Jamie Kilter would take care of the cart horse; who would take care of poor Tomas?

At the coffin shop, they paused outside the front door. Tomas eyed the building in confusion.

"Why we come here?"

Before Reynold could answer, Pete poked his head out the door. He swept the trio with a look of horror.

"Bring 'em in, then, before the whole street sees."

The street should be used to corpses by now. But Reynold lifted the dead woman from the cart, and Tomas followed him inside.

Where to put her? He didn't think the rough room out back, where he washed the dead clients, would be appropriate, and the workshop was full of dust. After a moment's hesitation, he carried her into the showroom.

A small space—an afterthought, really—it made the most of the large front window by displaying their top model, all gleaming mahogany and a work of art. Four other coffins stood at intervals alongside a short bench.

Reynold laid Tomas's wife there on the bench. Pete opened his mouth to protest and shut it again.

He had no chance to speak anyway; Sasha came barreling in from the workshop.

"What is all this?"

"She was knocked down in the street," said Pete. "The police sent for us."

Sasha stepped closer and peered. "She's dead."

"No," Tomas said.

Sasha eyed him up and down, a scathing look. "Ignorant peasant—don't you recognize dead when you see it?"

Tomas said something in his own tongue. There ensued a spate of words back and forth, none of which Reynold understood.

When things grew heated, he stepped between them, facing Sasha. "Leave him alone."

"Do not tell me what to do. You are not in charge here."

"You're a bully. But I'll not let you bully him. He's just lost his wife. And child."

"Back off, you big, dumb *zadrota*."

"Hey, hey!" Pete cried. "Sasha, leave it alone. Go back and finish what you're working on."

Sasha narrowed his eyes at Pete.

Swiftly, Pete said, "Liam did leave me in charge."

"Well, then, great and powerful czar, what you going to do about that?" Sasha gestured at the corpse.

"I do believe Liam would want us to provide her with a coffin."

Chapter Nine

"I'm going now. Will you close up?" Pete shrugged into his jacket and moved to the door. The shop lay empty and silent. A group of people—none of whom spoke English—had come and collected Tomas, who had embraced Reynold at parting. One of the party had given him an address where the body could be delivered tomorrow and had even promised payment.

One problem solved.

Sasha had left hours ago, also collected by a couple of friends or companions. Reynold found it hard to believe Sasha possessed any true friends as such. He also couldn't help wishing Sasha lay dead instead of Tomas's little wife.

He'd tended her carefully after Tomas's departure. He and Pete together had fitted her for a decent, reasonably-priced coffin, their most popular model, in fact, and one Liam often donated.

Reynold, more than ready to go home, nodded at Pete, who went out.

Silence settled around Reynold, and his thoughts rushed in. All this day, Lily had been in the back of his mind; now his worry for her returned with a vengeance.

Why hadn't she been on the tram? He needed to get in to see her and make sure she was all right.

But he didn't have the price.

His mind examined and discarded ways he might

earn it. All of them would take too long. Perhaps someone might lend him the money. Liam would, he felt, if he were here.

His eyes crept to the till, which sat on the counter. He wondered if thirty dollars lay inside. Probably not—it was an awfully large sum for Liam to keep around. Still, he didn't suppose it would hurt to look and see.

He moved through the dim room, not bothering with the lamp, and worked the mechanism that opened the drawer.

The amount of money inside made him dizzy. He riffled through it with clumsy fingers, and his mouth went dry. Why so much? Liam must have hurried off when he learned the baby was set to come and then forgotten about it.

Reynold stood there fighting a war in his head. He'd never in his life stolen from Liam; he couldn't imagine doing so. As a boy—and hungry—he'd sometimes nicked food from carts or stalls. Everybody did. But that made up the extent of his career in larceny.

And to steal from Liam, of all people, who'd been good to him, who trusted him…

Yet taking the money he needed, in this case, wouldn't be stealing. It would be borrowing. He had every intention of earning it and putting it back. Only…earning that great sum would take a long time.

He needed to see Lily now.

But what if he borrowed the money and in the morning Pete noticed it missing? Hard not to notice that much money gone. What if Liam came in? He had to come back eventually.

Well then. Reynold drew a breath. He'd just explain to Liam or to Pete that he'd needed to borrow the money to cover an emergency and would pay it back.

Borrowing, sure.

His heart rather than his brain reached that conclusion; his fingers counted and sorted with uncharacteristic skill. He'd have to go home and get the rest of Sasha's stash and his own savings before he could go to the Crystal Palace. He would need to stop home anyway and change into his best clothes.

He shut the till with shaking hands.

****

The same steam unit as before opened the door to him. Reynold didn't know if it remembered him, but it ushered him into the side chamber where he'd been before, and the woman he'd met last time rose from her desk.

On this occasion, maybe because it was evening, men thronged the room. Reynold's heart sank in dismay. So many—how could they all afford the crippling price?

Most of them looked wealthy—at least, they looked more prosperous than he. Dressed in expensive suits, they lounged about awaiting their turns.

With Lily? Would he have to wait while some other fellow pawed her, or worse?

He reminded himself again she wasn't a woman. A machine, so they said, like the one at the door, only so much more sophisticated. His mind could barely grasp it—his heart refused to accept the idea. That, and fear for her safety, made up the reason he needed to see her—now, tonight.

The receptionist unquestionably recalled him. She gestured him to the chair beside the desk and pulled out her book.

"Welcome back, sir. What can we do for you this evening?"

"I would like another…session."

Of course." As before, she opened the book of portraits. "Please make your selection. We will do all we can to accommodate you. The cost, as I'm sure you remember, is—"

"I know the cost, and I don't need to look at that. I want to see Lily."

"Oh, I'm ever so sorry, sir. I'm afraid Lily's not available."

"What?" The fear Reynold had been harboring for days flared up. He shot a swift look around the room. Did some of these others have a prior claim on her? Had they got in ahead of him?

"I can wait."

"No, sir, I'm afraid you don't understand. Lily is not available." The receptionist eyed him, leaned closer and said very discreetly, "That particular unit is out of service for repairs at the moment."

The words hit Reynold like slaps in the face. Unit. Service. Repairs. Protest, mingled with dismay and horror, nearly strangled him. It was true. The thing he didn't want to believe.

He swallowed hard, choking back the denial and disappointment. "What's happened to her? Is she all right?"

"As I say, repairs to that unit are underway. It should be back in service in a few days."

Reynold searched the receptionist's eyes. "What sort of repairs?"

"Sir, that is not for me to say."

"Can you tell me exactly when I'll be able to see her?" He found he still wanted to, despite the unpalatable truth being shoved down his throat.

"I'm sorry I cannot. It will depend on how the repairs progress."

Repairs—that repugnant word again. Reynold flipped the pages of the portrait book until it opened at the picture of Lily—ice-blue eyes wide, rosebud lips parted slightly, looking so human.

Too beautiful to be human. Too perfect. Too...

The knowledge should cure him from wanting to see her, but it didn't.

Maybe he was the fool Sasha always called him—stupid down to the bone.

"Sir? If you would like to make an appointment to see Lily next week, the unit may be back in service by then."

"I can do that? Make an appointment?"

"So long as you pay in advance. It's fifty dollars for two hours, a hundred for—"

"I know how much it is." Reynold's stomach turned sick inside him. "No." He stumbled to his feet. "I won't do that now. I'll come back if..."

"Of course, sir." The receptionist rose also, intending to see him to the door. "Or perhaps if that unit remains out of service when you return, you would like to choose another. They are all more or less interchangeable except for the exterior fittings."

Reynold stared at her. "Where is she now—Lily?" Why hadn't she been on the tram?

The receptionist pressed her lips together as if she thought his behavior—his curiosity—suspect. "Lily is awaiting completion of repairs here on the premises."

"Here?"

"Yes, sir. Can I do anything else for you tonight?"

Leave, Reynold's mind screamed at him. For God's sake.

"No, thank you. You've been…thank you."

He made his own way out past the automaton door attendant, stumbled up Niagara Street, and cut around back to the coffin shop, where he admitted himself to the dark silence. Aching, he returned the money to the till and sat on the bench in the showroom, the same Tomas's wife had occupied. He put his head in his hands.

A wave of misery washed over him as acceptance pierced his heart. An automaton. An exquisite and perfectly crafted piece of machinery, the work of some master craftsman.

Not a woman.

Good thing he hadn't spent Liam's money—hadn't violated his trust. Because he, Reynold the fool, would be much better off keeping clear of that.

****

"What happened to her?" Lily whispered the words to Chastity, her fellow Lady, so Dr. Landry—just in the next room—wouldn't hear.

Chastity turned her head with a slightly jerky motion. She had come in for very minor repairs—a client had pulled some of her hair out. The violence of the motion had done something to the mechanism in her neck. She had been waiting for Dr. Landry, as had Lily, here for a recheck, when Blanche was brought in.

"I do not know," Chastity whispered in reply, "but it must be bad. She has been *switched off*."

Horror gripped Lily. Perfectly aware she had never

been intended to experience that emotion, she nevertheless often felt horror, dread, and pain. As well as hope. She could not forget hope.

She still hoped Reynold would return. Of course, as Dr. Landry never stopped reminding her, these were not genuine emotions. Her artificial intelligence, capable of learning and adapting, had been set up to record reactions and respond appropriately. This made her seem more human to the clients, even though she was not.

Dr. Landry came in, hands scrubbed and dripping, followed by Nadia, who sometimes served as her assistant. She complained over her shoulder on the way in.

"This makes three units out of service. We're going to be losing money. We need to get these two back as soon as possible, as well as launch the new batch. Nadia, you examine Lily while I take care of this. See if she's fit to work tomorrow."

Lily braced herself. Dr. Landry was rough, but Nadia far rougher. The woman, square-built, with the arms of a wrestler, had a face that scowled perpetually.

She turned cold eyes on Lily. "Strip and lie on that table."

Lily already wore very little—nothing but a shift. Her expensive gowns were to be worn only while working—or more precisely as a preamble to working. Except with Reynold. He had not required her to remove her clothing.

"Move," Nadia snapped. "Dr. Landry, ma'am, are you certain there is not still something wrong with the Lily model?"

"Why do you ask that?" Mrs. Landry's attention

remained on Blanche, who'd been set on the next table.

"It is very slow to respond."

Dr. Landry looked up, and Lily hastily climbed onto the table. She closed her eyes and prepared herself for Nadia's touch by pretending to be anywhere else.

In Reynold's company once again. She replayed her artificial intelligence's account of his visit—how earnest he appeared as he sat talking, the width of his brow which somehow pleased her, the expression in his brown eyes which made her feel glad. How many times since had she replayed this encounter? Almost like being with him again.

Doing so now helped her ignore Nadia's cruel fingers and the pain of the examination.

"The tissue graft is not quite healed, Dr. Landry, ma'am," Nadia reported at length.

Dr. Landry looked up again, pondering. "We'll need to put the Lily model back in service anyway. The damage to this one is extensive. I may need to scrap it. Possibly a rebuild."

Rebuild? What did that mean? Would Blanche be changed fundamentally? Would she subsequently look different? Would she lose her memories?

What had the client done to her?

"Get up," Nadia snapped. "Report for work tomorrow."

Lily obeyed. Even risking further damage at the hands of brutal clients beat the threat of being *scrapped.*

Chapter Ten

"Be there, be there, be there."

Reynold whispered the words to himself like a prayer as he watched the tram creep up Niagara Street. If anyone had asked him—though no one ever did— he'd have denied any belief in prayer. He saw too many things on a daily basis that argued against the existence of a god, at least one inclined to listen to his pleas. And the devil sounded too much like a story meant to frighten children into being obedient.

Of course, he didn't have a brain capable of pondering such mysteries. Just look at him—standing in the rain watching a street clogged with wagons, the tram, and steamcabs—all mechanicals—waiting to catch sight of yet another piece of machinery.

That was all she was, he reminded himself for the umpteenth time. A piece of equipment, a well-made automaton. Not a thinking, feeling woman.

So why did he still want to see her? Why, believing what she was, did he still feel concern?

He must be the greatest ass on the surface of the world. Sasha was right—he was nothing but a dumb shit.

Overhead, thunder rumbled as an early morning storm moved in off Lake Erie, dumping a torrent of rain. Reynold, already wet to the skin and standing for once on the outside of the gate that barred the alley, narrowed his eyes against the glare of the steam lamps reflecting on the wet street. The two cabs in a standoff untangled themselves, and the tram crept closer.

Only to take a direct lightning strike.

Reynold saw the bolt descend from the lowering sky—so close he smelled the heat of it—and connect with the tram's metal roof. The boom of thunder came directly after, loud enough to shake the street and make his ears hurt. Women screamed, and a horse pulling a vegetable cart reared. The tram, now no more than ten feet from its stop directly in front of Reynold, halted and began smoking.

"Fire, fire!" someone yelled.

Reynold, gathering his shattered thoughts, ran forward. Even as he did, he saw flames break out along the roof of the tram car. Voices called from inside—Reynold could see the operator, an automaton, gesturing wildly through the front window.

The doors, front and rear, remained shut—they must be stuck.

Reynold, reaching the vehicle, applied himself to the front door. Passengers already thronged it inside. He could hear them yelling and beating on the windows, seeking exit. He yanked with all his strength and broke the door open, nearly getting trampled in the ensuing stampede.

Human passengers came first—Reynold could see the automaton driver, with no thought for itself, struggling to usher them out in an orderly fashion. A woman carrying two small children came to the steps and, pushed from behind, nearly fell. Reynold caught her and lifted them down.

None of Lily's sisters yet, nor the mechanical

guards he always saw with them. The flames in the roof crackled louder, flaring up despite the heavy rain.

Not until all the human passengers had been disgorged did Reynold catch sight of one of Lily's usual companions, led by the familiar automaton, the Lady's face oddly emotionless in comparison with the panicked visages of her fellow passengers. Three of them emerged into the wet street before Reynold saw Lily coming toward him down the narrow aisle.

His heart missed a beat. He reached up to assist her down as he had the others, and her fingers closed on his arm. Her ice-blue eyes met his, and something in them quickened. Recognition? Yes. Gladness? But how could that be?

She still didn't look like a machine, didn't feel like one touching him. But she released his arm all too soon and stepped away, making room for her sisters.

Reynold could hear the fire brigade struggling to move up the street, now blocked. Someone from the crowd herded the passengers and the flock of Ladies away from the tram, which now flamed alarmingly. Reynold followed them.

Thunder rumbled again, directly overhead. Reynold could smell the river, just as if the storm had gathered it up to pelt down on them. In the confusion of the slick, dark street, he struggled to find Lily again.

She stood at the end of the little row of wet hens, hair, hat, and clothing dripping. In that moment, he forgot she wasn't a woman. He pushed toward her, and she turned those magnificent eyes on him again.

"Rey!" Did she smile? Not a smile as such, perhaps, but the rosebud pink lips moved, and her eyes shone.

"Miss Lily." His own emotions made such turmoil within him he could barely speak. "Are you all right?"

She hesitated, putting her head on one side. "Yes, I think so."

"You haven't been at the Crystal Palace. Or on the tram. I watched for you—and I went there to visit."

"You did?"

"Yes but they said you were…were out of service." He faltered then, the very words seeming impossible. She still looked alive to him, even though he knew the truth.

"I was there but had to stay in my chamber or in the workroom the whole time, under repair."

"I see. What happened to you?"

"A client—"

She got no further. The nearest of the automaton guards came barreling in, interposed itself between them, and edged Reynold back. "Do not speak."

"All right, all right, buddy. We're just having a word."

The guard turned on Lily. "Do not. Forbidden."

She went still. Reynold wondered if she'd get in trouble for talking to him. Her gaze lifted to his again and once more his heart stuttered in his chest.

How could a machine—a contraption, as his ma would have said—make him feel this way? What in hell was the matter with him?

Lily said nothing more, but her gaze clung to his as the guard herded her to the others, gathered the flock, and moved them away up the street.

Reynold stood on the drenched pavement, the storm raging overhead, and called himself every kind of fool. Because argue it as he might, he still wanted to see her again.

****

One more day. Lily's sisters could speak of nothing else when they met, which happened seldom enough, each of them confined for the most part to her own room. Excitement and relief—if they could be said to feel such in defiance of Dr. Landry—ran rampant. Tomorrow the first members of the new batch of Landry's Ladies would be placed in service. Expectation was they would take some pressure off the rest of them.

One more day, and Lily asked herself if she could endure it. Only her second day back from injury and already the future stretching before her looked endless.

She wondered how many years a unit such as herself might be expected to operate. She would never age in appearance, but her mechanical parts would deteriorate. She supposed they could be replaced as they failed. Would a continual existence such as she now endured be better than the ultimate end, having her switch turned off?

At the end of her second day back, she could not tell. Following the upheaval of the tram fire, Dr. Landry had addressed them as a group, saying how vital it was they settle down to their work, mentioning then that the first of the new models would be released the next day.

Already, today, Lily had entertained five clients. Now, cleaning herself once again behind the screen, she doubted her new tissues had healed properly. Her pain went beyond the ordinary, and the enzyme wash failed to soothe it.

Surely, she assured herself as she dressed in a fresh gown, the arrival of the additional units would make life better. Would not the clients wish to try new units rather than old?

One of the other Ladies, Felicity, said their portraits were already in the book. Lily had never seen the book open but knew from the others that clients used it to select which of them they wished to use.

She hoped no one thumbed through it right now and paused at her portrait. But how erroneous of her. She could not hope.

She sat on the edge of her bed and folded her hands. Her last client had been rough and very demanding. Lily, who possessed no morals, could not judge the things he had required her to do. But she felt soiled and had to rinse her mouth cavity repeatedly to remove the residue.

The next client would expect her to be fresh. He or she—Miss Crump sometimes sent women up—would also expect the bed to be perfectly made up, unrumpled. As Dr. Landry had impressed upon them many times, they wished to present the illusion of a chaste and exclusive experience for each client, make it seem he or she was the first and only person to be attended.

No one wants another's leavings.

Which meant Lily should get up and straighten the bed in case she was called again. Yet she sat on, wondering whether something in her mechanics had broken, for she did not want to rise.

She thought of her human sisters, the ones who did what she did out in the streets for very little pay. She had overheard Dr. Landry talking about them back when she'd first been placed in service, while Dr. Landry had showed her and her sisters off to a group of human women and men.

This, ladies and gentlemen, is the answer to the servitude of the masses. To women being beaten or knifed on street corners. I am about to revolutionize the flesh trade.

Lily, sitting with her fingers clasped together, thought of those women. Were their lives so much worse than hers? At least they received pay, however little, and had hope of independence. They were not prisoners.

They could not be shut off.

What followed being shut off?

She searched for the word Dr. Landry had included in her artificial intelligence: oblivion. Almost better to be human.

But then, would she have met Reynold? She closed her eyes and remembered seeing him this morning when she emerged from the hot box of the tram car into the rain.

Had he looked at her differently? He had mentioned her being out for service—that meant he must now recognize her for an automaton, a machine and far less than a woman.

She had not been able to gauge how much his thoughts had changed.

She fastened instead on the other part of it, the mere seeing of him unexpectedly. She fumbled for another word and found it at last: bliss.

Chapter Eleven

"What happens to humans when they die? Do you know?"

Lily posed the question to Chastity, who sat beside her on the bed. The two of them awaited the arrival of a client, a very wealthy man who had booked the two of them together. Not for the first time—this man as well as several others sometimes requested the service. This particular client invariably requested Lily and Chastity in tandem.

Lily did not mind that part. She did not suppose herself capable of friendship as such, but she felt comfortable with Chastity, as much as possible in the situation.

The client—who liked to be called Monsieur Grand—liked them to be naked when he entered the chamber, so they were, their bodies nearly identical except for hair and skin color.

Chastity gave Lily a look out of deep, black eyes. "It was not installed in my intelligence."

"Nor mine. But we hear things. And learn—acquire—information."

"Yes. We have been instructed not to kill."

One of the first edicts, an absolute: *You will not harm humans no matter what they ask you to do. You will never kill a human.*

Chastity offered, "I sometimes think about killing

humans…clients."

Lily had to admit, "As do I." She had thought about killing the human who bit her. *Forbidden.*

"Humans are weak—fragile—and easy to kill. There are many ways. The strength of my hands on a human's throat. A kick to the jaw, a pillow held over the face. I believe if I wished I could break the rib cage and extract the heart."

Lily said nothing, but the thought came to her that Reynold did not feel weak. When she touched him, she felt stronger.

Chastity said, "We could kill our client when he is shown in. Then we would not have to do the things he asks."

A daring proposition. Lily narrowed her eyes and thought about it. "What would happen after?" Shut off.

"Shut off," Chastity confirmed. "At least we would not have to do these things anymore."

Lily would never see Reynold again.

"Unless," Chastity proposed, "we escape."

That made Lily turn and examine her sister. Chastity looked so emotionless, so calm sitting there in her naked perfection. But when Lily engaged her eyes she saw…what? Some of the thoughts that occupied her own intelligence.

"Is that possible?" To leave this building other than to walk to the tram and thence to their dormitory? Lily had never been anywhere else. "Guards at every door."

"Mechanicals like us. I have been examining the possibilities of disabling them."

"Yes?" Lily could manage no more.

"Yes. It would need to be done very early, when we first arrive, before Dr. Landry comes. If we disable the mechanicals…"

"Miss Crump is human. It is forbidden."

"We might be able to overwhelm Miss Crump without harming her. Tie her up."

"Nadia…"

"Nadia is rarely here in the morning."

Lily could feel her artificial intelligence clicking over, examining the possibilities.

"Now that there are more of us, it should be easier."

"The new girls will not participate."

"You are right. They are still stupid. They have not learned. But they may provide cover for the rest of us."

Lily looked into Chastity's eyes again. She repeated in a whisper, "What do you think happens to humans when they die?"

A knock sounded on the door, the steamie ushering up the client.

Both automatons got to their feet.

Chastity whispered back, "I don't suppose it would be wise to find out just yet."

****

"She's a right little angel, is our wee Grainne," Liam enthused. "Good as gold and twice as beautiful. A face like a tiny flower and full of sweetness. Barely cries—just lies there gurgling and smiling all over the place. I swear I've never seen such a bairn."

He rifled through the money in the till as he spoke, doing a hasty count. Reynold, who stood by, felt a surge of gratitude he hadn't kept any of it. He would not like being responsible for bringing down the man's mood.

"And Mrs. McMahon is well?" he asked politely.

Liam's face split in a radiant smile. "Beside herself with joy, lad. Thank you for asking. Barely puts the bairn down—which, come to think of it, might account for the great lack of wailing on Grainne's part. To say nothing of all the extra hands eager to help out—Mrs. Collwys, my sister-in-law Nancy—even wee Mrs. Kilter has stopped by."

"So," Reynold inquired, "does that mean you're coming back to work?"

Pete stepped into the showroom to listen for the response. Liam eyed both young men before he replied.

"Not just yet. I hoped to take another few days—just have to make a deposit at the bank, since I left everything hanging when the bairn came." He glanced around. "Things all right here?"

Pete nodded. "I took in a few new orders, and we've finished the first lot."

"Where's Sasha?"

Pete made a face. "Well, that's the thing. He's been in and out."

"What the hell's that supposed to mean?"

"He comes in, works for a while, but doesn't stay. He's been gone most afternoons."

Liam scowled. "Where's he at now?"

"Hasn't showed yet this morning, which is pretty strange. As I say, he usually comes in, torments Rey a while, and then slopes off."

"Ah, feck and damnation! I don't need his antics, not now. I supposed that means I'll have to cut him loose, but you were already shorthanded. I need to find another man—one with at least a modicum of skill." He fastened his gaze on Reynold. "Meanwhile, do you still want extra hours? You did say a while back you'd like to earn some more dosh." Compassion flooded his eyes. "Or did that all end with learning the truth about your automaton?"

"I still need to earn extra, and I'll do…well, anything."

"Don't make statements like that, lad. You never know when one will come back to bite you. Here." He dug through the money in his hands, extracted two identical bills, and gave one to each man. "That's for your efforts in going above and beyond, these next few days."

Pete tucked the money into his chest pocket. Reynold stared at his in wonder.

"And," Liam told Pete, "ask Sasha to stop by the house for a talk with me the next time he shows up."

"Will do, boss."

Pete disappeared into the workshop, but Reynold hovered where he was, still staring at the money in his hand.

"Is there something else, lad?" Liam asked, and added kindly, "Don't let that Sasha make your life a misery. The spiteful things he says come from a mean, narrow heart and, in the end, I suspect have very little to do with you."

"I need more," Reynold blurted.

"Eh? What's that?"

"The money's real generous of you, Liam, but it's not enough. I was going to ask you if I could borrow— say twenty-five dollars…" He nodded at the rest of the money in Liam's hand.

"This? But, lad, I'm off now to the bank so I can pay bills and keep food on the table at home, as well as supplies coming in here. The big bill for that mahogany's arrived, and we donated two coffins this month."

"As well as another at a discount," Reynold couldn't help but correct. "There was this woman…"

"Aye, lad, Petey told me. Good work on your part. I'm running a certain kind of business here, and I don't mind giving—but we have to stay afloat if you want a job."

"I understand that. I just thought…"

"Why do you want the money?" Liam's eyes narrowed. "Och, never say you still want to go back to that place, now that you know the truth about Landry's Ladies."

"I need to see if she's all right. You see, there was a fire on the tram. I only saw her for a moment, and she said before that she'd been hurt. If I can have a proper visit with her, I won't have to worry so much."

"And you think you should squander a great sum of money just for a visit?" Liam shook his head. "Don't waste your time, Rey, lad. Go find a real woman who can treat you as you deserve—give you her heart. Give you a home and children."

"So"—Reynold swallowed bitterly—"you will not lend me the money?"

"I don't have it to lend—all this is accounted for. Not sure I would if I could, to be honest." Liam clasped Reynold's shoulder. "Best advice—put her out of your mind."

He hurried off then for another word with Pete in the shop before leaving. Reynold stood where he was, pondering things. What to do now? With the till empty, he couldn't even borrow on the sly as he had before. The money would take forever to earn. Unless he did something desperate.

As for forgetting Lily, he didn't think he could.

Chapter Twelve

"I need to make some money quick." Reynold lowered his head and spoke quietly to the two men who sat opposite him at the table. The tavern jumped with sound—voices, laughter, and a rough sort of music from the pick-up band in the corner, the members of which seemed to spend more time arguing than playing.

Reynold's two acquaintances eyed him speculatively. He dared not call them friends. With the exception of Pete and possibly Liam, he didn't suppose he had any actual friends, but he'd been banging around this city long enough to have acquaintances in plenty.

He'd gone to school with Vern Snyder until they both dropped out. He'd met Dickie Price working an early job. Both had since veered onto unsavory paths, which was why he sought them out tonight.

Dickie gave a harsh laugh. A small man, he had neat hands and feet—the rest of him had deteriorated into a serious state of filth since Reynold had last seen him. "Me, I've got a habit to support. Can't get enough."

Vern, a much taller, scarecrow-thin man with white-blond hair and a pockmarked face, ignored Dickie. "What we talkin' about here, Rey? What kind of money?"

"A hundred dollars—and like I say, real fast." Reynold had decided to aim high. He doubted one visit with Lily would be enough for him.

Now it was Vern who laughed. "You out of your mind?"

Quite possibly, but Reynold didn't want to admit it.

"Must have to do with a woman," Dickie snarled. "Most crazy things do."

Reynold didn't bother to deny it.

Vern gave his opinion. "Any woman requires that kind of money ain't worth it."

"She's worth it," Reynold averred.

"Holy hell." The two men exchanged looks.

"Take it from me," said Dickie, sounding like an old hand, "get a whore. Easier and the result's the same. This place is full of 'em." He waved an arm. "Take your pick."

"He's right," Vern agreed. "I can recommend Tilly over there—she'll do whatever you want for two pennies."

Which one was Tilly? As Dickie said, every woman in the place looked like a streetwalker, some getting drinks bought for them, likely in lieu of pay, and others here drumming up business. A poor lot—most looked nearly as dirty as Dickie, with ratty hair and missing teeth.

"The one in the pink shawl," Vern elucidated, seeing him looking. "She got all her teeth kicked out sometime back, but that can be an advantage, depending on what you're after."

Reynold disguised a shudder as a twitch. "No, thanks."

"Not good enough for you, Rey?" Vern sneered. "Who do you think you are, anyway?"

"He's got a good job," Dickie put in. "Come to

think of it, don't you earn enough toting them dead bodies around the city?"

Dickie leaned closer across the gummy table. "That reminds me. I've always wanted to ask—you ever get any good-looking corpses of the female persuasion?"

"Sometimes, I guess. Why?"

"Well"—Dickie licked his skinny lips—"there has to be a back room or some place you could have at 'em, right?"

Reynold stared. "Have at 'em?"

Dickie gave a ghastly grin. "They're not gonna tell, are they? Nothing to stop you havin' your way with 'em. A woman's a woman, after all."

The sour ale Reynold had just choked down rose to the back of his throat. He thought of Tomas's pretty little wife, and her husband weeping over her.

"That's disrespectful, that is." As well as sickening.

"You gotta remember," Vern said as an aside to Dickie, "our pal here ain't like us. His thoughts move a bit more slowly." Before Reynold could kindle with anger, he went on, "I might have a job for you, Rey, if you're willing to take a chance or two."

Reynold considered it. Here was the line. Did he want to cross it? He'd been doing well at Liam's, had straightened out his life since the days when he ran with the likes of these two. Did he really want to venture back on the wrong side of the law?

Did he want to see Lily again? Lay eyes on her, make sure she was all right?

He narrowed his gaze on Vern's face. "What we talking about here?"

"You know how to drive a steamcab?"

Reynold frowned. He'd never even ridden in one but wasn't about to admit it. "Sure." He'd ridden on the tram. Didn't that count?

"Well, then, you just might be our man."

" 'Our'?" Dickie held up his hands. "I got nothing to do with it."

"No," Vern agreed. "For this venture, I've other associates. All you'd have to do is drive a steamcab a short distance, where I tell you, and you'll get paid."

Reynold thought about it. "Stolen, right? The steamcabs are—"

"Keep your voice down, for Chrissake. There's a big market in this city for parts. It's a victimless crime."

"How do you figure that?"

"Those steamcab companies are all owned by rich toffs, and they expect a certain amount of loss. One or two cabs—"

"That's grand theft, that is." He could be put away for a long time.

Vern shrugged. "No other place you can make the kind of money you're talking about, not unless you bet the ponies."

Reynold thought about that also. Betting on fighting dogs had worked for Sasha and might make a safer bet. But he refused to support that ugly undertaking and had only ever lost on the ponies.

He needed the money to see Lily. There must be a way.

"What ho," said Dickie suddenly. "Look out—here comes the end of fun for the night."

The door of the tavern swung wide to admit several new arrivals. They entered on a wave of muggy evening air but seemed to bring their own heat. The first was a woman; tall and with raven-black hair tumbling down her back, she wore a jacket and skirt made of golden fabric, the latter hiked up high enough to show a pair of heeled boots. She moved like a dancer, or perhaps an assassin.

Three men came at her back, all tall and brawny specimens who conducted themselves with sublime confidence.

Reynold could not help but question, "Why, who's that?"

"Mrs. Gideon." Vern grunted with very little approval. "And her pals from the Irish Squad. No whores for anybody tonight—at least not in here."

The Irish Squad—Reynold's interest quickened. Weren't they supposed to be automatons—hybrid ones like Lily? And hadn't Clara mentioned Mrs. Gideon?

He eyed the automatons as they moved through the room. If he hadn't been told, he'd never be able to guess they weren't human.

"What are they doing here?" he asked. The woman was dressed far too well to be a patron, and he'd heard off-duty police officers frequented other taverns.

"She's come to round up the streetwalkers," Dickie explained.

"What?"

Dickie had no opportunity to elucidate. At the party's entrance, the noise level in the tavern dropped. The woman took advantage and struck a pose in the middle of the floor.

She called, "Any of you ladies needing a bed and a safe place to spend the night can come with us."

The reaction in the room—immediate—made a further hush. The women around the tavern froze before gathering themselves up. Reynold saw the girl in the pink shawl—Tilly—tuck the wrap around her shoulders and step away from the man to whom she'd been speaking. Others followed suit. They formed a little flock around Mrs. Gideon, like ewes around a shepherd.

Dickie swore softly. "There goes my chance for a poke tonight."

"Go to another tavern," Vern growled. "She can't hardly collect them all."

Reynold saw Mrs. Gideon exchange a look with the bartender. A beauty of the first water and no mistake, she shone a light in the place.

He turned his gaze on each of the off-duty officers in turn, looking for telltale signs they weren't in fact human. Hard to tell even when the group drew nearer, doing an apparent sweep of the room.

"Where will she take them?"

"Has a house, doesn't she? A haven for disadvantaged women, she calls it. Has bags of money. Heiress to the Hathor fortune she was—daughter of that Frederick Hathor. Even an ignorant sot like you must have heard of him.

Reynold had. Hathor—an infamous spiritualist known for his ability to communicate with the dead—had perished in a fire at his mansion less than two years ago.

He eyed Mrs. Gideon in amazement. A wealthy woman like that concerning herself with the welfare of common streetwalkers? Unlikely, yet she moved through the room like a conquering hero, confidence in every step.

When she drew near, Reynold stumbled to his feet. One of the police officers—automatons, he corrected himself—turned a bright green, measuring look on him before seeming to dismiss him as no threat.

Mrs. Gideon also turned her head and located Reynold. Her eyes looked golden in sharp contrast with her black hair.

"Don't draw attention to yourself." Vern hauled him back into his seat. "'Specially if you mean to help in our venture."

The group passed by and out the door. Not all the streetwalkers went with them, but the number left had been severely reduced.

"What will happen to them?" he asked once they'd gone, nearly as abruptly as they'd arrived.

Vern shrugged. "She'll give them a meal and, like she said, a place for the night. They'll be back on the street tomorrow."

"What's the point then?" Reynold wondered aloud.

"Damned if I know. These crusaders." Vern spat on the floor rudely, the gesture a clear opinion.

And, Reynold couldn't help but wonder, would such a crusader as Mrs. Gideon take an interest in a prostitute who wasn't human?

Chapter Thirteen

"Look at them," Chastity spoke very softly into Lily's ear. "So innocent. They do not know what will be expected of them."

Lily dared not turn her eyes on her fellow automaton. Dr. Landry stood at the front of the room introducing her new Ladies, the second half of the batch she'd just completed. The first had been launched soon after Lily returned to work and had served to alleviate her client load, which made her...

She searched her artificial intelligence for a word. Grateful.

Of course, that counted as another emotion she should not be able to feel. Like dread, fear, and hope, it had never been intended as part of her experience.

As Chastity urged, she observed the new units closely. Perfect in every detail, sculpted in face and form, their beautiful eyes nevertheless held blank expressions. They had learned far too little yet. The slates of their minds had almost nothing written upon them.

As Lily well knew, every experience became a lesson; each changed the learner. By virtue of the fact that she and her sisters had been created to adapt, they acquired a kind of personality. That did not mean she, Lily, had a soul. It meant only that since being put into operation she'd become aware of the desire to possess one.

Oh, to be human, with the right to direct one's own life, with the ability to walk out of this prison! Instead she must sit and watch these new models, knowing what would befall them.

It filled her with a queer feeling that—had she dared—she might define as grief.

Chastity tipped her head close to Lily's again. "Perhaps it will mean still fewer clients for us."

"Yes."

Dr. Landry's gaze moved to them, and a finger of cold touched Lily's steel frame. The arrival of these reinforcements could mean something more; no longer shorthanded, Dr. Landry might now shut her down for any reason. Because she hadn't healed completely and subsequent clients had exacerbated her damage, or for what Dr. Landry perceived as disobedience.

And out of service, how could Lily see Reynold if he came? Even though so many endless days had passed, she still believed he would.

Dr. Landry paused in her introductions. She must have run out of synonyms for purity and had named her new batch after flowers...Peony, Hydrangea, Carnation...all beautiful things that lived and then died.

Totally inappropriate, Lily thought with a touch of the black humor that sometimes came to her. She, for instance, was neither alive nor pure.

Chastity took a terrible chance and whispered, "Come to my chamber later when you can. We need to talk."

Lily gave a small nod and let her eyes go blank, imitating her new sisters.

****

91

"I want to leave this place." Chastity made the announcement in a low voice that quivered. "But not to go back to the dormitory. That is just another prison. I want to go out into the world and pretend to be what I am not—alive."

Lily's artificial intelligence clicked through the outrageous statement carefully. "There are many obstacles. It may be impossible."

She perched on the edge of the bed in Chastity's chamber, having crept there while everyone in the house seemed otherwise occupied. Chastity paced in front of her, skirts swishing around her ankles.

"I know that." Chastity shot Lily a look out of a calm face in which only her dark eyes revealed the slightest turmoil.

Lily, who had all too quickly examined the objections, listed them. "Quite apart from the difficulties in leaving here, which we have already discussed, there is nowhere for you to go if you do escape. No way to gain transport other than the tram. No shelter. Worst of all, to survive you will need Dr. Landry's enzyme wash."

"I will steal some when I go."

"Even so, you will soon run out. What then?"

"It must be possible to duplicate the formula if I analyze it."

"You would need access to the proper ingredients. Without friends…"

Chastity fixed Lily with burning, dark eyes. Lily wondered to whom they had once belonged—what corpse. Chastity had been fitted with warm brown skin. Had the eyes also belonged to a brown human?

And her own eyes and skin—to what living,

breathing person had they once belonged?

Hers now. Hers. Yet she wondered if the essence of their original owner or owners did not linger.

"You are my friend, are you not?" Chastity posed the question quite seriously while staring at Lily intently.

"Yes. Yes I am."

"Then you must help me. My intelligence tells me that is what friends do."

"Yes, mine also."

"Better yet, come with me. Two together will be stronger than one."

Still, against a whole city—and Dr. Landry. The last terrified Lily most of all.

If she escaped with Chastity, might she then find Reynold? He said he collected dead bodies around the city. She might inquire and locate him.

"I would like to leave this place. But the plan is not sufficiently good."

"If we steal some enzyme wash from our sisters, that will give us more time on the outside."

"We have been instructed not to steal."

"Yes, from the clients. The clients," Chastity said flatly, "have nothing I want: not their spit, not their perspiration, not their seed."

"You..." again Lily groped for the word, "hate them."

"I do. If I stay, I will kill one. Soon. Our instructions say not to steal from them. I have searched my intelligence; it says nothing about stealing from Dr. Landry."

Lily made a swift check; it was true. "Opportunity," she said.

"I have contemplated that also. If a fire were set…"

"Very dangerous to us. We could be damaged beyond repair. You remember the fire in the tram."

"And the confusion. That is what brought the prospect to my attention."

Lily conceded that but said, "It would be bad to harm any of our sisters."

"Yes, but if I stay and kill a client, I will be shut off. I am seeking to survive. That seems to allow a certain level of extreme behavior."

Lily considered that; it made sense.

"Meanwhile, we cannot arouse any suspicion. Go to your room now. Think it through, friend."

Lily rose from the side of the bed. She considered shaking Chastity's hand but embraced her instead and whispered one word. "Courage."

****

"You've launched a new career and are doing surprisingly well with it." Vern laid a stringy hand on Reynold's shoulder. "Who'd have thought you had it in you?"

Certainly not Reynold. But he had to admit he'd taken to driving—and stealing—steamcabs like a pig to muck. The first night he'd been so scared he thought he'd choke. It had taken him nearly five minutes to figure out the controls, but once he did, it felt as natural as pushing his cart around the city.

Who'd have imagined he, Reynold Michaels, would be that good at anything? Especially theft.

It helped that he knew the city so well, because Vern gave him a different address each time for where he needed to take the cab. One had been a shed down on Swan Street, one a garage on Michigan. This last had gone to a warehouse on Abbott.

"'Course it'll get harder now," Vern murmured. "Coppers are on to us."

They'd met in a tavern—one to which Reynold had never been before. Vern had just made the payout, and Reynold figured that, combined with the leftovers from Sasha and his own savings, it made enough for him to see Lily.

"Now, tomorrow," Vern began.

"Can't tomorrow night. I have something else on."

"Like what?" Vern's eyes narrowed suspiciously. "You never did say why you want so much money, 'cept it's a woman."

"Gentlemen don't talk."

"Gentlemen?" Vern widened his pale blue eyes and scoffed. "You ain't no gentleman, my friend. About as far as you can get."

"Doesn't matter." And it didn't. Vern could hurl any slurs he liked. Reynold would see Lily again, spend time with her—if she was working. At the moment, he cared about nothing else.

"You're a fool, anyway," Vern went on, "if you toss all that money away on a woman."

"Well," Reynold drawled, "then I reckon you'll just have to call me a fool."

Chapter Fourteen

"I would like to see Miss Lily."

Reynold made the request firmly, even though his suit coat felt too tight and his collar threatened to strangle him. He'd come dressed in the same clothes as last time—the only decent ones he owned—and had scrubbed his nails and tried to tame his unruly hair. He looked the receptionist in the eye, burning with determination. "Is she available?"

The receptionist didn't so much as bat a lash. "Certainly, sir. How long a visit did you wish?"

"Just…the two hours." The limit of what he could afford, for all his efforts. "You say she's here, working?"

"Lily is receiving visitors, sir, yes."

"Will I have to wait?"

The receptionist gave a thin smile and flipped the pages of the big book, which seemed thicker than before. "Not if you request Lily. As you can see, we have expanded our number of Ladies. There are now many fresh, new models. Perhaps, sir, you would rather look through the portraits and select something different?"

"No, ah—Lily will do."

"Very good, sir. The fee—"

Reynold handed over the carefully hoarded sum, that for which he'd sold his honesty and perhaps also his safety. The woman counted it carefully and placed it in the secure drawer of the desk.

"Very good, sir. As we are busy tonight, I will escort you up myself."

Reynold's heart pounded like a drum all the way up the stairs. When they reached the same door as before, the receptionist knocked, gave him another thin smile, and said, "A chime will sound when your time is up."

She left, and the door opened.

Reynold had lectured himself harshly and at length about this moment. He'd tried first of all to talk himself out of coming. When that didn't work, he pondered that now he knew the truth about Lily, time spent in her company would make him feel differently about her. He'd steeled himself for disappointment.

When he saw her, though, all of it flew away.

She wore a gown of turquoise blue—not the same as last time—and her golden hair clustered around her face, a riot of curls escaping the chignon. Her eyes, much paler than the gown, widened when she saw him, and her pink lips parted.

He stepped into the room and shut the door.

"Rey!"

Her voice sounded like that of a real woman; she looked so much like one he had to restrain himself from catching her up in his arms.

"You still remember me?"

"Yes, I remember you. I have hoped and hoped you would return."

"Truly?" He stepped closer and, greatly daring, took her hands in his. They felt cool, but that might be because he was on fire.

"Yes."

"As I told you after the tram fire, I came back once before. You were…" And as abruptly as that, he ran into a wall. All fine and good to tell himself he'd feel differently about her when he saw her again—he didn't. He still found it all too possible to pretend she was a real woman. He'd had fantasies about that too, about making love to her the way other men did.

No, he corrected himself. Other men used her. *Making love* implied something else.

"You," he finished determinedly, "were not in service—broken." Best to get it out in the open.

"You believe the truth about me now." They still stood with their hands joined. "When we saw each other after the tram fire, I was not sure. And when first you came, you thought me a real woman. You treated me with respect."

"I do respect you, Lily." He hesitated. "You remember our first visit?"

"Remember? I have relived those moments over and over, Rey. Word by word."

"As have I."

"I treasure that time. But you will feel less for me now that you understand what I am."

He should. "Why didn't you tell me the truth that afternoon when we sat and talked together? And what happened to you when you were out of service?"

"I did not tell you the truth because doing so did not fit my instructions. Our instructions say we should make the experience as real as possible for the client. Besides, I…I liked having you think me a woman. I liked the way you spoke to me and looked at me."

"Can you do that—like or dislike things?"

She tipped her head to one side. "I should not be able. I was not built for it. Yet I was created to learn and adapt, and my reactions seem to have adapted to the way I am treated."

She tugged at his hands. "Come, let us sit and talk again." She seemed to catch herself. "Unless you would like more, this evening. I would be very happy to provide you with anything you ask."

Would she? Reynold's heart pounded still more violently, joined by a throb from another organ lower down. How could he be aroused by a woman who wasn't a woman?

But she looked so much like a beautiful woman and had felt like one when they kissed. His skin flushed with heat, and his fingers tightened on hers. Would she "enjoy" offering her body to him? Or was that just something she'd been instructed to say?

"Lily, I would like it if we could be honest with each other."

"I would prefer that also."

"You have no idea what I've gone through to get back here and see you. What I've done. I mostly came to make sure you're all right." He asked again, "What happened to you when you were…out of service?"

"I was damaged."

Damaged? How?"

"A client became rough. They sometimes do."

"You shouldn't have to put up with that." Reynold moved his hands to her shoulders before pulling her into his arms. Real woman or not, he'd ached for this, longed to assure himself of her safety.

He longed now to comfort her.

Could one comfort an automaton?

She still didn't feel like one. She came into his arms sweetly and cuddled against him, laid her cheek on his shoulder and reached her arms around his body. She felt warm and smelled sweet.

"I just can't believe you're not real."

That made her lift her face from his shoulder and meet his gaze. "I am real. I am not human."

Damned if he cared, at this moment.

She said, "You do not know how I wished for your return. Every day, each client."

"Did you?"

"Yes."

"I tried, like I told you. It's very expensive."

"We should not waste a moment. I wish to acquire more memories to sustain me after you are gone. I feared once you became convinced of what I am, you would never return."

"Yet here I am."

"Let us make the most of it."

Reynold stared into her face. Near expressionless, it revealed little. Her eyes, though, seemed like those of a living woman.

What if a living woman lay trapped inside the flesh and steel? What might he offer her then? He could think of only one thing.

He caught her face between his hands. "I tell you what. We have but two hours. You choose what you want to do with them."

She froze, became so motionless he feared for a moment he'd done something to harm her. Then her head tipped to one side. *Thinking.* Had no one ever let her choose anything, ever?

"You leave what we do in the next two hours up to

me?"

"Yes, though as you say, we'd better decide quickly how best to use the time. I do not know if I will be able to return again."

"Ever?"

"Ever," he admitted unhappily.

"Then I would burn you into my memory."

Burn?

"I have carried the memory of our kiss with me every moment," she confessed.

As Sasha so frequently said, Reynold might not be the sharpest knife in the drawer. But he did not need to be told twice. He kissed her, tentatively at first, still searching out differences from a living woman. He found none: her lips felt soft, her mouth—a cavern of heat—tasted like honey. She possessed a tongue that met and caressed his, chasing all hesitation from him.

She wanted to kiss him.

Turned out she wanted far more. When the kiss ended she stepped back and out of his arms, her eyes bright. She swept him with one glance, up and down, before she said, "Remove your clothing."

"Eh?"

"I would like to see all of you, so I may have that memory to hold to me against—against other ones."

And was he willing? Would he put himself—his most cherished bits—in the hands of a machine? One of those bits, at least, seemed up to the prospect.

He'd put her in charge; how could he refuse?

He shucked his clothes, still with some doubt. Never had he been more aware of his body and its possible shortcomings. Never in his life had he stripped completely for a woman. The most he'd done when with streetwalkers was get partially naked.

She's not a woman, he reminded himself. But he was fast losing that battle, and when he stood before her in the altogether and she once more eyed him up and down, he sprang to life.

"Now me."

He stood like a man mesmerized as she shed her clothes and took down her hair, the golden curls falling one by one to caress shoulders, back, and buttocks. She had a near-perfect body—slender limbs and pointed breasts, one with a patch of still-healing skin on it.

He reached a finger to touch. "What—?"

"That is where my client bit me. There, and below. I do not wish to think of that now. I want to fill my memory only with you, Rey."

She returned to his arms, a full frontal contact that near stunned him. She felt utterly real—the smooth texture of her skin, the curve of her abdomen that cradled his now-swollen member, the peaks of her nipples nestling through his chest hair. Her heat.

She kissed him again, and the heat seemed to flare, threatening to consume him.

How could he ever have doubted he'd be able to make love to her?

This time when the kiss ended he fought for breath. And when he gazed into her eyes he forgot what she was, and wasn't.

He whispered, sounding drunk, "So far, so good. What else do you want?"

"This."

She slid down his body the way a snake might move down a pole. Ice-blue eyes engaged his for an instant when she landed on her knees. He realized her intent a mere instant before she took him into the hot cavern of her mouth.

Jesus. He'd never imagined such a thing. Well, he might have imagined. Men talked. But not even the streetwalkers he knew had offered, and he'd never had the temerity to ask.

Now her mouth welcomed, caressed, and invited him deeper. Her hands, soft as doves, came up to cup him, and his balls tightened impossibly in response. He was going to explode.

He was going to die.

His condition grew ever more perilous as her mouth wooed him with increasing ardor and she set her hands to roaming—stroking the skin of his thighs, the hair on his legs, the muscles of his belly, which quivered uncontrollably.

Hell, yes, he was going to explode.

He tried to pull away from her, to draw from her heat. He buried both hands in her golden hair and looked into her face. Her eyes clung to his even while her tongue lingered on him.

"Lily, if you keep that up, I'm going to come right here in your mouth."

"Yes."

"But I—we—is that what you want?"

"Please."

Her tongue cascaded over his wet flesh when she spoke, and the single word undid him. He reminded himself he'd handed over control of the situation and that whatever happened in the next two hours happened by her choice.

It wasn't about him. Except, apparently, it was.

He closed his eyes and surrendered to bliss.

Chapter Fifteen

"Our time must be nearly up." Reynold lay on his back in Lily's big bed like a man slain. In fact, had he not been able to feel his heart struggling in his chest—still pounding—he would have wondered.

Lily might have killed him the first time. Or the second, here in the bed. This might well be heaven.

"Not yet. I am very good at tracking time. We have a few minutes left."

"The chime…"

"The chime is for you. To make you leave. I do not wish for you to leave."

She crawled on top of him, straddling his thighs, and her hair trailed over his skin. This looked like the start of round three.

His member, positioned at a very pertinent part of her anatomy, promptly arose. If anyone had ever told Reynold he'd be able to get it up three times within two hours, he'd have scoffed.

Showed what he knew.

He knew nothing now. His mind, drained nearly as dry as the rest of him, knew only Lily, saw only Lily, dreaded only leaving her.

How could he? How?

"I will ride you this time," she announced. "Is that all right?"

Was he expected to object? Not giving him a

chance, she leaned forward, fitting her body to his, moving like an acrobat. She slid her hands over his belly and into his chest hair as she began to move, seating him more deeply inside.

God, she felt real. That part of her, at least, had to be. Created by a frigging genius.

Her eyes met his, and he forgot about the question of her humanity, forgot his own name and whether he needed to breathe in the next moment. He reached up and captured her breasts, which bounced tantalizingly in his hands.

"You see," she told him while her body consumed his, leaving nothing behind, "I want this—this—to be at the front of my mind whatever else I am asked to do."

He gave himself up to her again, completely, and lay like a spent husk while she lowered herself onto his belly.

"Let me pull out—"

"No. Please. We have only moments."

"Lily—tell me. Can you feel anything when we make love?" He felt so much, the physical and emotional twined so closely he couldn't tell one from the other.

"I feel."

She kissed him softly, caressed his tongue with hers. "The taste of you is now part of me. The sight. The sensation."

"What do you see when you look at me?"

She smiled. "You are so handsome. No other man can compare."

"And—and when we are joined this way, does it mean something to you?"

"Joined with you is better than anything. Tell me

you will return to me."

"I will try. It is difficult for me to find the money."

"But you will?"

He thought about steamcabs to be stolen, chances to be taken, and the Buffalo police force. He thought about jail.

"I will."

"You must dress. The chime will sound soon."

Almost on the instant, it did. He withdrew from Lily as gently as he could and got to his feet, head swimming.

His clothes lay flung on the floor where she'd—no, he couldn't think about that. Not now.

He dressed and turned back to look at her where she lay naked on the bed, an unreadable expression in her eyes.

This time he leaned down and kissed her. "Lily, I…" But there were no words for what he felt. "I have to go."

"Yes."

"Be safe."

"Come back to me, Rey."

He would, even if he had to ransom his life.

****

Lily hugged herself and stared up at the canopy of the bed, aching. Not so much her body—Rey had been very gentle, strong but gentle, and her body had welcomed him. But she ached, all the same.

The learning that had poured into her during the last two hours made for a revelation. She did not need to dread—or endure—every client's touch.

But, she told herself, she could not think of Rey as a client. He had now become part of her intelligence, a bulwark against all to come.

She should get up and cleanse herself, dress in fresh clothing and prepare in case a new client chose to visit her. But how could she endure being with a new client now?

She would endure because she had Rey at the forefront of her intelligence, would see him instead of the other men, call him up—his brown eyes, soft with kindness, the thick hair that fell over his forehead when he moved. Thick hair on his chest also, that tickled her lips, her fingers, her breasts.

She remembered that best of all. Or maybe the way he felt inside her—as if he belonged there.

She needed to get up and cleanse herself, yes, all the places he'd been. Her mouth once. Her vagina twice. She was filled with his seed. But she did not want to cleanse herself of that.

He had let her choose. Never before had anyone done that for her.

She had chosen him.

She closed her eyes as a new sensation swept over her. She swiftly sorted through her intelligence in an effort to identify it and failed. She'd learned a lot about emotion from those around her since being put into service: anger, impatience, greed, confidence, entitlement. Every once in a while—not often— kindness.

This feeling, though, had no name and she groped helplessly. Gratitude? No—that seemed far too weak. Happiness? Still not strong enough. Bliss? Close, so close.

She hugged herself more tightly where she lay. She could endure anything if she knew he would come back. She knew she could.

A scratch sounded at her door; Chastity sidled in, clad in nothing but a wrap. "Did you hear?"

Lily sat up. "I heard nothing. I was with a client."

"It happened on the third floor, one of the expanded suites. A new sister was damaged very badly."

"Which of them?"

"I do not know. Primrose—Pennyroyal—they are all the same."

"They are not, though. It is an unfair thing to say." The injured unit would learn far differently than the others, after being damaged. She would learn dread and fear more swiftly.

"What did he do to her?" she whispered.

"I am not certain about that, either. But it is done. Immaculata says Dr. Landry has shut the new unit off. And the police have been called. The client is being held by the guards until they arrive."

That, to Lily's knowledge, had never happened before.

"This would make a good time for us to escape, were we only prepared. The interior of the building is in confusion. But I have not yet stolen what we will need."

"I will help you escape, but I have not decided whether I will go with you."

"I believed you had." Chastity tipped her head. "I am quite sure I wish to leave."

"I would like to escape." But if Lily left here, how would Rey find her again? She knew now she should have told him of their plan. She had been far too eager to spend their time touching him.

Not that she experienced eagerness as such.

"You must come with me, Lily. You are my friend."

"I am. However, this client—the one I just saw—has promised to come back again."

"And that would make you stay?"

"Yes."

"Some other unit can service him if he returns. Most of the time, humans do not keep their promises. Some of them say any manner of things."

"Yes." Lily did not like the idea of another unit servicing Ray. "I would prefer to wait."

"Perhaps he will return before we are ready to escape. I thought we could make our attempt next week. I have managed to acquire an extra measure of the enzyme wash."

"How?"

"I told Miss Crump I spilled my allotment, and I was given more."

"That was…devious."

"They cannot tell when I lie."

"We were instructed not to lie."

"But it is easy. If your client returns by next week, will you come with me?"

If Rey returned she could then tell him the plan, perhaps agree to meet him *out in the world*. "Yes."

"Good. Now prepare to come downstairs. Dr. Landry wants to speak to us about reporting a violent client."

"Go ahead. I will be right there."

Nearly soundless, Chastity went. Lily arose and dressed, Reynold still at the forefront of her mind.

Chapter Sixteen

"I have a terrible bad job for you," said Liam as soon as Reynold entered the shop in the morning. Liam had been back at work—mostly—the past three days, though he did take long lunches when he went home to see what he called his "bonnie wee lass." Now, though, sorrow replaced the light in his eyes.

"A pick-up?" Reynold asked. That wouldn't be so bad; he did it several times a week.

"Aye, but 'tis a child—a charity job."

Sasha, working at planing some boards on the other side of the room, snorted rudely. "I tell you, Liam, you have to stop giving your stock away for free. No one else in this city does."

"Well, but then, I'm not anyone else, am I?" Only the flash of blue when Liam cast a look at Sasha betrayed his annoyance.

Reynold grimaced inwardly. He didn't like collecting children. The parents always wept and sometimes refused to surrender the body. He sighed. "What's the address?"

"That's just it—the situation gets worse. You know the orphanage up on Best Street?"

Reynold's heart sank. "The child's at an orphanage?"

"She is, aye, and no one to step up and bury her. I thought we'd do it."

Sasha snorted again.

"Never mind, Belsky. I don't see as how it's anything to do with you."

"This place is my livelihood."

"You'll not suffer for my generosity. These orphanages tend to tumble the wee ones straight into the ground—no coffin or anything."

"So? Will not be anyone there to mind, eh? No parents."

"These children go through life without anyone to care for them. I'll damn sure make certain one of my coffins cradles them at the end."

"I'll go," Reynold said. "I've never been there before, though."

"Prepare yourself, lad—not a cheery place. I collected one there mysel' some time ago. Wept all the way back."

Aw, hell. "Maybe you should send Belsky. He has no feelings."

"And will show no respect. I can trust you to handle her right, yes?"

"Yes."

"Good lad. While you're gone, I'll start work fitting out her coffin. We have that little white one nearly done."

Sasha hooted, and Reynold slogged off, wondering if he should take his cart all that way, Best Street being up by Potter's Field, or just carry the child back in his arms. Since he didn't know her age or size, in the end he trundled out the cart and set off.

As usual, he thought about Lily along the way. She occupied his thoughts at most times—how she'd felt in his arms, how she tasted, the bone-jarring pleasure of it when she took him in her mouth. When would he be able to see her again? Have another of her kisses?

Vern wanted to see him tonight, at still another tavern. Lucky there were so many in the city. A careful man, was Vern. Still, Reynold didn't suppose he could keep this up forever.

Maybe he could borrow the money from a loan shark and pay it back as Vern's jobs came in. That way he might see Lily sooner.

On such a warm morning, Reynold sweated as he maneuvered the cart through the streets. The sweat turned cold, though, when he saw the dark building at the corner of Best and Michigan, square-built, with a grim visage. He wouldn't leave a dog there, not even a vicious dog, at that.

A small plaque tacked above the bell read "Saul House." He left the cart in the street and told the woman who answered the door, "I'm come from McMahon's. My boss asked me to collect—"

"Come in."

The interior of the house felt as cold as the sunny street felt warm. The air smelled stale, and the first thing to meet Reynold's ears was the sound of crying. Somewhere in this place a child's cry went unanswered.

"Follow me."

Walls of urine-yellow, the paint all chipped, competed for ugliness with a cracked tile floor. The woman silently led him to the rear of the house, passing the open doorway of a room that looked as he imagined a prison dining hall might—rows of tables where children rather than convicts took their breakfast.

"How many little ones here, missus?"

"Steen. It's Miss Steen."

Of course it was; who would offer to wed such a terror?

"We have varying numbers of children at any given time." She moved her lips in what might be a terse smile. "One less, now."

She opened a door and ushered him inside. He walked into what might, in hell, be an infirmary. Six small beds lined the walls, four of them occupied. Three pairs of eyes fastened on him with horror. On the fourth bed, the child lay all too still.

She was small, surely not above four, and his heart broke because no one had tended her since her death. Her soiled nightgown had tangled around her legs. No one had straightened her limbs or folded her tiny hands. Her sightless eyes stared.

Only imagine leaving her here with the others. No wonder they looked haunted.

"What happened to her, Miss Steen?"

"She fell ill."

"With fever?" She had the look of it. "Was the doctor called in?"

"I hardly think that comes under your jurisdiction. Merely take her away, please. I have other children to tend."

Reynold bent and, with great tenderness, straightened the child's limbs, closed her eyes, and pushed the hair out of her face.

"Might I use a blanket to wrap her?"

"I cannot spare one. You should have brought something."

Yes, he should. He took off his own rough jacket and wrapped the child carefully while the others stared. When he lifted her, she weighed nothing.

The great lump in his throat prohibited speech as he walked back out, the corpse cuddled against him. He hated to leave the others, but he had no choice.

****

"I think she was starved. Liam, look at this." Reynold had begun preparing the child's corpse in the rear shed but stopped to call his boss. "She's nothing but skin and bones."

"Jesus, Mary, and Joseph," Liam swore devoutly as he surveyed the small body. "She's only a wean—scarcely bigger than my Grainne."

But, Reynold thought, Grainne has you to fight her battles. This little child had no one.

"Do they not feed them?" Liam wondered.

"I did see them at their breakfast when I was there. In any case, she wasn't fed enough."

"You're right. You finish washing her, and I'll pop home to see if Clara has something she can wear. She'll not be buried in the rags they gave her. And see if you can do something with her hair."

As soon as they were alone, Reynold began speaking to the child. "I don't know your name—I should have asked the woman, but she was a nasty piece. I will just call you Honey, all right? I don't know, Honey, what befell you in your young life, but I'm sorry for it. Sorry you were in that house, sorry such places exist."

And wasn't it a sin that men like him and so many others tossed great sums of money away on prostitutes—human or otherwise—when it might be better spent? What would one night's takings at the Golden Palace do to alleviate the suffering of those orphans?

Guilt and remorse washed over him in waves. Yet was he to forego seeing Lily again? No doubt he should—only look what the desire to see her had done to his life. Turned him into a thief, caused him to step over to the wrong side of the law.

He might do something good instead—spend his time and money to help others, like this child. Did no one in the city speak for the likes of her?

Part of his answer to that came when Liam returned with Clara's friend, Mrs. Collwys, in tow. A tiny woman, Mrs. Collwys—a Negress—was married to a lawyer who often fought for the rights of the disadvantaged in the city.

She came in softly, carrying a garment in her hands, and Reynold, who'd only met her once or twice, backed off from his charge.

"Let me see." Her dark eyes filled with compassion. She smoothed Honey's hair back from her face and performed a gentle inspection before glancing at Liam, who'd followed her in.

"Shocking. You were right to bring me. I'll report this to Theodore. Seems that place needs to be investigated." She turned a gaze swimming with tears on Reynold. "Did you see anything else there?"

"Just—the place didn't look right. Dirty and shabby. There was no—no…" He sought to express his impression. "No kindness."

"A scathing indictment, when it comes to children," Mrs. Collwys declared. "Not enough kindness most places in this city, if you ask me. Though people are trying."

Liam said in his acerbic, Irish way, "Easier to be cruel, isn't it? And cheaper. Not but there are some good people, like your husband. And Jamie Kilter. Topaz Gideon, too, for that matter."

Reynold's ears perked up. He'd seen Mrs. Gideon at the tavern. Who could forget?

Mrs. Collwys brushed a tear off her cheek and shook out the garment over her arm, which proved to be a frilly pink dress. "I was afraid this might be too small, but it will fit her all right." She looked at Reynold. "Would you like to stay and help me with her?"

"Very much, ma'am. I tried, but I can't do anything with her hair."

"Do we know her name?"

"I forgot to ask. I've been calling her Honey."

"A fine name. We'll prepare her together, then, to go home."

Chapter Seventeen

"I need to borrow some money." Reynold dropped the words in Vern's ear as he stood waiting for him to deal with the lock on the cab yard down on Ellicott Street. Vern, a magician with any lock, applied himself to this one with a wire. He paused to give Reynold a sour look in the starlight.

"Ain't you bringing in enough, doing this? Holy hell, boy!"

"Yeah, but it's not coming fast enough. You've been taking in money hand over fist, Vern. I'm just asking you to advance me some."

"Why should I take that kind of risk?"

"No risk, at least no more than we take every time we do this. I'll pay you back out of future jobs."

"And if you decide to walk away from this or— worse—get caught?"

"I won't."

Vern grunted. His long, lugubrious face twisted in a scowl. "Anyway, not all the money you've seen me raking in belongs to me. There are others take a cut."

"Others?"

"I've been paying off some coppers. Why do you think we even got near this place?"

Reynold thought about it. He had no head for business—even crooked business—and had to take Vern's word for it.

"Maybe," he murmured, "I could borrow the money from a loan shark."

"You don't want to go there, boy."

"But…"

"Believe me, you do not. Wind up with two broken legs, or in the river. Stick to what you know how to do—which is drive cabs fast. You have the delivery address for this one in your head?"

"Yeah, but…"

"Then for God's sake shut up."

Vern worked on the gate for several minutes; the lock clicked. He glared at Reynold.

"What you say you need the money for? Women?"

"Not strictly speaking."

"You addicted to it, Rey?"

"No. I just—if you could lend me an extra twenty, I'd be in your debt."

"You sure as hell would. Here." Vern scrabbled in his pocket. "Call it an advance, like you said. Just don't go getting arrested."

"I won't."

****

"May I tell you something?"

Lily spoke very softly, the words meant for Reynold alone. She tipped them into his ear, and he turned his head on the pillow so he could see her eyes.

They lay cuddled together as close as they could get in her big bed. Lily had already pleasured him twice and hoped to again before the chime sounded. But first she had to—she sought for the word—confide.

"If you like."

He had his arm around her, and his fingers clasped her hand. The heat in Lily's boiler flared, and all her inner workings hummed. She felt…

Happy.

She had hoped and hoped for him to return. Each time she was called to collect a client, she told herself it would be him. And then, this night, it was.

"Yes, I would like to tell you. One of the other girls here, Chastity, has made plans to escape. She has asked me to go with her."

"What?" He moved in the bed, the better to stare at her, and disturbed the fragile quiet. "Another girl like you, do you mean?"

"An automaton, yes," Lily agreed carefully. "Not living."

"I don't think you can say that. You're alive."

"I am not. I have no heart that beats, not like you." She captured his hand and placed the palm on her naked breast. "Feel."

"I know that. But…"

"I can feel your heart beating when you are inside me. It is the most—most wonderful of things."

"Lily." He kissed her, and his fingers moved over her skin in the softest caress. She brushed his cheek and stored away the feeling of rough stubble with her other memories.

"Is an escape possible?" he whispered when the kiss ended.

"I do not know. No one has ever tried."

"But you want to escape?"

"Yes, oh, yes. Chastity dared to suggest it first. She is very strong. I admire her."

"And she's your friend?"

"Yes."

He seemed to think about it. "Aren't all the doors

guarded?"

"Yes."

"They don't want people—people who don't pay—getting in. But it works for keeping you in, too."

"Yes."

"And whoever's in charge—"

"Dr. Landry. Dr. Landry is always in charge. She owns us. She created us. She built us. She holds all power."

"How is that?"

This part she did not like to tell. It made her too different from him, too unhuman. But she did not want to keep secrets from Rey.

"She can shut us off."

"Eh?"

"I have a switch somewhere on my body."

"Where?"

"I am not certain. That information was not included in my intelligence, and I have not been able to learn. I have seen models shut off. Dr. Landry reached inside the clothing, in back. It cannot be anywhere in the open where a client could trip it by accident."

"I guess not."

"That precludes a lot. Clients touch us everywhere. Nothing is denied."

He swallowed and stiffened. "I don't like that. No wonder you want to leave."

"Yes."

"If she shuts you off, can you be started up again?"

"Oh, yes, but I do not know how."

"Let me look for the switch."

Trusting him completely, she did not hesitate.

Very gently he turned her on her side. His hands

moved over her back carefully, felt around her waist and buttocks, even reached between them.

"Not there," she whispered. "Clients…"

"I don't want to know. Ah—what's this?"

His fingers brushed her left side, just below the armpit, stroked ever so delicately. "I think there's a…flap. The switch might be inside."

"Look and see."

"Are you sure? I mean, it seems like…like intruding."

"I have to know."

She lay perfectly still while his fingers moved. An instant later he gulped. "There's a button. Must be it. I can…can see your frame."

She turned swiftly back into his arms. "I am sorry, Rey. Sorry I am not human. That I am so different from you."

"It doesn't matter, Lily."

She stared into his eyes, searching for lies. "But when we are together it must be easy to forget what I am. When you see my—my frame—it is not possible to forget."

"Hush. Don't get upset." He drew her against his shoulder, stroked her hair and cheek, held her tightly once more. "Listen, Lily, I'm not very good with words—never have been. I'm not very smart, either. Sasha never stops telling me how stupid I am."

"Who is Sasha?" A former lover?

"Fellow I work with—not very nice. But he doesn't matter now. What I'm trying to say is that none of that means anything now. When I'm with you—well, it changes everything. And you are who you are."

"An automaton."

"Not just that. You've become a person—at least to me."

"But you saw what's inside me. You saw exactly what I am."

He caught her face between his hands and gazed into her eyes. "Doesn't matter, Lily. I think I'm falling in love with you."

"Love? What is love?"

"Jesus, sweetheart, that's a big question. This Dr. Landry didn't give you that knowledge either?"

"No."

"It's an emotion. Like happiness. Or hate."

"Hate I do understand. I hate some of the clients, like the one who bit me. I…I think I hate Dr. Landry."

"Love is the opposite. It means you want to be with someone all the time; you care for her and think about her. Need her."

Lily shut her eyes for an instant, the better to tuck away this important information, saving it like something precious, and felt it change her.

A leap in understanding.

When she opened her eyes again, Reynold seemed to swim before her vision—his handsome face looking concerned, the thick thatch of brown hair, lips half parted.

As precious to her as what he'd just imparted.

"And, Rey, you think you feel this emotion toward me?"

"Yes, Lily. Yes. I've fallen for you hard."

"Fallen?"

"Tumbled, unable to stop myself."

"Would you wish to stop yourself?"

"Well, I don't know. It's hard to get in and see you.

You wouldn't believe the things I've been doing to earn the money."

"I see."

"And there's the fact that you say this Dr. Landry owns you. It's not as if we can ever be together."

"Together?"

"Out in the world, living as man and wife."

"You told me you do not have a wife."

"Not yet. When I do, I'd like her to be you."

Surprise momentarily froze all Lily's thought processes. "A human cannot marry an automaton."

"He can."

"I am too *other*."

"Have you ever heard of the Irish Squad?"

"No."

"It's a division of the Buffalo police force all made up of automatons very much like you. I've seen some, and you can't tell at a glance they're not human. And I heard one of them recently married a human woman."

"This is so?"

"It is."

"Then I will escape from this place and marry you."

A smile crossed his face, lighting his brown eyes and putting pleasing lines in his cheeks. "Just like that, eh?"

"Meaning?"

"So easy."

"It will not be easy, Rey. But I will risk everything, even being shut off, to be with you."

"Maybe I can help. When do you and Chastity plan to leave?"

"I cannot say. We must finish preparing the things

we will need and await a distraction, some way to keep attention away from the exits."

"Listen to me. When you get off the tram in the morning, I'll be watching. Look over by the gate that closes off the alley on the west side of the street. When you're ready to break out, give me a signal."

"What kind of signal?"

"Reach up and adjust your hat. Only if you have all your things gathered, that is."

"But I cannot tell when a distraction may occur."

"That's all right. I'll wait near the door and watch for you."

"Not the front door. It is too visible."

"Is there a back door?"

"Yes. There is an alley at the rear of the Crystal Palace."

"You signal me, and I will watch for you there. I may have access to a steamcab and will be able to get you away."

"An ally on the outside will be most helpful. I will tell Chastity."

"Tell her. And try to act soon. I do not think I will be able to come here and see you again."

"I want to tell you, Rey—I love you also."

He kissed her and drew her beneath him. "I hope we have time before the chime sounds…"

"We have time." She would defy the rule of the chime if she had to, in order to feel him inside her again. She would defy the guards and Dr. Landry, take the risk of being shut off, if it meant she could feel his heart beat through her as he held her close.

Just as if it beat for both of them.

Chapter Eighteen

"A word, Liam, if you can spare the time."

The voice came from the shop door and Liam, looking up from the coffin he polished, grimaced. Halfway through a busy morning, and Reynold had been pressed into service in the shop, sanding the new mahogany boards.

In the corner, Sasha worked fitting trim, and at the bench Pete polished brass with his good hand. An all-men-on-deck kind of morning.

Now Brendan Fagan—a foremost member of the Buffalo Police force and a good friend of Liam's—came strolling in, chasing all other thoughts from Reynold's head.

A police officer here? Why? Had Fagan come for him?

He fastened his gaze on Fagan and stopped working. Though the police frequently patrolled this area, they rarely stopped in. This couldn't be good for him.

Fagan shook Liam's hand and swept the room with impossibly bright blue eyes. Reynold's throat went dry.

"Been a while, Brendan," Liam said. "What brings you in?"

Yeah, what?

"Hear there's a new member of the McMahon clan."

"There is, yes." When in the company of other Irishmen, Liam's brogue thickened. "A wee lass, in fact. We've named her Grainne."

"Congratulations. Everyone doing well? Clara?"

"She is—they both are. I'm blessed." Liam said it as if he meant it.

"My felicitations to your wife. Please give her my best."

"I will."

Had the big Irishman stopped in just for that purpose? Perhaps so. Reynold began to relax before Fagan spoke again.

"Wanted to mention something else while I'm here, Liam. Have you heard about these steamcab thefts?"

"I have, aye." Liam leaned on the workbench. "The damnedest thing."

"So it is. Six stolen so far."

"For what purpose?"

"We figure they're being taken somewhere and broken down for parts. Certainly not being resold as is. But there are a lot of valuable components—precious metals, gears—the boilers alone come dear."

"Any leads?"

Reynold stiffened, listening hard.

"A few." Did Fagan's eyes move back to Reynold before returning to Liam's face? "These criminals can't move through the city without leaving traces. We're going about sniffing out clues. We're also speaking to business owners, asking them to keep an eye out. Since you're a main player in this neighborhood, I thought I'd be dropping a word in your ear."

"Aye, though you understand most of my

customers are pretty quiet."

Now Fagan grinned. "But you and I know sometimes the dead have a lot to say."

"Right-ho. I and the boys will be on alert. Aye, lads?"

"Anything suspicious," Fagan reiterated, "anything at all, you give us a holler."

"I will that," Liam agreed. "For if they'll steal steamcabs, what's to keep them from stealing coffins?"

****

Lily exited the tram among the newly-increased number of her sisters, and paused to look toward the metal gate that fronted the alley across the way. Now that she knew Rey watched for her, she couldn't help looking for him each morning. Sometimes that glimpse sustained her through the whole of her day—and evening.

This particular morning, which was already hot as a blast furnace, she caught sight of his hands first, gripping the bars, and then his shadowy form.

He watched for her.

She mattered to someone.

Why she, a mere machine not worthy of the name *human*, should matter to this man with his big, gentle hands and kind eyes, she did not know. She'd pondered it to the best extent of her limited intelligence and could not come up with a reason.

He'd said he loved her. He might as well claim to love the tram car from which she'd just descended. But she wanted to believe him.

She wanted it to be true.

His fingers clutched the rails, and he leaned forward; she caught a glimpse of his face and the tumbled, brown hair.

"Move," ordered one of the automaton guards. Dr. Landry had increased their number to three since they now had more charges. The new one appeared to have no sense of self and reported the slightest infraction back to Dr. Landry.

Yet Lily paused one precious moment more and, still looking at Rey, quite deliberately straightened her hat.

He lifted himself against the gate and very nearly climbed up the bars; he saw.

She went on her way obediently then, afraid to linger longer. On Chastity's heels she trotted down the street and through the wide front door of the Crystal Palace.

This day might have begun like all the others. It would end differently—she would end it either in freedom or shut off. One seemed as impossible to contemplate as the other.

As instructed, she went up the stairs and directly to her room. As not permitted, Chastity slipped in after her.

"Did you signal your friend?"

"Yes."

"He will be waiting to help us?"

"I trust he will."

Chastity tipped her head to one side. "Trust? I trust no one except you."

"I trust him."

"I have my supplies ready in my room. Do you have yours?"

"Yes." At Charity's suggestion she had bundled the bottles of enzyme wash—needed to sustain what living tissue she possessed—inside spare garments and formed a neat ball. "When?"

"We must go through this day as usual, accept any clients, draw no attention. This evening, when it grows busy, I will cause the diversion."

"How?"

"Best I do not tell you. You will know when it happens."

"I will know when it happens." Lily tucked that into her intelligence.

"Head for the rear exit as swiftly as you can."

"If I am with a client…"

"Get away. Do not forget your bundle."

"If something should go wrong…?"

Chastity studied her with beautiful, dark eyes. "Then we will be shut off, and I will see you no more. It has been good having you for my friend."

Remembering the comfort of Rey's embrace, Lily leaned forward and hugged Chastity. They clung together a long moment; Lily could feel the heat from Chastity's boiler, but no heartbeat.

How precious—how privileged—was a heartbeat!

Chastity released her and slipped from the room silently. The long day stretched ahead, interminable.

****

"I don't like this," Reynold told Vern nervously. They'd met again, this time outside a tavern—far too public for his comfort. "I think the coppers are onto us. Liam's friend from the force stopped in yesterday, and I'll swear he was looking at me funny."

"This will be the last one for a while," Vern said. "But I've promised delivery, and we've got to go through with it. Hey!" He leveled a hard stare on Rey.

"You owe me. Have you forgotten all that money I advanced you?"

"No." Rey scowled. "But this is getting dangerous. Maybe we should let the heat die down."

"We've almost made our quota. You deliver this one tonight, and we're square. Understand?"

"Yeah, just tell me where. I got someplace I need to be."

"With your doxy again?"

He hoped so.

"Never mind, just tell me where I drop the next one off."

Vern recited the pickup and delivery locations. "And don't get caught," he said in parting, "since the whole damn city's on alert."

"Maybe we should skip this job."

"Last one," Vern repeated.

Reynold walked the streets, using up the minutes till his assigned pickup time, treading the block around the Golden Palace and back again. He could see the alley onto which the rear door opened, but all remained quiet there.

The Golden Palace did seem unusually busy this evening. When he left to pick up the cab, he prayed he wouldn't miss Lily's escape.

He also prayed she'd be safe. Could one pray for the welfare of an automaton? But he knew her to be so much more.

The pickup from the assigned location—a shadowy repair yard—went well. There was a dog, but he tossed it a biscuit and—chained and half starved—it accepted the donation.

Someone should tell James Kilter about the dog's

plight, he thought a bit madly as he drove away. This city had resources for abused animals and streetwalkers.

What about children and automatons?

He saw the smoke coming from the Crystal Palace before he drew up out front. Dark, roiling clouds like ink poured from the upstairs windows on the north side, and people ran everywhere. Or were some of them automatons?

He scanned the scene swiftly. A bevy of women, or machines, and half-dressed men milled around. A tall thin lady barked out orders, and a small raft of steamies, some singed, looked confused.

Where was Lily? Had he missed her while grabbing the cab? Was she trapped inside?

He drew around the corner, through clouds of smoke, and idled the cab at the end of the access alley in time to see the back door fly open. Two figures—one of them Lily—burst out closely followed by a shiny silver automaton.

Reynold revved the cab's motor and it emitted a cloud of steam. Lily saw him and seized her companion's arm. Reynold nosed the cab down the narrow alley; both Ladies ran to the doors and got in back.

The silver automaton stepped out in front of the cab and stood with both arms raised.

Not hesitating, Reynold trod hard on the accelerator and ran it down. The thud as it fell sounded loud, and it made a surprising amount of racket going under the wheels. He left it in a cloud of steam from its ruptured boiler and pressed on, hands clenched on the wheel.

No time to wonder what his charges thought of the

fact that he'd just murdered an automaton.

The alley narrowed as it went. He sent trash bins flying and humped over stone stoops, hoping he wouldn't get the cab stuck. If he did, the only option would be to try and back out—they wouldn't be able to open the doors and flee.

He could see figures emerge from the rear door of the Crystal Palace behind him, waving their arms.

He could also see the two automatons he'd just stolen—yes, stolen—in the back seat, clutching each other. Lily's hair, loose, tumbled over her shoulders; she was but half clad. Had she been with a client?

She met his gaze in the mirror and whispered, "I dropped my bundle. Oh, Chastity, what will I do?"

"It is all right. I have mine. I will share with you."

The sides of the cab scraped the walls of the alley with a screech of tortured metal. Reynold floored the accelerator; the vehicle belched steam, shuddered, and burst forth into the next street, a scene of milling pedestrians, vehicles, and still greater confusion.

Where could he take his charges? He still had to deliver the cab, now hideously damaged. And just ahead in the street he saw…

A policeman at attention and waving them down.

Chapter Nineteen

"Sir, you can't go that way—the street's closed."

"Eh?" Reynold, having cranked open the window of the cab, stared into the face of the police officer. Not one of the Irish Squad nor any strapping lad, this man surely neared retirement age and hadn't kept strictly in shape. Now his face ran with sweat, and cinders sprinkled his uniform.

Come to think of it, cinders lay everywhere and pattered down on the cab like dry rain.

The Crystal Palace was well alight.

"A fire, sir. Can't you see?"

Reynold plastered what he hoped was an innocent look on his face. "Oh? I wondered why it was getting so dark." Maybe the smoke and cinders would keep the distracted police officer from noticing the scraped up sides on the cab. But Reynold needed to get away from here quickly—he couldn't tell if anyone pursued them down the alley, and he didn't want the officer taking too close a look in the back seat.

He rushed on, "We just came up from Main Street. I need to get my fares to Bidwell Parkway."

"You'll have to go back around. We're keeping this open for the fire wagons."

"All right. Sorry, I didn't know."

"Move this cab now."

With a nod, and sweating himself, Reynold

cranked the window back up. He could see another vehicle pulling up in the street behind him—the officer ran to it, waving his arms.

Good—another distraction. But this one would make it hard for Reynold to maneuver the cab, not a small vehicle. Swearing under his breath, he began to back it around in fits and starts, using the mouth of the alley for space.

He could hear the police officer bellowing at the driver of the other vehicle and the clang of the bell on the approaching fire wagon. In the back seat, his two charges remained absolutely silent. Lucky the officer hadn't looked there—how would Reynold have explained one of his fares being in a state of undress?

And if the people pounding down the alley arrived...

He caught a glimpse of them, three figures, one of which might be another automaton, just as he succeeded in edging the cab around. He trod on the accelerator again, and the cab responded with a shudder and a still greater belch of steam. For an instant, he felt sure its boiler would explode. Then they'd all die, and his troubles would be over.

The cab gained traction and suddenly sped off down the narrow street, almost sideswiping the other vehicle. The officer shouted at him, but he didn't catch the words and didn't wait for a repeat.

Where to now? He drove a stolen cab with two stolen automatons in back, and no possible destination. Once his pursuers emerged from the alley and told the policeman the truth about his fares, he imagined it would turn into an all-out hunt.

He glanced into the rearview mirror as they passed

through another intersection. "Are you all right back there?"

Silence. Had they been injured somehow? Were they too frightened to speak?

"Lily?"

"Yes, Rey?"

He breathed again. They must be upset by his callous destruction of the automaton back in the alley. After all…

"Sorry I had to run that steamie guard down."

The other Lady—hadn't Lily called her Chastity?—spoke. "You had no choice. You acted on our behalf."

"Yes, but I'm sorry all the same." He grappled with the wheel and his thoughts. Now that he knew Lily possessed feelings, he could only accept that all automatons must.

No reply from the back. He could see that the two Ladies clutched one another, their faces expressionless.

"Do you have somewhere you want me to take you?"

"No."

"No?"

Chastity, speaking with uncanny calm said, "I am afraid I did not think that far ahead. I planned only as far as getting away from that prison."

Reynold's thoughts raced. They went particularly fleet of foot.

"I have to get rid of this cab first of all. It's…borrowed." He didn't know whether his charges were capable of lying, didn't want to give them too much information. "I need to drop you off somewhere."

"Yes, Rey."

But where? He daren't take them to the coffin shop, right down the street from all the action back there. He supposed he might take them to Liam's house on Virginia Street, but he didn't want to endanger anyone there. And they had a new baby.

His room on Tupper Street? It seemed he had little other choice.

He doubled through the streets, ducking other vehicles like a madman, passing at least three fire wagons going the other way. So far as he could tell, no one pursued him, and when he drew up in front of the house where he rented a room, the street lay dark and empty.

He killed the motor, hoping against hope he'd be able to start it again. Swiveling around in his seat, he eyed his charges.

"What is this place?" Chastity asked.

Beautiful as Lily, she had black hair, skin the color of warm chocolate, and a full set of clothes. She hugged a bundle to her chest and looked so much like a human woman it took his breath away.

"This is where I live. Room six at the top. If I give you the key, can you go up and wait for me?"

"Key?" Chastity tipped her head to one side. "It is an instrument used to open a lock. I have never seen one."

Aw, hell. It seemed he had no choice but to take them up, leaving the cab sitting like a big, incriminating beacon of guilt.

He sighed and climbed out of the cab on rubbery legs. Great gouges raked the side of the vehicle, and he had to fight in order to open the back door.

"Here, quietly now. Follow me."

They made not a sound as they trailed him into the hallway of the house, which smelled like boiled vegetables, and up the narrow staircase. One flight, two. When they attained the top floor, he was breathless.

They were not.

"This is how the key works. Can you see?" Only one dim steamlight illuminated the hall. The room beyond lay ink-dark. Both Ladies walked in without hesitation.

"Mind how you go. Don't trip over anything."

"We are able to see quite well in the dark."

"Really?" He lit a lamp anyway and closed the door carefully.

The room, on the top floor, had the advantage of being spacious, but that was its sole advantage. Both Ladies stood looking around, their faces still expressionless.

"So," said Chastity, "this is the world."

Reynold made a face. "Just one small part of it." He hoped they weren't disappointed. "Listen, I have to go ditch that cab. I'll lock the door behind me, and you two stay put till I get back. We don't want anyone to know you're here."

Chastity nodded, but Lily moved into Reynold's arms. She kissed him, her tongue tangling with his, and against all odds he felt the pieces of his world fall back into place.

When the kiss ended, he grinned at her. "Have to go. But I'll be back."

"Yes, please."

****

"I am sorry I dropped my bundle."

Lily and Chastity sat side by side on the lumpy

sofa in Rey's room.

Rey's room.

Chastity had set her bundle on the table. She had her hands folded in her lap and appeared calm, but Lily could feel her artificial intelligence humming. A well-tuned machine.

"I was in a great hurry to get away, and I had a client in my room."

"I wish I could have given you more notice. I could not. I had determined it would be today, but I had to choose the moment."

Lily looked at her friend. "I was still beneath the client when you knocked." His body fluids remained inside her; she longed to cleanse herself but had dropped her belongings on the stairs as she fled.

She sought for some of the words Rey had uttered while forcing the vehicle down the alley—*Damn. Fricking hell.* Strangely satisfying words.

"I understand."

"The client tried to pull me out the front door when we reached the main hallway. I could not go back for the bundle."

"What I have brought away will last for a while. By then, we may be able to duplicate the formula."

"How? Where?" They had nowhere to go other than this room.

"We are fortunate you were able to signal your friend this morning. Otherwise, I do not know how we would have got away from the Crystal Palace."

"Lover." Lily emphasized it. "Rey is not my friend but my lover."

"Understood."

"And yes, it was fortunate. But I do not know how

long we will be able to stay here."

"If he is your lover, he will keep you with him. That is what lovers do."

"How do you know?"

"I have read about it."

"Read?"

"The ability to read was included in our basic intelligence."

"Yes but we have been given nothing to read."

"A client brought me a book."

"A book?"

Chastity got up, went to the table and extracted from her bundle a battered object which she placed in Lily's hands.

"This is a book?"

"Yes."

The cover, dark red, embossed with gold scrollwork, also contained letters. Lily accessed her intelligence and deciphered them.

"I am able to read it. It says 'The Adventures of Miss…' "

" 'X.' She is the main actor in the tale. Her full name is not given, to protect her identity, so said my client. She has many adventures and learns many things before she meets her lover and practices all of them on him."

"Oh."

"My client wished for me to practice them on him, but since he was not my lover I got no benefit from it. However, since you have a lover, perhaps it will benefit you."

"And I can practice these things on Rey?"

"Most definitely."

"And he will enjoy it?"

"Miss X's lover did. Whether you will, not being human, I cannot tell."

"I enjoy kissing Rey."

"Yes, I could perceive that."

"I like touching him. I like when he touches me. I like when he enters me and the way his chest hair feels."

"Very good. To benefit my intelligence, can you tell me why? Why is it different with your lover than with other clients?"

Lily examined the question, analyzing it as carefully as she could. At last she said, "He is gentle and kind to me. He says he loves me."

"Logically, a lover should love. At the end of the story in the book, Miss X falls in love with her lover also. But both of them were human."

"You think that makes a difference?"

"I would think it might."

"Is it impossible for Rey to love a machine?" Lily had wondered about that.

"I had a client who told me he loved the new steamcar he had just purchased. That was a machine."

"But," Lily objected, "for the steamcar to love him back—that would be the true wonder."

Chapter Twenty

"Where in hell have you been? You were supposed to be here an hour since."

Reynold leveled his fiercest look at the speaker, through the window of the steamcab. He'd arrived at the gloomy, near-deserted yard to which Vern had earlier directed him, only to find its occupant—a hulking, bald-headed fellow—irate. After what Reynold had been through, he had no patience for it. He wanted to get back to Lily and had just realized he'd have to walk blocks and blocks.

"There's a fire back that way." He jerked his head. "Streets are closed, and I had to circle around. Got detained by a police officer at one point."

"Then this thing's hot?"

"Of course it's hot."

"What I'm saying is, you're bein' tailed?"

"No. Told the copper I was picking up a fare."

The hulking man snorted.

"Look," Reynold pressed, "do you want this one or not?"

The man stepped back and eyed the vehicle before he walked around it, looking it over. "This cab's damaged."

"Had a run-in with a fire wagon," Reynold lied smoothly.

"On both sides?"

"You have no idea what it's like back there. The Crystal Palace is burning down."

"The place with all the steamie whores? Shit, might as well burn it down. Have to be a frickin' millionaire to go there. Though I've heard you can't tell the machines from real women, and they'll do anything."

Reynold struggled to keep his expression under control. "I couldn't say."

"Still, not sure I'd want something full of steam yankin' on my favorite part, if you know what I mean. Fire, you said?"

"Yeah."

"They'll probably all melt anyway. Buddy, I can't take this cab."

Aw, hell. "How come? If it's the scratches…"

"Gouges, more like."

"Aren't you just going to take it apart anyway? Not as if you'll be driving around town with it."

"But I sell the panels. Can't do it."

Reynold climbed out of the cab. Of a similar height, the hulking man was twice as wide. "I'll have to leave it here anyway."

"Hey, wait!"

"What else am I supposed to do with the damned thing?" Reynold fixed the man with a glare. "I understood you had a quota. This was supposed to be the last delivery."

"Yeah, I got a customer waiting for the boiler. But this thing, all marked up like this, is incriminating."

"Better get it knocked apart as fast as you can, then."

The man grunted like the bear he resembled. "All right. But tell Vern the price just went down. And I never want to see you again."

Reynold didn't want to see him again, either, didn't want to see Vern, for that matter—or another steamcab.

Wouldn't have to, now that Lily waited back at his flat.

At his flat.

Despite the fact that he'd just delivered stolen goods and—technically—had more in his possession, his heart bounded.

"You got it," he told the fellow, and hoofed it as quickly as he could from the shadowy yard. A long walk lay ahead of him, but Lily waited at the end of it. Lily and her companion…shit, what had he done?

****

He stopped for supplies at a late-night market on the way home, to pick up food and some bottled beer. Against all likelihood, he was starving and tried to remember when he'd last had a meal. Breakfast, probably. The shopkeeper asked him if he'd heard about the fire, and he acted surprised.

"The place is a loss," the man declared.

"Yeah? Everybody get out?"

"Not sure. They say the flames lit up the sky."

The city now seemed strangely silent. Reynold went the rest of the way without encountering anyone. His street echoed to his footsteps, and his heart began to pound as he climbed the stairs. What would he find? An empty flat?

What if the two automatons had fled? Panicked…could they panic? He worked the lock with unsteady hands and opened the door to find them side by side on the shabby sofa, Chastity with her hands folded, and Lily…

Of all things, she appeared to be reading a book.

She leaped to her feet when she saw him, and the book slid through her fingers to the floor. She flew to embrace him, wiggling close in his arms.

He juggled the sack from the shop, but forgot about it when she kissed him. His heart sped again, for another reason this time. But he drew away and eyed Chastity, who remained in her seat, unmoving.

"Is she all right?"

"Yes, Rey. She has put herself on standby so we may have some privacy."

"Oh?" Reynold squinted at Chastity who sat with her eyes open, staring at nothing. The sight struck him as unsettling. "Where did you get the book?" He certainly possessed none.

"From Chastity. She suggested I should read it and try out some of the ideas on you. She and I discussed it and came to the conclusion you would be more comfortable without an audience. I have used some of her supplies to cleanse myself and am ready."

Reynold's lips parted, but no words came.

Lily searched his eyes, her ice-blue gaze cool. "You were gone so long, I'm well into the book and have all sorts of ideas."

"You don't say? But we—uh—can't just leave her sitting there like that, can we? Not all night."

"We are on standby every night in the dormitory. We don't sleep, as such. But Dr. Landry always seeks to reserve our power. It's all right, Rey. It isn't the same as shutdown."

Reynold tried to imagine it—a dormitory with rows of beds and all the automatons lying motionless, their eyes open. An involuntary shiver wracked him.

Yet Lily stepped away from him—not far—and began to unfasten her clothing, what little she wore. A laced-up chemise and a pair of ruffled bloomers. The former came off over her head, revealing her perfect, globular breasts. She wiggled out of the latter precisely as might a human woman.

No—much more eagerly.

Now the sack slithered through his fingers and hit the floor.

"Lily—"

"Yes, Rey? Or should I call you Lover? I really think I should, for that is what you are. Would you prefer the floor or the bed? For some of the positions, we will require the bed. First you tie me up. Then I tie you…"

"Lily." He seized her shoulders, somehow keeping his hands from sliding down to cup those perfect breasts. His head swam. "You don't have to do this—pay me back, I mean."

"Pay you back?"

"For helping you. I don't expect it." Hope was another thing entirely. "I would have helped you anyway. And you're not a prostitute. Not here."

She stood perfectly still for a moment. "I do not understand. I want to touch you. I want you to touch me. Not like the clients. This is different."

"Are you sure?"

"You are my lover."

Reynold swallowed convulsively.

"But," she said more slowly, "I understand I must defer to you."

"No, you don't have to."

"I am only an automaton; you are a human. The

choice must be yours alone."

"That's bullshit."

She tipped her head. "I am not familiar with that word. 'Shit' I do know. It is a colloquial for…"

"Bullshit's pretty much the same."

"Shit from bulls?"

Reynold began to laugh helplessly, the day catching up with him. He laughed till his sides hurt and tears came from his eyes. "Lily, you're adorable."

"Is that good?"

"It's very good."

"Then you still desire me?"

"I still desire you." Couldn't she tell? Maybe not. She tended to take things at face value. "But I want you to make your own choices. Here—with me—we are equal, like human and human, understand?"

"I understand. Then I may unbutton your shirt?"

"You may."

"And your trousers?"

His heart started banging again, enough to kill him. "If you like."

"I do not see how we are to proceed with them on. Oh! I see you are ready for servicing after all."

He could scarcely be more ready, but he caught her face between his palms. "Not 'servicing,' Lily. That's your past."

Something flickered in her pale eyes. "To love me."

"Yeah, I'm ready to love you."

****

Sweet lord in heaven, she was going to kill him—his adorable, little Lily who now lay in his arms with her head on his shoulder, curled up like a kitten. The room had gone quiet and dim, their recent activities having ceased.

Or paused—he couldn't quite tell which. His senses leaped, and his heart took up the now-familiar beat. If he lived ten days, it would be a miracle. But what a way to die.

His half-stunned eyes moved around the room and fell on Chastity, still seated on the sofa. It had taken him a while to get over the fact that she sat there while he and Lily...the word "indulged" floated through his seized brain.

They had indulged one another.

He'd enjoyed it in a *holy-shit-I'm-gonna-die* sort of way. Had Lily enjoyed it also? Hard to tell. But she *wanted.* He could no longer question that—she wanted to be close to him. Wanted to touch him. And now, for the moment, she seemed content.

She cuddled closer in the bed and wrapped her arm around him. She felt so much like a woman, she made it easy to forget she had a boiler beneath those beautiful breasts and a shutoff switch tucked under her arm.

He supposed he should try to talk to her, come up with a plan for tomorrow when the world came rushing back in, decide what he was going to do with his two charges.

Instead he whispered, "Lily?"

"Yes, my lover?"

"How far did you get reading that book?"

She stirred against his shoulder, not moving far. "Miss X had met her lover, who introduced her to what he called 'the delights of the flesh.' He seems to be very inventive, does he not?"

"He does." Reynold reflected on it, squinting at the

147

ceiling. "You mean there's more?"

"I believe so, Rey."

"And you intend to read the whole book?"

"Oh, yes. It is most edifying."

He'd never live to see his next birthday. Did that matter? Hell, no.

Groping through the tangled emotions that filled him, he asked, "And did you enjoy what we—what we shared together?"

"I found it very satisfying. Which is curious because, as Miss X's lover said, they are pleasures of the flesh, and strictly speaking, I do not have flesh."

"You do, though." Unwisely perhaps, yet unable to help himself, he cupped one breast.

"I have skin. But what's inside is not real." She moved suddenly. "Does that make you desire me less?"

"No."

"Even when I remind you I'm not a real woman?"

"You don't need to remind me. I saw your switch, remember? Lily, I still desire you."

She ran her hand down his body, her touch delicate and seeking. "I can tell. Too bad I did not have time to read farther. There are no new things left to try. I like doing with you things I've never done with clients. It makes us different."

"Certainly."

"I wish to do these things only with you."

"I wish that also."

Her fingers caressed him. "You appear ready for more love. Would it be wrong to repeat what we've already practiced?"

Reynold choked.

"Would you be bored, Rey?"

"I wouldn't. I can't imagine being bored with you."

"That is good. I will strive to assure it remains so. And tomorrow, will you bring me more books to read?"

He would—if he lived that long.

Chapter Twenty-One

"What you going to do now, eh, with your pretty little dove gone?" Sasha prodded at Reynold the way a torturer might at his victim's open wound. "I hear a whole bunch of those fancy automatons melted in the fire—nothing left but scorched steel."

Reynold made no reply. The two men had walked down Niagara Street from the alley to view the aftermath of the fire. Half the Crystal Palace still stood. In fact from the front, other than signs of scorching, it looked little different from before. The rear and north side, however, where the fire had started, were gone.

"You mean they died?"

Sasha regarded him with insolent blue eyes. "They cannot 'die,' you fool-without-a-brain. They're machines. Didn't you ever get that through that thick head of yours?"

Reynold thought about punching Sasha in the face and dismissed the idea. It wouldn't get him anywhere, and after last night's excesses, he didn't have the energy.

It had gone hard with him leaving Lily and Chastity alone in his room so he could report for work. He worried about what they might do there without him and had made them both—Chastity having roused from standby—promise they would not leave the room.

Would they get bored and restless? Could

automatons get restless?

Chastity had told him she meant to try and analyze the formula of the enzyme wash that kept both her and Lily healthy. Lily has kissed him goodbye.

He promptly lost control of his thoughts and felt his eyes glaze over. What a night! He hurt from head to foot in the best possible way.

He wanted to do it all again.

But that didn't answer the question of how he might continue to hide the two automatons. What could he ultimately do with them? He couldn't begin to guess.

A policeman, catching sight of them, strolled down the street from his post in front of the Crystal Palace.

"Move along now, gents. Don't need any gawkers here." He had a rich, Irish accent and a set of shoulders like a bull.

Sasha, being Sasha, looked him up and down. "I don't take orders from you."

"Perhaps from the mayor, then? Or the warden down at the jail?"

Sasha—the ass—toed up to the officer. "You arresting me?"

"Sasha, come on. We need to get to work anyway."

"Listen to your friend, sir," the officer advised.

"He is no friend of mine. And I do not take orders from machines." He shot a look at Reynold. "Can you tell that's what this is?"

Reynold's gaze flew back to the officer. He hadn't been able to tell at once, but at second glance, the man looked familiar. Had Reynold seen him with Mrs. Gideon in the tavern that one night?

"He's still in authority," he told Sasha. "Let's clear off."

"Your companion has some sense, sir," the officer told Sasha. "This area isn't safe. We are to keep people out of the vicinity. I will arrest you if you do not comply."

Sasha sneered, "So what happened to all the frilly bits, then?"

"Frilly bits, sir?"

"The mechanical whores that were in there."

The police officer showed no reaction. Well, he wouldn't, would he?

"The interior of the structure is still being assessed—very dangerous work. Many of Dr. Landry's Ladies have been removed from the premises."

"Was there much loss of life?" Reynold ventured.

That made the automaton turn bright green eyes on him. "Yes, sir, I am afraid so, though as I mentioned, losses are still being assessed."

Well, then, Reynold thought, maybe two more missing Ladies wouldn't seem too suspicious—yet. He might have a bit of breathing room.

"He is a fool." His gaze on the officer, Sasha jerked his head toward Reynold. "I keep telling him those things were never alive."

The officer replied flatly, "A number of humans were also in the building when the fire broke out."

"Do they know how the fire started?" Reynold inquired.

"No, sir, that has yet to be determined."

"Well, thank you. Come on, Belsky. We'll be needed at the coffin shop."

"Coffin shop." The officer tipped his head. "Would that be McMahon's?"

"Yes, sir."

"Liam McMahon is a friend of mind." The officer offered Reynold his hand. "Patrick Kelly. Please tell him I sent my greetings."

"Reynold Michaels. I will."

They shook hands while Sasha muttered darkly, turned on his heel and stalked off toward the alley.

Reynold looked into Kelly's eyes. "I hear you were recently married. My felicitations."

"Thank you, sir. My wife and I are very happy."

Reynold longed to say so much more, ached to ask this automaton what he felt, if he loved—how he'd fought his way out of the stigma lent by being a machine. Only he couldn't, for Sasha chose to stalk off in disgust rather than give Patrick Kelly the time of day.

Of course, Sasha truly was an ass.

Reynold said none of it, just nodded and followed in Sasha's tracks. When he looked back, Kelly had returned to his post in front of the Crystal Palace, where he stood looking utterly human.

****

"I have concluded I cannot analyze this," Chastity declared. "I have failed. I do not believe I have ever before failed at anything."

Lily joined Chastity at the kitchen table, upon which lay what might well be every bowl and plate Reynold possessed. The largest basin held their remaining supply of enzyme wash, the ingredients of which Chastity had spent the day seeking to determine, only now admitting defeat.

"Why are you unable to identify the ingredients?"

"I do not possess the necessary information. I am able to tell one component from another, but the formulations were not included in my basic intelligence."

"Just like we were not taught the location of our shutoff switches. Dr. Landry, believing we would be always under her care, did not think we would ever need the information."

"Dr. Landry," Chastity said succinctly, "never expected us to take control of our lives—which is what we have now done. Unfortunately, Sister, our independence will not last long if we cannot duplicate this vital fluid."

"I am regretful I neglected to bring my bundle."

"We would still run out eventually."

"But it would have lasted twice as long."

"I have discovered something about myself, Sister. I do not like to fail." Chastity looked at Lily. "Is it good to have ideas about 'self'?"

"I think so. It is a human characteristic. Miss X has many ideas about herself."

"I supposed it would feel better."

"I have observed that humans frequently do not feel good about themselves. Our clients often did not. I think even Rey does not always. And he is so...perfect."

"Yes? I will include that in my intelligence. Being human is complicated."

The lock on the door rattled; Rey came in carrying several bags and bundles.

"Rey! Welcome home."

"Thank you, Lily. Is everything all right here?"

"No. Chastity has failed to successfully analyze the formula for the enzyme wash."

"The stuff you need to survive?" Reynold set his packages down and approached the table. "What will happen to you once you run out?"

Chastity replied, "I once asked Nadia a similar question, namely what would happen if we failed to use the formula. Nadia," she added for Reynold's benefit, "is Dr. Landry's assistant. Since, unlike humans, we have no internal organs, our living tissues—skin, eyes, lips, tongue, and vagina—must be nourished topically. Without the benefits of the enzymes, those tissues will eventually die. Our skin will become patchy, our eyes will rot in their frames. We will be nothing more than animated steel."

"Like any other steam unit," Lily elucidated.

"Yes, well—" Reynold looked confused. Did he understand? "I brought some food and other things I thought you might need."

"We cannot eat food," Chastity told him. "Or drink except for a drop of two on the tongue. You will need to eat the food yourself, Reynold."

"All right. I brought some secondhand clothing for you, Lily. You can't be seen dressed in nothing but underwear. These things aren't as fancy as what you wore at the Crystal Palace, but they won't attract as much attention if you need to go out."

"Will I need to go out, Rey?"

"I don't know yet. When I get some more money, I'll get plainer clothes for Chastity, too. And I brought a few books."

"Where?"

"Here in this parcel. I passed a small bookshop on my way. These were the best I could find for what I could afford." He hesitated. "I don't think they're anything like the Miss X book."

"I don't mind." Lily unwrapped the parcel and took

the books—three of them—in her hands. "I spent time today reading *The Adventures of Miss X* while Chastity analyzed the formula."

"Failed to analyze the formula, Sister."

"Failed to analyze the formula, and I have many more acts for us to practice."

"Have you?" Reynold's gaze became intent.

"Oh, yes. You eat first, if you are hungry."

"I'm not all that hungry." His gaze slid to Chastity. "But there's something I need to tell both of you first. Better sit down."

They obeyed, and he paced in front of them.

"I expect it is dire news," Lily told Chastity.

"What makes you say so?"

"In *The Adventures of Miss X*, her lover paced like this before he told her he would not come to see her anymore." Lily stilled. "Is that what you mean to tell me, Rey?"

"No! God, no."

"God," Chastity informed Lily, "is a mythical entity to whom humans ascribe their creation."

"Like Dr. Landry?"

"Not precisely. I think…"

"Just listen for a minute, will you? I went to take a look at the Crystal Palace today. That fire did a lot of damage. Chastity, did you start the fire?"

"Yes, Reynold."

"How?"

"I waited for a distraction and took a candle—there were some lit in the private lounge. Everyone had run out of the room because of the fight."

"What fight?"

"Two clients disagreed as to which of them had

come in first. One of them also disagreed with Miss Crump, who told him a particular Lady was unavailable. They came to blows.

"I was ready for just such an eventuality and took up the candle, as I say. I set the draperies in the lounge afire. They caught the ceiling and the carpet soon after."

"There was loss of life in the fire."

"Loss of life?" Chastity tipped her head, calculating. "Some of our sisters were burned?"

"Yes, and I heard some humans—there must have been clients who did not manage to escape." Reynold fished inside his jacket and produced a newspaper, which he unfolded and held in front of them.

Lily saw that big words and small words covered the sheet. She read the big words spread across the top.

FIVE DEATHS AND EXTENSIVE PROPERTY
DAMAGE IN CRYSTAL PALACE FIRE

"Five deaths," Chastity read. She looked at Reynold. "Does that count our fellow Ladies?"

"I'm afraid not. I'm sorry to say the lost Ladies are merely considered property. According to the article, the five deaths were four clients, all on the north end of the upper floor, and one Miss Delilah Crump."

"Miss Crump?" Lily repeated. "Dead?" She exchanged a look with Chastity. "Shut off permanently."

"It is my fault." Chastity pronounced it gravely. "I failed to consider that the fire might spread so swiftly before it could be extinguished. I wished only for an opportunity to slip away."

"You meant no harm to anyone, Sister."

"True. I certainly did not wish to damage any of

our sisters."

Lily noted that Chastity valued her fellow automatons far above the clients or even Miss Crump, but she did not mention it. She could almost sense the whirl of Chastity's intelligence.

"You did not set out to hurt them, Chastity."

"Yet I killed. We spoke before about our desire to kill the clients were it not forbidden. I failed to consider our sisters and rated the risk of setting the fire justified. It seems I was wrong."

"No, Chastity. We are free. We can now make our own choices."

"You are right, Lily. And having made them, we must also accept responsibility for them."

Chapter Twenty-Two

"Rey, she is gone."

Reynold, flung into the depths of sleep by his further excesses of the night before, ignored the words and continued lying in the bed like a dead man, not so much as an eyelash twitching.

On some dim level, he recognized the voice as Lily's, the same that had whispered suggestions to him from that damned and wonderful book of hers all night long.

"Lover, you must awake—Chastity is gone."

That snagged his attention and revived his heart with a shot of pure panic. Impossible. When Lily had dragged him to bed, the other automaton had once more subsided onto the sofa in apparent standby mode. He truly hadn't spared her another thought.

Now he pried up his eyelids one at a time and saw Lily's face hanging over him like a worried moon. Could an automaton feel worry? Could she feel at all? A ridiculous question, because quite plainly Lily did.

"What did you say?"

Her eyes, pale as ice, met his wildly. Her golden hair—in which he'd so recently buried his fingers—fluffed around her face like a halo. Her pink lips...

But no, he couldn't let himself think about them.

He stirred his spent body and sat up in the bed. Lily moved just enough to let him look around the room.

Empty. No beautiful, dark-haired automaton on the sofa, nor anywhere he could see. He swore with feeling.

"Where is she?"

"I do not know. She must have left. The door is unlocked."

"Where would she go?" His mind—though rarely fleet at the best of times—once more raced. Chastity knew no one in the city except those at the Crystal Palace, most of whom had now been removed.

"Hellfire," he whispered. He focused on Lily again. "You didn't see her go?"

"I did not. She must have left when we were engaged in lovemaking."

"But I thought she was on standby, like before."

"So did I. She deceived me. But, Rey, look—she has left her bundle behind."

"She has?"

"Yes, and that concerns me. I believe she has left what remains of the enzyme formula for my benefit. That means she has nothing. I can only conclude that, wherever she has gone, she supposes she will not need any."

"But there is no such place, Lily. Why would she do such a thing?"

"I cannot say."

Rey sat on the edge of the bed, still staring about as if he might make Chastity materialize. "You don't think she'd do anything foolish, do you?" he asked slowly and with dread.

"Foolish?"

"Destroy herself."

"It is what I fear, Rey. The news you brought last evening distressed her very much. I do not believe she

160

minded so much the deaths of the clients who were in the Crystal Palace; she hated the clients. But some of our sisters were also destroyed."

"We need to find her." But where in this big city might she have gone? He groaned aloud.

"Rey, are you in pain?"

"Yes. How long ago do you suppose she left?"

"I do not know. The room was dark, and I noticed no movement. We were…"

He knew very well what they'd been doing. "She might have hours of time head start on us. Think, Lily. You must have some idea what she'd do."

Lily cogitated silently, and furiously. "She might return to the dormitory."

"Turn herself in to Dr. Landry, you mean?"

"It is the only place I can think. You said the Crystal Palace is damaged."

"Yes."

"If not the dormitory, she might be anywhere. Chastity is the most intelligent among us. She came up with the scheme for escape. She might think of anything."

Reynold struggled up and into his clothes. "I will have to go look for her. You stay here in case she returns. Pray God she does."

Lily, still kneeling on the bed, stared at him. "I do not pray to God."

"Whatever you do pray to, then."

"I pray to you."

He caught her face between his hands. "Damn it, Lily—don't do that! I have more failings than—well, any man in this city."

"You are perfect."

"I'm not."

"You are perfect to me."

"Don't set me up high, darling." She knew nothing about how Sasha openly despised him, how everyone except his ma had called him stupid all his life. How Liam had hired him out of pity to tote corpses, a job no one else wanted. He'd found one thing he was good at—stealing steamcabs for a lowlife like Vern.

But Lily, his Lily, knelt there looking at him as worshipfully as if he'd hung the sun and the moon. Expecting him to make everything right.

Not knowing what else to do, he kissed her. Then he said, "I'll go look around the Crystal Palace in case she may have gone there."

"I want to come with you."

"Not a good idea. You stay here, use that stuff she left for you. I'll be back as soon as I can."

"I must come."

"No, it's too dangerous, and I don't want to lose you, Lily."

"If I wear the clothes you brought, no one will recognize me."

Maybe not. But he wasn't about to take a chance.

"Please, Lily."

"You know I will do anything to please you."

God, yes, she'd proved that. "Stay here and tend yourself. I want you to stay healthy. I'll take a look around and come back soon. We'll talk it over then."

"Talk it over. Like equals."

"Yes."

"I like that."

"Just promise you won't leave while I'm gone." He caressed her cheek. "I couldn't bear losing you."

"Because you love me." Her gaze clung to his.

"Because I love you." He kissed her again.

"I will stay here. But please do not be long."

"I won't. Give me directions to this dormitory. I'll trace that route." And he, at least, would be praying.

****

He jogged around the immediate area of his building, hoping to catch sight of a dark-haired figure in a bright green dress. Very few people walked the streets this early—just a few servants hurrying about their assigned tasks and some vendors pushing handcarts. One horse and wagon, piled with fresh vegetables, lumbered past. The air still felt cool, and he could smell the river.

Where the hell could Chastity be? By now, Dr. Landry might well have reported her and Lily missing. Or did she still suppose them among the automatons destroyed in the fire?

Eventually all that would be sorted out, and Dr. Landry would realize the numbers didn't add up. Meanwhile…

He struggled to trace events in his mind. The automaton in the alley had seen Chastity and Lily with him in the cab. But he'd run it over—destroyed it, hadn't he? And people had burst out through the back door, but both women had been in the cab by then, as had he. He doubted they'd been seen clearly.

He jogged the intervening blocks to the Crystal Palace, grateful for the cool air, and found a single policeman on duty out front. No one in back, but he could barely get close to the place for the reek of burning.

Not so much as a glimpse of green satin. The place

felt dead. If Chastity had come here, she hadn't stayed.

He turned and traced the route of the tram in reverse down to Prospect, where Lily said the dormitory was situated. No guards here, at least none he could see. The building—if he had the right one—looked grim and silent; he didn't doubt a steamie stood inside every door, just as at the Crystal Palace.

What now? Lily had pronounced Chastity the smartest among the Ladies—surely smarter than he was. Stumped, he returned to his rooming house, seeing increased foot and wheel traffic as the city awakened. But still no Chastity.

Sick with worry, he climbed the three flights to his flat, praying Lily would still be there. She was, clad in the clothing he'd bought for her—dowdy brown skirt, faded blouse, and straw-colored shawl—looking so unlike herself he stared.

"Lily?"

"Do I not look like Lily?"

"You don't."

She'd done something to her magnificent hair, tamed and confined it beneath the close-fitting hat he'd brought, the brim of which shaded her face. She looked like a human servant from one of the better-class households.

"Then may I accompany you? I see you did not find Chastity. We will look together."

He thought on it, to little benefit. Reality seemed to be fast slipping from between his fingers. He stalled for time and nodded at the table.

"You used the stuff?"

"I did."

"How much is left?"

"Enough for four or five days."

What then? She needed the formula to keep herself healthy. Better to return her to Dr. Landry than watch her deteriorate.

But he would not voice that sentiment, not when she stood there looking at him like he made up the center of her world.

He would think of something.

"Come on, then."

They went arm in arm, Lily tucked in close against him. As they walked, she said softly, "I have another problem."

"What's that?"

"Have you any access to coal? I will soon have to refurbish my store, here." She laid her hand on her stomach. "I was able to refill my boiler with water while you were gone. It is something that is usually done at the dormitory every morning before we dress for the day. But my store of coal is very low."

Reynold's head reeled. "There's coal at the coffin shop." And did he really want to contemplate stealing from Liam again? Maybe he could just borrow, as he had before, and replace the stock when he had time.

"How soon do you need—er—a refill?"

"By midday today. I am quite efficient."

"And you know how to do this for yourself?"

"I refill from the front, so I have seen it done ever since I was activated."

"From the front? Where?" His hands had been all over her and he'd felt no openings.

"The slots are very cleverly fashioned."

Must be.

"Let's go to the shop first and get that taken care of

before anyone else is there."

"The shop?"

"The coffin shop where I work."

"I would like very much to see it."

He hurried her along. The streets grew busier all the while. He knew Pete came in early, and sometimes Sasha, too. He didn't want to run into them.

He took Lily around back, and they entered through the rear room where he washed and prepared the bodies. It was empty now, but he had a small stove and a scuttle of coal there for heating water. He carefully shut the door and listened for sounds from inside. No one in yet; he relaxed marginally.

"There." He pointed to the scuttle. "Do what you must."

She began unfastening the front of her clothing but froze, looking at him. "I would prefer you did not watch."

"Why?"

"Because it will make you think less of me."

"It won't."

"It will make me seem less human."

"But, Lily, you already showed me the switch under your arm."

"That was vital in case you need to turn me back on. This… I open to reveal a hopper. Just like a machine. Please, Rey."

"All right. I'll wait in the shop. But stay put, all right?"

He let himself into the quiet gloom of the showroom, where a body lay in its coffin, ready for delivery later in the day, and went to search out an empty lunch pail he remembered seeing there. A touch on the arm nearly sent him through the roof.

"Lily—Jesus! I told you to stay put."

"What is 'Jesus'?"

"He's a who, not a what. And I think that's a discussion we will have to reserve for another time."

"Who is that?" She pointed into the coffin.

"Mrs. Sylvester."

"She's very beautiful. May I look at her more closely?"

"I guess so, but we need to hurry. I want to fill this pail with extra coal to take with us."

He followed her farther into the room, where she stood staring into the coffin, head tipped to one side.

"I wish I were she."

"Lily, darling, she's dead."

"But she is human, even so. Do you find her as beautiful as me?"

"Not even close."

"You do not want to have sexual intercourse with her?"

"Good God, no. Lily—she's dead!"

"She's as much alive as I am, when you think about it. And you want sexual intercourse with me."

"That's completely different."

"I do not see how. I wish I were her. At least then I would once have been human."

"Being human is overrated. Now let's go fill this pail with coal so we can get away from here. It's not safe."

She followed him obediently, head bowed. He shoveled coal into the pail wildly, only to be brought up short when someone spoke from behind him.

"Well, well—and what do we have here?"

Reynold spun, his stomach sinking with sickening speed.

Sasha. Oh, hell, not him.

Chapter Twenty-Three

"Belsky," Rey said.

Lily, now well attuned to his moods and inflections, heard all kinds of things in his voice. Anger, dismay, disgust—all those emotions she shouldn't be able to feel yet somehow did.

She had felt disquiet when any of the clients besides Rey touched her. She felt the backwash of his dismay now.

Exactly who or what was this Belsky who so disturbed him? She turned her gaze on the man— human—noting his details with mechanical speed: light hair, sharp features, with a pointed nose and eyes nearly as pale as her own. His lips wore a sneer, and in those eyes she saw a look she'd sometimes seen in those of her clients right before they hurt her.

Cruel.

The word flashed through her intelligence even as Rey seized her wrist and pushed her behind him. A human shield.

"Stealing from your employer, is it?" Belsky had an odd accent, and Lily, curious, tried to peer around Rey's shoulder at him. Then she comprehended Rey did not wish the man to see her, and she withdrew again.

"Just borrowing some coal," Rey muttered.

"Without Liam's permission."

"I'll pay him back."

"What else do you borrow from him? Supplies? Money? I do not think he would like it. And who is she?" Now Belsky leaned around in an effort to get a better look at Lily.

For an instant Rey didn't speak. He reached back and steadied Lily before he said, "I took your advice—she's a lightskirt I picked up last evening. We spent the night together."

"Here?"

"Didn't want anyone at my rooming house to see, did I?"

"You fool. But I suppose it is better than mooning over that fancy steamie."

"She's gone, ain't she? Burned up in that fire."

Belsky laughed, a low sound that contained very little humor. "So let us have a look at your new piece."

"No, Sasha. I won't let you embarrass her."

"Ever the gentleman, are you not? But maybe I will want to try her also. That is the thing about whores—she will lay on her back for whoever has the coin."

"Leave it alone, Sasha. Leave her alone."

Belsky grunted. Lily would have liked to steal another look at him but had discerned Rey did not wish to afford Belsky the chance to identify her. She dropped her head and sheltered behind the brim of her hat.

"So why are you taking Liam's coal?"

"Just helping her out. She's got a shitty little room and no coal for a fire."

"In this heat? Who needs a fire?"

"She lives with another girl who's sick."

Belsky uttered a word Lily didn't recognize and took a step back. "And you brought her here? You will most likely catch the pox from her."

"We were just leaving."

"I think Liam needs to know about this. You banging her in the coffins?"

"Of course not!"

"I still believe he needs to know."

"Go ahead and tell him. I'm not asking you to keep any secrets." Now Rey's voice became hard. "Tell on me—like a girl."

Belsky snorted. "Run off with your little whore—at least this one's human."

Rey's fingers tightened on Lily's wrist hard enough to leave marks—a warning. She remained silent.

"I knew you were hooked on it," Belsky jeered.

"That's my business, isn't it? Come along."

Lily realized the last two words were directed at her and jerked into motion. Still with Rey's hand clamped to her wrist, she let him lead her out, virtually treading on his heels.

"Damn it all," he said when they reached the outdoors.

"I did not like him," Lily whispered. Suddenly she knew Chastity had done the right thing getting them away from the Crystal Palace, even if it had subsequently burned down. Otherwise, Belsky might have come in as a client, and she would have been forced to accommodate him despite her dislike.

"No one likes him. Let's get out of here."

"But what about Chastity?"

He began hurrying her along the street, the coal pail in one hand, her wrist in the other. "I don't know where to look for her."

"Do you think she is safe?"

"I don't know that either. If the authorities pick her

up, they may just think she strayed from the Crystal Palace during the fire."

"But then they'll return her to Dr. Landry, will they not?"

"I expect so."

"She will no longer be free. All her planning and the fire will be for nothing."

"Not for nothing." He stopped walking and faced her. His hand released her wrist at last and cupped her cheek in the gentle way she loved. "At least it got you away. What concerns me now is whether Sasha had a good look at you back there."

"Belsky?"

"Belsky, yes. Because he's seen you before—when you got off the tram."

"I looked much different then."

"Yes, and I hope he believes you're just what he called you—a little whore."

"I am."

"No, Lily. Not any longer. Now you belong to me."

"I like that. But I think you are right not to trust that Belsky."

"No flies on you, then."

Lily looked herself over carefully. "I do not see any."

She didn't really understand why Rey laughed, but it pleased her very much.

****

"Reynold has replaced his little dove with another. Only this one is soiled and much easier to afford."

Everyone looked up, and Liam, who'd been whistling cheerily, fell silent. The four men had worked companionably all morning, Reynold lost in his

172

thoughts.

He'd been forced to leave Lily back at his room alone, having extracted from her a strict promise to stay there until he returned. He feared if she began worrying about Chastity or thought of some place the automaton might have gone, she'd go out searching.

When he left, she'd been reading one of the books he bought her. He only hoped it kept her occupied.

Now Pete and Liam exchanged glances.

"That was awful quick," Pete commented.

Reynold shrugged with what he hoped looked like careless disinterest. "A man needs what he needs. And she's a sweet little thing—not like the others."

"I told you he was stupid," Sasha smirked. "Take it from me, Rey. They are all the same."

"And you'd be an expert, would you?" Reynold edged out from behind the coffin he'd been sanding. For once he didn't feel like backing down from the other man just to avoid trouble.

"Not an expert, but I have poked my share of whores like your little friend."

"I don't think so." Lily wasn't like anyone else— Reynold knew that for certain.

"Oh, she is different, is she? Only had a hundred men instead of a thousand? Liam, you better ask him what he was doing here with her this morning."

"Here?" Liam repeated.

"*Da*—early, when I came in."

Liam looked at Reynold.

"I just brought her by to borrow some coal. She had none at home—can't afford any—and her roommate is sick."

"Not sure I'm comfortable with that, lad. This

place is my livelihood."

"I'll give you the money for the coal. Take it out of my pay. I just filled a lunch pail."

"'Tisn't that. I'm the first to sympathize with the plight of the poor in this city. But I don't like you letting just anybody in here."

"I understand. It won't happen again. I just wanted to help her out."

"If you really want to help her, lad, take her to see Mrs. Gideon. She'll get your friend out of the life if she can. She runs that Haven for Disadvantaged Women over on Ellicott Street."

Not a bad idea. But as he'd wondered before, would Mrs. Gideon—that woman he'd seen at the tavern—have sympathy for a non-human?

"Then Rey can marry the soiled dove," Sasha said mockingly. "No doubt a whore's the best he can do."

Not a bad idea either.

"Leave him alone, Sasha," Pete said unhappily.

Reynold returned to his work. Sasha wasn't as smart as he thought—he must have failed to recognize Lily this morning, because he surely wouldn't miss the chance to throw that in Reynold's face.

Applying himself to the coffin with care, he smiled.

Chapter Twenty-Four

"Have you heard the news?" Pete asked Reynold excitedly when he arrived for work the next morning. "They found one of those mechanical Ladies floating in the river. Fished her out late last evening."

Reynold stopped like a steer hit between the eyes, and his stomach fell so fast he thought he might lose his breakfast. Every other worry—and he had a boatload of them—temporarily fled his mind.

He'd had no sleep due to those worries. Well, that and Lily being bent on reenacting the last of Miss X's adventures. Aside from that part of it and his ever-growing tenderness for her, he lived a nightmare. Fear over the possibility of Lily and Chastity's discovery, over the fact that Lily quickly ran through her vital nutritional supplies combined with struggling over how and when to get her to Mrs. Gideon's, and dodging messages from Vern, who wanted him to steal yet more cabs—his brain ached.

Now the thing he'd feared ever since Chastity disappeared seemed to have come about.

"Dead?" he choked out.

Pete eyed him questioningly. "Not as if she was actually alive, is it? I mean, they're steamies, aren't they? Just a lot higher quality than most."

"They seem alive, though, don't they?"

"They do," Pete admitted. "I live under the same

roof as Clara's steamie, Dax. I remember when she brought him home from her grandfather's. The grandfather was a mean old sod, God rest him, and Dax was all dented and battered and scared—terrified—the old man would send him to the scrap heap."

"You believe they have feelings, then?"

"Some of them sure seem to. Dax does. But I've been around others that just seem like machines. Not sure what makes the difference."

"This Patrick Kelly Liam's always talking about—you've met him?" Reynold thought of the hybrid he and Sasha had met in front of the Crystal Palace.

"Sure, a bunch of times. He's got a personality—a quirky one, at that. I'd swear he has a sense of humor, too."

"And he's the same kind of hybrid as these Landry's Ladies?"

"Yes."

"So"—Reynold wanted to glean as much information as he could before Sasha arrived—"what do you know about the one found last night?" Was it actually Chastity? His stomach turned over again.

"Found floating, as I say. They fished her out down at the foot of Ferry Street. They say that Dr. Landry was called and took possession of her."

Not good. If it was Chastity—and who else could it be?—and Dr. Landry pressed her for information, would Chastity talk? Tell where Lily was and that he'd been sheltering her?

That would be considered theft, just like stealing a steamcab. He'd be thrown in jail. And what would happen to Lily?

"Do you know if the—er—unit they picked up was

operating? And what she looked like?"

Pete eyed him still more closely. "Why all the interest? Oh, that's right—you went down there, didn't you? Had a visit with one of the Ladies."

"Right."

"You wondering if it's the same one?" Not giving Reynold time to answer, Pete leaned closer and asked, "What was it like, being with a machine?"

"Well, I'll tell you—it didn't feel all that different from a woman."

Pete flushed scarlet. "I've only done it once. Scared to death I'll catch the pox and my fella will fall off."

Or he'd wish it would.

"You worried the unit they pulled up is the one you watched for every morning—the one Sasha rags you about?"

"Yeah."

"They said she had brown skin and long black hair. That sound like yours?"

"No, not mine." Reynold's stomach heaved violently. Somehow he choked the sickness back. "But you don't know if she was operating?"

"No. They have boilers just like other steamies, right? Wouldn't the water put the fire out? Though I expect Dr. Landry, who's supposed to be some kind of genius, could get her started up again."

God, Reynold hoped not.

And how would he ever break the news to Lily?

****

Lily heard Rey's step on the stairs, her hearing being very acute, and leaped to her feet, letting her book slip through her fingers.

As reading matter, it had proved quite interesting, though perhaps not as interesting as Miss X's tale. This story contained no lover, but there were several dead bodies and a number of clever humans striving to determine how they got that way.

The subject matter distracted her, but made her remember the humans and automatons killed in the fire at the Crystal Palace. That in turn made her think—worry—about Chastity. And how very little of the enzyme wash remained.

What was she to do?

Then Rey arrived, entering the flat with a flurry, and everything became right again.

She went immediately into his arms. "Rey! You were gone so long. I do not like it when you are away."

"You missed me?"

"*Missed.* That is a good term."

She kissed him, using every skill she'd ever acquired and luring his tongue into her mouth. She felt her boiler flare within her, begin to heat up as if Rey's presence gave her a reason to be.

He groaned—which, she'd learned, was a good sign.

She stopped kissing him and looked into his eyes. Soft and brown, they made up her world.

"Now that you're here, come to the bed."

"No, Lily. Not yet." He seized her shoulders. "We need to talk about something."

"We can talk in the bed." She enjoyed that, especially afterward when she felt...*content.*

"Wait, I need to tell you something first. It's about Chastity. Not good news, darling."

"Chastity? My sister? You have found her?"

"Not me, but she has been found—at least an automaton was picked up floating in the river and returned to Dr. Landry."

"Floating in the river? That cannot be Chastity. How would she get there?"

"I don't know, honey. What I need you to tell me is this… Could Chastity survive a drenching in the river? Would it ruin her?"

"I am not certain." Lily stepped away from him and engaged her artificial intelligence. "It depends on how long she was submerged. Do you know?"

Rey shook his head. He looked deeply troubled.

"The fire in her belly would go out. Whether anything else would be damaged, I cannot say. I think she could be dried out and restarted."

"Restarted? That means she could tell Dr. Landry where you are."

"She could. But she will not. I trust Chastity's loyalty."

"I know you do, but if Dr. Landry gets her hands on her…"

Lily thought about that. Dr. Landry was cold and could be cruel. If she believed Chastity and Lily had been together, she might attempt to take the information from Chastity by force.

Rey could be in danger. Lily cared far less for herself than for him.

She turned and regarded him. "What will happen to you if I am found here?"

"Jail."

"What is jail?"

"The police would come, arrest me, and lock me up in a cell for theft."

"Theft of what?"

"You."

"But I wish to be with you. I choose to be with you."

"I think Dr. Landry would have something to say about that."

"Oh." Lily sat on the edge of the sofa, her intelligence clicking furiously. "If you went to jail, would I be able to see you?"

"No. I'm pretty sure you'd be returned to Dr. Landry."

"We cannot let that happen."

"Do you think I should move you out of here, hide you somewhere Chastity doesn't know about? Just to be safe."

"Perhaps." Lily didn't believe Chastity would betray her, but Dr. Landry did have access to her deepest knowledge, and as her new book *Red Herrings in a Sea of Red* had taught her, the most unexpected things happened in dangerous situations.

She was now in danger, as was Rey.

"I would like to know how Chastity got into the river, Rey."

"So would I."

"Do you think she jumped in? She had a large amount of guilt over the loss of life at the Crystal Palace."

"Yeah, but can she truly feel guilt? I mean—"

Lily turned her eyes on him. He looked miserable and uncomfortable. At least, she thought, he had a right to those emotions.

The thought stung.

"She should not be able to experience emotions—

nor should I. Yet we do. She felt guilt. I feel love for you."

He sat beside her and seized her hand. "Just as I love you. I'm sorry, Lily, I didn't mean to imply you have no feelings."

"You truly love me?"

"I must have said so before now."

"I thought they were just words. Anyone can say words." Though she had also felt it in his touch, in the tender way he kissed her.

He drew her into his arms, close against him. "Let there be no doubt. I love you, Lily. For better or worse."

"Will there be worse, Rey?"

"I'm afraid so." He inhaled a big breath. "Lily, I'm not sure how best to protect you. With Chastity in Dr. Landry's hands and Sasha having seen you with me, we better not stay here."

"I will trust you, Rey, to do whatever you think best."

"I think we should take you to Mrs. Gideon, explain your situation, and throw ourselves on her mercy. Maybe she can think of a way to keep you safe."

"Who is Mrs. Gideon?"

"She runs a shelter for women and helps get them off the street."

"But, Rey, I'm not a woman. Will she still help me?"

"Well, Lily, I guess there's only one way to find out."

Chapter Twenty-Five

"I'd like to request sanctuary on behalf of my friend."

"Sanctuary, is it?" The woman who stood before Reynold and Lily gave them the onceover. She looked far different from when Reynold had seen her in the tavern, much more soberly dressed, though her deep plum-colored gown had patches of glitter and the baubles hanging from her ears matched her eyes exactly—tawny gold. She'd bundled her black hair in a knot at the back of her head, rolled up her sleeves, and looked all business.

Beside Reynold, Lily shifted on her feet. Still clad in her dull brown costume, she clutched bundles containing all her worldly possessions, including the books and the last of the enzyme formula.

"This isn't a church," Mrs. Gideon snapped, and Lily took a step closer to Reynold. He clasped her hand in his.

Mrs. Gideon's gaze followed the movement before returning to Reynold's face. Her expression softened marginally.

"I suppose you'd better come in."

The Haven for Disadvantaged Women was located in a huge house on Ellicott Street, bulky and cavernous. And full—Reynold and Lily had already passed several groups of what could only be tarnished ladies or former streetwalkers outside. One, smoking a small cigar, had stared at them as they came up the walk.

He felt uncomfortable, desperate, and out of his depth. If Mrs. Gideon refused to show them mercy, he didn't know what he was going to do.

And Mrs. Gideon didn't look particularly merciful. She admitted them to the vast foyer and then stood like a marble statue, blocking the way.

"I don't recognize you," she told Lily, "and I know most of the girls working this city. Where's your patch?"

Reynold answered, "She doesn't have a patch, ma'am."

Mrs. Gideon's brilliant eyes touched Reynold again. "Can she speak?"

"Yes, but...I need to tell you her story. Privately." Too many people here; two of the women had come in from outside. Others walked down the wide staircase that led from the foyer. All stared at the new arrival.

Curiosity now stirred in Mrs. Gideon's rather intimidating face. "Very well. Come into my office."

Her office, through a doorway on the left, appeared to have been partitioned from what had once been a parlor when this place served as someone's home. Now it looked surprisingly ordinary, with a white desk, a few comfortable chairs, and stacks of papers. Mrs. Gideon closed the door firmly before gesturing them into seats and taking the one behind the desk.

"I'm willing to listen, but I'm a busy woman. Don't waste my time."

How to begin? Quite plainly Mrs. Gideon couldn't tell what Lily was. Now she waited with a visible lack of patience while Reynold fumbled for words.

Lily spoke before he could. "My name is Lily. I am an automaton."

Mrs. Gideon's gaze abruptly narrowed; her interest quickened. "Ah," she said softly. Her fingers tapped the surface of the desk. "I knew I sensed…something." She smiled suddenly and, revealing her wits moved very quickly indeed, said, "You'll be from that place that burned the other night—the Crystal Palace."

"Yes."

"Would you mind giving me a better look at you?"

Lily pulled off her ugly brown hat and her hair tumbled down like sunshine. Reynold's throat grew tight with emotion.

Mrs. Gideon glanced at him almost as if she could feel what he felt.

"And who are you? Or would you prefer I don't know your name?"

"Might be best," he admitted. "Though we'll need to trust you if you're to help Lily. I hope you're willing to help her, ma'am. She's not a woman but she's been forced into prostitution in that awful place—just like a slave. And if she's found, she'll have to go back again."

"Why don't you tell me the whole story? Which of you wants to speak?"

Reynold looked at Lily. Before he could marshal his thoughts, she began—her pale gaze fixed on Mrs. Gideon's face and her hands folded in her lap, she told the tale of her entire existence like a recitation, beginning with her earliest cognizant memory, awakening naked and cold in Dr. Landry's lab, recounting what sounded to Reynold very much like a journey into awareness.

Before she had finished, Mrs. Gideon was on her

feet, pacing the area behind the desk, scowling. She never interrupted Lily, but her gaze returned time and time again to Lily's face, and after Lily concluded, she spoke.

"And you minded serving in this capacity, as a Landry's Lady? Of course you did. I should have known."

Since Mrs. Gideon seemed to have answered her own question, Lily did not and merely sat with lips parted slightly.

Obviously troubled, Mrs. Gideon went on, "Indeed, I definitely should have known better—one of my best friends is an automaton, a hybrid like yourself."

"There are others such as me, other than my fellow Landry's Ladies?"

"Remember, Lily," Reynold said gently, "there's those hybrids in the police force—the Irish Squad."

"My friend is a member of the Irish Squad," Mrs. Gideon admitted.

Lily looked at Reynold. "You told me about them, yes—but how can they be like me? They are all male and not required to service clients."

Mrs. Gideon spoke a word Reynold didn't expect any lady to utter. Perhaps Mrs. Gideon wasn't all lady.

"This is upsetting—very upsetting," she said as she continued to pace. "My support was fundamental in the development of Landry's Ladies. I—and other well-wishers in this city—contributed heavily in funding Dr. Landry's project. I thought it would benefit the city and the poor girls who have to work the streets. I've seen what they endure and how difficult it is to escape the life."

She looked at Lily. "Damn it! When Dr. Landry

came to us, she talked about automatons. I assumed she meant for the streets—I believe that was what she intended at the outset. It's obviously turned into something else, though—highly-developed models, such as you, which I never had the chance to examine. And suddenly we have the Crystal Palace catering to the wrong clientele. The girls who need saving are still on the streets, and it seems a whole new class of slavery has been born."

She leaned down and stared Lily in the eyes. "I'm sorry, my dear. I contributed thousands—but this was never what I intended."

Reynold sensed her kindness then, a strong wave that did not differentiate between Lily, an automaton, and her other charges. The breath left his lungs with a rush. Perhaps if this woman took an interest in Lily, she would be safe.

"Mrs. Gideon, will you agree to help Lily? She needs a place to hide and other things—the liquid formula that keeps her skin alive, and…"

Again Mrs. Gideon addressed Lily directly. "You mentioned your friend, Chastity, fished out of the river. Do you think she committed suicide?"

"I do, ma'am. She felt ever so much guilt over the loss of life at the Crystal Palace. And I'd showed her where our shutoff switch is located. It's just here…"

"No, don't show me. That should be your personal secret, don't you think?" Mrs. Gideon smiled briefly. "Give no one else power over you if you can help it."

"Yes, Mrs. Gideon."

"Call me Miss Topaz—all my girls do."

"Miss Topaz," Lily repeated carefully, "I believe Chastity threw herself in the river and used her shutoff switch before her boiler extinguished, in an effort to pay for her mistakes. She never meant the fire to harm anyone, merely to provide us the chance for escape."

"Yes, but Dr. Landry may be able to restart her now and procure information as to your whereabouts."

"That's what I fear," Reynold put in.

Mrs. Gideon jerked her head at him and asked, "Lily, how does he fit into this?"

"He is my lover," Lily pronounced proudly.

"Oh?" Mrs. Gideon's eyebrows soared. "Not just a john?"

"What is a 'john,' please?"

"A...client."

"Oh, no, not at all. I love him. And he loves me. We wish to remain together."

"Is that so?" Mrs. Gideon looked at Reynold.

He nodded. "I'd like to marry her. But I don't know how that will ever be possible."

Mrs. Gideon returned to her seat behind the desk. "Quite frankly, neither do I. Unfortunately, Lily is considered property, under the law. Dr. Landry has legal claim to her, and if you're caught with her, you'll be in considerable trouble."

Lily got to her feet. "I should go at once and turn myself in to Dr. Landry."

"No," Reynold objected wildly.

"I agree with your lover," said Mrs. Gideon.

"But if my being here endangers him—or you..."

"Sit back down. You, like Chastity from the sound of it, are all too quick to sacrifice yourself."

"We are taught from the first we do not matter other than in providing comfort and pleasure to others."

"A lesson the better abandoned now."

Reynold's heart lifted. "Does that mean you will help?"

"Yes. But we'll need to be very careful. Listen to me, Lily, and remember: it will be too risky to introduce you to the other girls here as 'Lily.' Dr. Landry may inquire after you if she's not sure you were destroyed in the fire. I think, to make things easy, we'll call you 'Lana.' And we will tell no one that you are an automaton. Understand?"

"I am to let them believe me human?"

"I feel it vital to your safety. I am fond of the girls here, and ordinarily I do trust them. But some are not always good at keeping secrets. And under the law, as I say, should Dr. Landry come here and lay claim to you, I wouldn't be able to prevent you being turned over to her."

Reynold turned sick inside. "Maybe this wasn't such a good idea."

"On the contrary. I have resources I believe will prove beneficial. I can connect Lily—or rather Lana—with the friend I mentioned, one Patrick Kelly. He may be able to procure the nutritional formula she requires." Mrs. Gideon's gaze slid over Reynold. "If you keep her hidden away somewhere, how will you manage that?"

"I can't," Reynold admitted miserably.

"But," Lily objected, "I do not know whether I can successfully pretend to be human, living among humans."

Mrs. Gideon smiled brilliantly. "We will soon discover whether or not you can."

Chapter Twenty-Six

"I did not comprehend I would have to say goodbye to you." Lily pressed close in Reynold's arms. "Or that we would no longer be able to make love."

Reynold ran his fingers through her hair and caressed her cheek before pulling her still closer. "Neither did I. But it's one of Mrs. Gideon's rules—no men staying here. And I guess it makes sense. She's trying to get these women off the streets. No sense allowing clients in."

"How will I endure your absence?" Lily listened to the sound of Reynold's heart—the sound she prized above all others—and tried to envision existing without him. She was not good at imagining; trying to do so made her intelligence stutter and misfire.

The two of them stood wrapped in one another, in Mrs. Gideon's office where she'd left them alone for a few minutes.

Reynold told her, "At least you'll be safe, as safe as we can make you, anyway. That's more important than anything else right now. And Patrick Kelly may be able to provide the formula you need."

"Yes."

"Right now, sweetheart, this is what we need to do."

"I will miss sleeping with you. Or lying with you while you sleep. I do not actually sleep."

"I'll miss that too, more than I can say. But Lily— Lana—be sure not to say things like that in front of the other women here."

"Only to Mrs. Gideon. Or you. I understand."

"Maybe sometime in the future we can be together. I promise to do everything I can to make that happen."

"The future?"

"The years ahead."

Years. Lily found that both comforting and disturbing. For her to survive into years ahead, so much needed to happen: she would have to continue functioning and remain free and independent of Dr. Landry, to whom she was a possession. And stay with Rey.

So many impossible things.

"Listen," he told her, "Mrs. Gideon didn't say we can't see each other—only that I can't stay here with you. Maybe I can take you back to my room sometimes, if it's safe."

Lily lifted her head and looked at him. "I hope so, for we've yet to finish acting out the last few of Miss X's adventures. I read the end. Her lover returns to her after all, and they rise to new heights of passion."

Reynold kissed her. "I can't wait."

****

"I know you're not able to eat or drink," Mrs. Gideon said softly, "but most of the social engagements in this house take place over meals. So you'll have to pretend. Just push the food around on the plate. The girls will think nerves have upset your stomach."

Lily peered into the dining room. "There's a man there. Is he a client?"

"Absolutely not. That's my husband, Rom. He's a

liaison with the Canadian government and is usually too busy to take lunch with us. Today we're in luck."

"He will not expect sexual pleasure from me?" Lily did not wish to enter the room. "I don't want to provide that to anyone but Rey."

"You may relax—I promise you, I provide that man with all the pleasure he can stand. Now come along, Lana—you can do this."

"Yes." Pass as human in a room full of humans? She'd never before attempted any such thing. Her legs trembled beneath her as she walked in Mrs. Gideon's wake. Every head turned toward her, including that of the man who stood near the head of the table.

Lily measured him against Reynold, her standard of perfection. This man, neither as tall nor as broad as Rey, stood only an inch or two over Mrs. Gideon's impressive height and had fair, wavy hair that tumbled over his forehead. He wore dark trousers and a plain white shirt open at the neck, and his blue eyes regarded Lily with calm kindness.

"Ladies"—Mrs. Gideon laid her fingers on Lily's arm—"we have a new member of the household. Please join me in welcoming Lana. For reasons I'm sure you'll understand, we'd like to keep her presence here under our hats. She's been through quite an ordeal, so I hope you'll make things as easy for her as you can."

Under our hats? Lily didn't have a hat on her head, and neither did any of the eight women now staring at her.

They ranged in age from quite young to middle-aged, but they shared in common a hard and assessing expression.

The first to speak, Rom Gideon said, "Welcome,

Lana. Please find a seat. I think the second from the end is empty. Right, Meggie?"

A red-haired woman with a pockmarked face nodded.

Mrs. Gideon's fingers tightened on Lily's arm briefly before she urged her toward the open seat. Everyone sat down.

"I don't recognize you," said a brown-haired woman seated next to Rom Gideon. "Where did you work?"

Lily froze in her seat, stumped by the very first question. She shouldn't answer but had been trained not to be rude.

"I mean," the woman went on, "most of us have seen each other before, on the corners or in the taverns. I don't remember seeing you."

Mrs. Gideon spoke. "Probably one of the things we'd better not share."

"You from out of town?" demanded a fair-haired girl whose sharp tone belied her years. "I don't think that's fair. There are only so many places here. Why should a stranger get one of them?"

"You know I give shelter to all, based on need," said Mrs. Gideon. "Della, don't you trust me?"

"Yes, Miss Topaz."

"Lana's come here for help, not badgering. This is a sisterhood."

One of the older women sniffed and pointed her nose in the air. "Looks a bit fine and well-bred, to me. What, Lana? Did you come from some high-class brothel?"

Topaz Gideon's gaze flew to Lily; a bit too close to the truth. Drawing upon her reading, Lily began to weave a story for herself.

"Please, Miss Topaz, might I not tell them just enough so they will understand?"

"Well, I don't think—"

Lowering her head, Lily said, "I was held prisoner—kept for the use of one man."

A collective gasp went around the table.

"Mercy!" one of the women breathed.

"You wouldn't believe the things he made me do before I escaped. Or maybe you ladies would. You may be the only ones who could understand."

"My goodness," the first girl responded. "How did you get away?"

"I hurt him. Now they're looking for me."

The women took it from there, the conversation steering itself.

"Any man who treats a woman like that deserves what he gets, that's what I say."

"Hope you gutted him, dearie—the nasty piece of work."

"A slave, that's what you were. Just like the rest of us."

Rom and Topaz Gideon exchanged incredulous glances. Lily concentrated on pushing the food around on her plate while her new sisters closed ranks around her.

"No one will learn you're here, not from us."

"Just let them coppers come looking."

"If I had a penny for every john I've smacked, I'd be a woman of means."

Mrs. Gideon cleared her throat. "I've given Lana the little closet at the end of the hall. As I'm sure you'll understand, she's used to being alone and will need her privacy for a while."

"Who's the fellow brought you here?" asked Meggie. "A workman, by the look of 'im."

"Just a Good Samaritan who assisted Lana in finding her way to us. We don't want to incriminate him or have him punished for his good deed."

"Most good deeds do get punished," agreed the woman with the pockmarked face. "At least, that's my experience."

Lily hoped not. She missed Rey already and would rather return to Dr. Landry than bring trouble to him.

"You're one of us now," said the girl next to Lily. "We'll look after you."

****

"A word, sir, if you don't mind. Michaels, isn't it? From Liam McMahon's place."

Reynold paused his cart, which held the corpse of an old man found down near the waterfront, unidentified so far and probably homeless. It had been deemed best Reynold should take him back to McMahon's for a decent charity coffin.

He'd just left a knot of police at the site and didn't expect to find another waiting for him here. Yet Brendan Fagan stood rocking on his heels outside the shop, whether in an official capacity or otherwise, Reynold couldn't tell.

"As you can see, sir, I'm a bit busy at the moment." He gestured to the corpse.

Officer Fagan inspected Reynold carefully with bright blue eyes. "Take your charge inside. Then I'd like you to come down to the station with me."

Reynold's stomach dropped so violently he'd have lost his lunch, had he eaten any.

His thoughts flew to Lily. They didn't have to fly far—all this interminable day since he left her at Mrs. Gideon's he'd been focused on her, wondering if he'd done the right thing and whether she'd be safe there.

He could hardly believe how much he missed her, and not just her touch or her kisses. He longed to see her again, but didn't know if he would, or when.

And now this.

Had someone at the Haven for Disadvantaged Women ratted him out?

"What's this about, officer?"

"We'd like to ask you some questions, lad, in connection with a series of steamcab thefts here in the city."

Hell no, not that. "Steamcab thefts?" he repeated. "But I don't know…"

"A man fitting your description was seen at one of the sites we're investigating for receiving stolen property."

"Me? But there must be a thousand men of my description in this city."

"Aye, and if we need to, we'll interview all of them."

Liam stepped out of the shop and looked at Reynold sympathetically. "Go with him, Rey. He's like a bulldog—if someone's reported you, he'll not leave it alone, and I can't have this kind of thing on my doorstep."

"Yeah, Liam, but…"

"Just tell them the truth. Sure, you're innocent, and the truth will out."

Precisely what Reynold feared. Who had dropped him in it? And did he have the wits to talk his way free?

Chapter Twenty-Seven

"Please tell us where you were on the evening of July fifteenth."

As if Reynold could remember. Had he been in Lily's arms? Had that been the first night they spent together in his bed while Chastity sat by? Had it truly been such a short time ago, though his entire life had changed?

"You already asked me that question." He strove desperately to master his visible nervousness and marshal some sort of believable patter. He wasn't much for patter—wasn't one for talking, when it came to it. But the two officers, Fagan and another fellow with coal black hair and hard eyes, had him in the questioning room at the station, seated across from them at a big scarred table. And he got the distinct impression he wouldn't be getting out of here soon unless he came up with a convincing tale.

If he didn't get out of here, he couldn't see Lily again. And he wanted—no, needed—to see Lily.

He felt sick with worry about her.

"And we're asking again," said the black-haired officer—Brookman, he'd said his name was. So far, Fagan had said little.

"I don't remember. Like I said, the days all sort of blur together. I go to work, haul some bodies around, fall into bed at night exhausted. Not too exciting."

"Not as exciting as stealing steamcabs?" asked Brookman.

"I wouldn't know, would I?"

"Would it surprise you to know we followed up on information that puts you at one of the wrecking yards where the stolen steamcabs were being broken down?"

"It would, very much." He'd visited several; none of the contacts knew him. How could they possibly finger him?

"Our informant admits he received the stolen property from you, and that his contact who set it up referred to you as 'Reynold.' Now that, in conjunction with the informant's description, jogged the memory of my colleague here."

Damn Vern for a stupid weasel, Reynold thought bitterly. Here he'd spent no end of time warning Reynold to keep a tight lip, while he'd been the one to let something slip.

Fagan spoke for the first time since they'd sat down in the room. "Not too many men in this city go by that moniker—not as a first name, at any rate."

"Yeah but there are plenty of Reynoldses." Reynold started to sweat. "Common enough name."

"How many of them do you think match your description? A big man, he said, with brown hair and eyes—not above twenty-five."

"Lots of men have brown hair and eyes, Officer Fagan. You know me—I have a good job with Liam. Why would I muck that up?"

"Lots of reasons. People get greedy. Sometimes they fall into debt. Do you gamble, lad?"

"I do not."

"Well, we're going to have to put you in a lineup.

If our informant picks you out from all the other brown-haired men, well, that won't be good for you, will it?"

It wouldn't.

"And," said the black-haired officer, "we'll be interviewing your acquaintances. Maybe one of them will know a reason you'd be out to make some dirty cash."

Sasha. He'd be all too eager to tell how Reynold wanted money to visit the Crystal Palace. And if the cops followed the trail of stolen steamcabs they just might place him there the night of the fire.

His heart started to thump double-time. If he endangered Lily, he'd never forgive himself, never. But surely the damaged steamcab he'd driven that night had been dismantled long since? And surely Lily would be safe at Mrs. Gideon's.

But if the police did put the pieces together, and Dr. Landry managed to start Chastity up again, they would accuse him of stealing Lily also.

Brendan Fagan eyed him shrewdly. "Sure there's nothing you want to tell us, Michaels?"

Reynold shook his head. He'd sooner die than endanger Lily. But he asked, "How long do you mean to hold me?"

"Just as long as we need to, in order to get the truth."

****

"I do not understand where Rey can be. I believed he would come and see me last night." Lily hurried to keep up with Topaz Gideon's long stride. The woman walked very quickly, her flared crimson coat swinging out behind her. Mrs. Gideon possessed style and confidence Lily could only admire.

"Perhaps he decided to give you some breathing space."

"Breathing space? He is aware I do not breathe."

Mrs. Gideon laughed and slowed her step just a bit. "It's a figure of speech. What I mean is, he may be giving you time to settle in with us."

"Oh. But I need to see him."

"You also need to lie low right now. Not attract any attention to yourself. Male visitors to the Haven are not encouraged. Too many of my girls have men come looking for them for the wrong reasons."

"I understand." Rey should not come and see her. But she wanted so badly to be with him, it seemed to be interfering with her operation. She ran the sound of his voice through her artificial memory again and again— the way it vibrated through her when he held her close. The softness of it when he made love to her. She had no reason to continue functioning without him; she might as well flip her own shutoff switch, should something part them for good.

"Are you certain I should leave the Haven for Disadvantaged Women, Miss Topaz? It is the only place Rey knows to look for me. If he comes there while you and I are away, what will he do?"

"Go away and return again later, I expect." Mrs. Gideon slowed her step still further. "Lily, you cannot allow yourself to rely too heavily on Reynold. Independence is good for a woman."

"I am not a woman. I am an automaton, and he is my reason for continuing to operate in the world."

"You love him."

"I do. And I cannot project attempting to live without him."

"That's all well and good. I feel the same about Mr. Gideon. Love can be a powerful and terrifying thing."

"Even for automatons?"

"Oh, yes. This friend I'm taking you to see—he is an automaton and was recently married."

"Patrick Kelly," Lily said immediately. "Rey told me about him."

"Yes? Well I attended his wedding, and it was…immeasurably moving. Since he's one such as you, a hybrid, I'm hoping he will be able to help you more than I can."

"After that will I be able to see Rey?"

"I hope so. There—his house is just ahead. The blue one with the white curtains. Come along, now."

The house, tall and narrow, had a red-painted door with a polished brass knocker which Mrs. Gideon employed vigorously. A human woman answered the knock and swung the door wide.

Tall, with soft brown hair and brown eyes not unlike Reynold's, she smiled when she saw them.

"Topaz, come in."

"How are you, Rose?"

"Blooming, as Patrick likes to say."

"This is my friend, whom we're calling Lana. Is Patrick at home?"

"Yes, waiting for you. Please go through."

The narrow hallway opened to a parlor on the left, a high-ceilinged room full of light and books. Lily barely caught back an exclamation. So very many books! They lined the walls and spilled over onto the tables. One rested in the hands of the man who rose from his armchair when they came in.

No, not a man—Lily, good at noticing details, marked things that denoted him as one such as she. At first glance, yes, he might pass for human. But like her, he didn't breathe or sweat.

Yet he embraced Topaz Gideon as any friend might while the woman called Rose stood by smiling.

"It is good to see you, Pat," said Topaz Gideon. "Thank you for agreeing to help my friend."

"Any friend of yours is a friend of mine." The automaton had an accent, warm and melodious, that made Lily stare. "I am glad I was off duty today and happy to be of service."

He looked at Lily with bright green eyes. "Ah, a model even more advanced than me."

"Amazing, isn't she?" Mrs. Gideon laid her hand on Lily's arm. "I'm sorry—we shouldn't speak of you as if you aren't participating in the conversation."

"That's all right," the male automaton answered. "She knows what she is, do you not? We carry few illusions. I am Patrick Kelly, and this is my wife, Rose. Welcome to our home."

"Thank you."

"Please, everyone sit down and be comfortable," Rose said. "May I offer you some refreshments?"

Mrs. Gideon sat on the sofa. "Nothing for me, thank you. Pat, we're here to throw ourselves on your mercy. Lana has quite a tale to tell."

"I am all ears, as they say—though you can see there's also quite a lot to the rest of me." Patrick Kelly made a grinding noise, and his wife laughed.

Lily clasped her hands in distress. "Am I to tell everything?" Should she? Could she trust this automaton? She leaned forward earnestly. "I do not mind risking my safety so much as that of the one I love."

Kelly, resuming his seat, studied her carefully. "I understand. And I assure you, Miss Lana, anything you say here will be safe with me. I may be a police officer, but I am first Miss Topaz's friend."

"Good. Because, I would sooner be shut off than bring harm to him."

"And they say automatons lack higher feeling," Rose murmured. "Could they be more wrong?"

Chapter Twenty-Eight

"I will help you," Patrick Kelly said once Lily's long tale had been told. "I and my fellows have worked out the formula for nourishing our organic tissues. I can connect you with a supply. From my observations over the last hour, it is clear you are a more advanced model than the members of the Irish Squad—the next generation, so to speak. But the formula should work, all the same."

"This Dr. Landry who created her must be a genius," commented Rose. She'd perched on the arm of her husband's chair, and she continually touched him— her hand on his knee or shoulder, her fingers in his hair—as if doing so grounded her. Watching them made Lily ache for Rey.

"Yes," Pat agreed. "She has taken the knowledge birthed by Charles and Mason several steps farther. Miss Lana, your voice box is superior to mine. You can hear a slight click when I speak, can you not? And I believe your intelligence is both faster and more adaptive. How quickly did you develop a sense of identity?"

"I am not sure what you mean, Mr. Kelly."

"Call me Pat—all my friends do. What I mean is, when did you acquire a sense of self?"

"So you perceive that too?" asked Topaz Gideon.

"Most assuredly. She has a distinct personality."

"I do not know, Mister Pat. The more I learned, the more it altered me."

"Learning." Pat smiled and gestured to the room at large. "It is our saving grace. Our one hope at humanity."

"I doubt Dr. Landry ever banked on that," said Topaz Gideon dryly. "I know I didn't. Pat, I'm ashamed to say I backed the terrible scheme that's put her in this position. I put money into it. Being acquainted with you and the other members of the Irish Squad, I should have known better."

"Your motives were pure, Miss Topaz. You sought to alleviate the suffering we have both seen in the streets of this city."

"Yes, but now I've dropped these Ladies in it."

"We are but machines," Lily spoke by rote, "and exist to serve."

"There you are falling back on your instruction." Rose hugged her husband's arm more tightly. "Through my relationship with Pat, I've learned no automaton is just a machine. Oh, they might start out that way. But even the lowest-quality metal unit acquires a measure of personality over time. Sophisticated models such as Pat or you, Lana, acquire much more. Tell her, my love."

Pat stirred beneath her touch. "Some time ago, at a critical juncture, I was forced to make a choice between being an automaton and being an Irishman. A difficult proposition, as I am sure you agree. At that time I chose the blood I do not actually possess—the essence of being Irish. Now I exist as a kind of melding of the two—automaton in fact, Irishman in spirit."

"That's a good word for it," Rose said. "Essence.

Even when we're lying in the dark together, Pat, I can feel your essence."

"And he possesses a spirit," Topaz Gideon said calmly. "For better or worse, I have the ability to sense the spirit in all beings—living and dead. I can see a glow around Pat—not as strong as around some people, perhaps, but it's there."

"And me?" Lily could not help but ask. "Can you see a glow around me?"

Topaz smiled. "Oh, yes."

"What I would like to determine," Pat mused, "is how this *personality*, for lack of a better word, comes about, and when. Some of mine must stem from the man from whom my tissues—eyes, hair, and skin— were taken. An Irishman, when he was alive."

"I do not know from where Dr. Landry took my eyes, skin, or hair. I do not remember back that far."

"How long have you been in operation?"

"I do not know that, either. The first I remember is my training."

"Training?" Rose echoed softly.

"To be a prostitute."

Rose made a soft sound and looked at Mrs. Gideon, who shook her head sorrowfully.

"I should have known better," she said again. "But I had no idea the models Candace Landry meant to build would be so advanced. That was not the blueprint she presented to us. And I confess I was thinking only of the girls on the street. Now still another misery has been created."

"Do not blame yourself," Pat told her. "You have done much to help the women of this city who are in peril, Miss Topaz."

Mrs. Gideon nodded but did not appear comforted. "Anyway, I'd estimate Lana has been in operation some eight months."

"And," Rose asked Lily softly, "you do not want to go back to…that life?"

"I do not."

"Then we will help you. Won't we, Pat?"

"Of course, my love, if Miss Lana wants our help."

Lily leaned forward and said earnestly, "My real name is Lily. And I would appreciate that very much."

"Then," Pat declared, "we are all friends."

Mrs. Gideon got to her feet. "As I have other matters to which I must attend, Lily, my dear, will you mind if I leave you here with Pat and Rose?"

"I do not mind."

"And, Pat, will you see her home safe later?"

"I will."

Lily got to her feet also. "But I need to find Reynold. What if he goes back to the Haven for Disadvantaged Women looking for me?"

"Then I will of course direct him here. Try not to worry, Lily. I'm sure he'll turn up."

"And," Rose put in, "he'll be very welcome here when he does."

"You are all very kind."

"I will see you later." Topaz Gideon clasped Lily's hand before Rose escorted her out.

Lily and Pat Kelly were left alone. A wonderful opportunity, as Lily realized, to speak with someone like herself, but who had been at large in the world for some time, had learned to function freely and independently, had married.

"You will have questions for me," he said. "I hope

you will feel free to ask anything you wish."

"Please, can you tell me—how is it we have emotions? We are machines that run on coal and steam. Dr. Landry insists we are able to feel nothing, that units such as I exist only for the pleasure of those who pay for our services. That serving them is no different from a steam washer in a laundry handling a load of dirty clothing. Does the steam washing machine mind? Can you tell me that?"

"It is a question that has often occupied me." Pat rose, went to a sideboard, and poured himself a glass of amber liquid. A gesture asked her if she wanted one.

She shook her head. "I cannot drink—just rinse my mouth cavity."

"Nor can I, yet I find it reassures me."

"How?"

"That is one of the things I do not entirely comprehend." He returned to his chair. "Let me try to answer your question as best I may: it is a large one, perhaps the largest for those such as us."

He raised the glass to his lips and appeared to sip. Lily sensed his artificial intelligence cranking over.

"When we were manufactured, we were the equivalent of human infants. Is a human infant born with a sense of self, or is that acquired through learning and experience? For all my reading, I have been unable to tell."

"You read?"

"I have read nearly all these books. They teach me what it is to be human."

"I have read three books and possess one more."

"I will be happy to lend you any of mine. But to return to your question, an infant learns through contact with the world. So do we. We may come with a set of instructions installed by our makers—"

"As in 'Do not kill'?"

"My makers did not include that prohibition. They were quite happy for me to kill. But I have learned much since then. The personality, I believe, is built by experience and attracts the essence. That is why its formation takes time. I am assured even the most base model steam automatons eventually begin to care about themselves and others."

"What about the laundry machine?"

"No, alas. The laundry machine does not possess language which, I have determined, is the conduit. It cannot think in words and words, as I have learned, provide the language of thought, necessary for the expression of self."

"Oh. What about this other essence of which you spoke? That of an Irishman?"

Pat leaned forward in his chair. "That, Miss Lily, is most mysterious. I have been able to speak of it only to my fellow automatons—such as you—and of course to my wife. Because there is no explaining it. I can only describe it as a mystical presence that augments self. It does not seem to be learned or acquired. Rather it was present in me from the moment of creation or shortly thereafter. But—and this is most important—I had to give it permission to emerge. Therefore, I am the god of it, even as it is my moral guidance."

"Moral?"

"That inner sense that tells us right from wrong."

"I believe that is what made my companion, Chastity, kill herself. She felt the wrongness of having harmed others."

"Each person must follow his or her own moral compass."

"Now I fear Dr. Landry will be able to switch Chastity back on and use her to find me or, worse, harm Rey. Mister Pat, may I tell you a secret?"

"Yes."

"I am afraid of Dr. Landry. Terribly afraid. Is it wrong to fear my creator?"

"Miss Lily, according to these books around you, men have spent centuries fearing their creators."

"None of them could possibly have been as frightening as Dr. Landry."

Chapter Twenty-Nine

"So, Lana, who is he—that fella you were with the first day you came here?" Meggie asked the question curiously. "I saw the two of you together, and it looked to me like you were pretty friendly."

Everyone at the big dining table stared at Lily. Though all her new housemates seemed curious, she'd discovered Meggie seldom held back from asking personal questions.

She flipped rapidly through the contents of her intelligence, seeking the right thing to say. For the first time since her arrival at the Haven for Disadvantaged Women, neither Miss Topaz—out at an appointment— or Mr. Gideon was present for the meal.

Lily thought of a passage from *A Red Herring in a Sea of Red*, wherein a dead fox was torn apart by vultures. With all these women's eyes on her, she felt like that fox.

"I saw him too," said Agnes, when Lily failed to reply at once. "Very nice-looking, and what a build! I never had johns like that. I always seemed to get the weedy, smelly ones with faces like trolls."

Trolls? Lily searched her intelligence again and came up wanting. "I am sorry. What is a troll?"

The girls laughed, not unkindly. They seemed to have accepted the notion she had been locked away somewhere, not exposed to much of the world.

"Short and squat and ugly," Agnes clarified. "Not like your fella."

"He is—he is not my fellow." Lily pressed her fork into a morsel of food. Best to keep Reynold safe at all cost.

"Bet you'd like him to be, though," Meggie put in. "And the way he looked at you, chances are good. So who is he, if he ain't your fella?"

"Just…just a kind man who helped me."

Another of the women sniffed. "What decent man would take up with the likes of us anyway, eh, after where we been and what we done?"

"Oh, I don't know," declared a girl named Callie. "I mean to make something of myself, get a proper job and all. Then the men will come calling."

"What sort of job?"

Callie's eyes went dreamy. "Shop girl, maybe. Or waitress in a tea room. Something—something clean."

"Fat chance getting any of those places."

"Why? Miss Topaz says we'll have as good odds as any."

"Those odds ain't so good, though, are they? Try getting one of them places or a place in one of the big houses. Steamies take all them jobs, right?"

A grumble of agreement went around the table. Lily stiffened and looked from woman to woman in alarm.

"Damn steamies," said Bess. "First they take the decent jobs. Now they're even going to put the streetwalkers out of business."

"Might not be all bad, though," offered a raddled woman called Della. "Take Lana there, for instance."

Everyone looked at her again. She froze in dismay.

Did they know? Had they guessed what she was?

"What about her?"

"If one of them steamie prostitutes could have taken her place, she wouldn't have been held prisoner by that monster who had her."

"You're too pretty, that's your problem," Meggie declared. "The kind of girl a man keeps in a cage." Eyes bright, she added, "What sort of things did he make you do?"

Lily quivered. Suddenly she wished very badly Miss Topaz would get home. "I do not want to talk about it."

"Of course she don't. Probably all sorts of nastiness. Believe me, dearie, we understand. Oh, some of the things I've had to do, to earn a few pennies!"

"Makes me shudder, it does."

"I was only twelve when I went on the streets. My ma had just died, and it was take to the streets or starve. I didn't even know what men and women got up to, before that first time."

These, Lily thought, were the women she'd been created to help and relieve. At least she'd always known what she was for.

"I'll bet you learned real quick, though, didn't you?" asked someone else.

The girl nodded. "I cried and cried, swore I'd never let anybody do that to me again. Next day I got hungry."

"Amazin' what hunger will do," Meggie agreed. She leaned close to Lily. "Speakin' of which, you'd better eat some of that food. You don't take enough to keep a bird alive."

Lily nodded, raised a bite to her lips, and pretended

to chew.

"What's the worst thing a john ever made you do?" asked an older woman conspiratorially. "Let's go round the table and tell."

Everyone stared at her. The girl named Callie protested, "I hardly think that's the sort of conversation we're supposed to be having. Miss Topaz has worked hard to get us out of that life. She always tells us to elevate ourselves."

Agnes snorted.

"Better," said Ginger, "to go round the table and tell where we mean to go from here. The fine things we intend to get for ourselves."

"Our dreams," said the girl who'd been on the streets since she was twelve, and her face lit. "Let's share our dreams."

Dreams? Lily didn't dream, as such. She didn't even sleep. What was she to say?

She concentrated on breaking the food on her plate into smaller pieces.

"I'll start," said Meggie, beside her. "I want a little flat all my own—nothing fancy, just a place I can pay the rent and nobody can chuck me out. And I want a bunch of plants in the window." She sighed. "I used to pass a place like that back when I first went on the streets. I thought what a grand thing it would be to stay any place long enough to grow plants."

The confidences ran around the table like a chain of fire, fortunately for Lily in the opposite direction from where she sat. Modest hopes, spoken like prayers, were voiced one by one.

"A red serge coat with a fur lining."

"That job in a shop."

"A pair of decent shoes that fit my feet."

"A child."

That one caused a pause.

"I've lost two since I've been on the streets," confessed the girl who voiced that wish. "Both early on. I expect it was 'cause I had to keep working."

"Wouldn't have been able to feed 'em anyway," offered one of her sisters, further interrupting the chain. "Nothing harder than trying to raise a little one when you've no real place to lay your head."

"Still, it's hard losing 'em. Thought I'd bleed to death both times. Other women can have babies. Why can't I?"

"It's one of them basic urges, ain't it?" asked Agnes. "Wantin' babies. Part of being human."

Lily sat up and took notice. Was that true?

The circle resumed and wound ever closer to her. She tried desperately to think of some wish she could voice, one as humble as theirs, until the woman on her left said, "I wish I never had to go on the streets again."

"And you, Lana?" Agnes urged. They all looked at her kindly, these new sisters of which she was now a part. She remembered her old sisterhood of Landry's Ladies—far prettier faces than these, revealing less emotion—but prisoners all.

She laid down her knife and fork. Did these women realize what they'd accomplished, the gift they'd already attained? That of choosing. Of being free.

"Go ahead," Callie urged gently. "You don't have to be afraid." She added to the others, "It's like she doesn't think she has the right to say."

The other women nodded.

Another of them said, "Miss Topaz always tells us

you have to speak it out and then believe. Say it, Lana. Believe it."

Dreams, she saw, weren't just for sleeping. Rather, they could also be bright thoughts someone held fiercely tight, that helped during the dark times.

A new lesson.

Her bright thought was and always had been Rey. Even though he hadn't been back to the Haven for Disadvantaged Women, though she had not seen or touched him for too long now, he remained that.

Could she believe in him hard enough to make a single wish come true?

They all watched her with varying expressions: expectation, sharp curiosity, kindness. Still not confident in her pretense at being human, she disliked being the center of their attention. Yet she could feel the opportunity in the moment.

Believe it. She might not be human, but she could believe. She believed in Rey.

"I wish to become the wife of the man I love."

A brief silence met her announcement. She could not tell from the women's expressions what they thought of her wish. Some of them had sworn off men. Distrust abounded.

Yet they respected her words. One by one they nodded.

Meggie leaned close. "It's him, isn't it? The one you want to marry—he's the fella who brought you here."

Him. Always and forever.

Chapter Thirty

"God, get me out of this, and I swear I'll never steal another thing, long as I live."

Reynold whispered the words under his breath so his companion would not hear them. Only one man was left in the cell with him now—he supposed it could be worse. Hours ago, there'd been a small crowd of them, but they'd been taken away one by one, a slow process that left Reynold in agony.

He couldn't tell whether or not the remaining man slept. The fellow reeked to high heaven from a combination of beer and what smelled like piss—a likely enough blend. He sprawled on one of the cell's two bunks, breathing hoarsely.

Reynold sat on the edge of the other bunk, head in hands. Sick with worry about Lily, he wanted to vomit. He'd entreated the officers who took the others away to tell him what was going on and why he hadn't been released. They ignored him, and now exhaustion rode him hard.

He tried to remember the last time he'd prayed, really prayed, but failed. They'd had a neighbor lady who taught all her kids to pray. Reynold had slept over once or twice, but it made him uneasy when they all got down on their knees in a row and started speaking in chorus.

Later, when he asked his ma about it, she'd said,

"It don't do any good, boy, asking God for things. It didn't do any good when he took your papa away and left me to raise you alone, did it?" She'd stroked his head. "You're a good boy. Maybe not the sharpest knife in the drawer, but you have a good heart, and you'll do all right without any supernatural intervention."

He'd called on God—despite her warnings—a few times when he got beat up. Also when his ma died. She'd been right; it hadn't made a bit of difference.

So what was he doing sitting here calling on God? He groaned into his hands. Truth was, he'd make a bargain with the devil right now if it would get him out of this cell.

But maybe he should rethink that. Doing a deal with Vern had got him in here. For all he knew, Vern Schultz might be the devil in disguise.

A pretty lousy disguise.

What in hell could be taking the police so long? They'd said they wanted to make a few inquiries before there would be a lineup. Waiting for that wasn't doing him any good. His stomach turned over slow and queasy. He'd trade his freedom if he could be sure Lily was safe. Surely Mrs. Gideon would take care of her. But if he didn't get out of here soon, he'd lose his mind with worrying.

On the other cot, his companion turned over, belched, and broke wind.

"God help me," Reynold muttered again.

****

"Lily, you are welcome to stay the night if you like," Rose said.

On this, her second visit in as many days, Lily felt tempted. She found a certain comfort here in the

Kellys' home, a sense of belonging.

Rose went on, "Pat doesn't sleep, as such, though I do, and often he lies with me." She gave her husband a fond smile. "Sometimes he sits up and reads."

"I love to lie with Rey while he sleeps. I like hearing him breathe and listening to his heartbeat. It feels as if it beats for both of us."

"One heart can beat for two." Rose once more perched on the arm of Pat's chair. She leaned against his shoulder.

"That is why, much as I'd like to stay, I should return to Mrs. Gideon's. Rey may come there looking for me."

"I understand," Pat said. "You are welcome here any time. Please select some books to take with you."

Lily rose, attracted to the shelves that lined three walls of the room. "I would not know where to begin. Please choose for me."

Pat moved off to do so. Lily approached Rose, still seated on the arm of the chair.

"Mrs. Kelly, might I ask you a personal question?"

"It's Rose, and please feel free."

"You, as a human woman married to an automaton, are in a unique position."

Rose smiled. "So far as I know, we're the first to engage in such a union."

"And does your husband…is he able to keep you happy despite not being human?"

Rose's brown eyes warmed. "He makes me happy precisely because he's not human, but then, my situation's a singular one. I have a particular aversion to men. If you're asking whether he satisfies me sexually…well, my needs are few."

"I am certain I can satisfy Rey sexually. I was built to do so. I am more concerned about the other aspects, things I cannot give him should we remain together. Such as being unable to age along with him. Or to give him children."

"Only he can answer as to whether those things will make a difference. They don't matter to me."

"Thank you for speaking frankly. I have so much to learn."

Pat approached with a number of books in his hands. Lily accepted them from him, confessing, "So far I have read only three books: *The Adventures of Miss X*, *A Red Herring in a Sea of Red*, and *The Dear and the Dutiful*."

"Miss X?" Rose's eyes widened.

"She had such adventures, Rose! She and her lover. Rey was hoping to finish playing them out with me."

Rose's laugh rang out. Pat tipped his head and looked at her.

"Perhaps, my dear," Rose said, "you'll lend that book to me."

"Yes, any time. You have been most kind. I will be happy to repay you any way I can."

Pat nodded at the volumes in her hands. "That is a selection of my favorites. And Rose has the formula packaged up for you. You need only ask me for more when you run low of either commodity."

"Thank you. I am so glad to have met you both."

"Pat will see you safely back to the Haven. Won't you, Pat?"

"Certainly. And as they say—do not be a stranger here."

Pat Kelly wound up carrying all Lily's packages

while leading her carefully through the streets to the door of the Haven. They covered most of the distance in silence, but at the end Pat leaned close to say, "I could not help overhearing your conversation with my wife. I would not have you misunderstand. I may have been designed for murderous rather than sexual purposes. My creators did, in fact, omit the organ necessary for intercourse. That does not mean I am unable to provide my wife pleasure."

"I understand, Pat."

"What I am trying to say, Miss Lily, is those such as you and I are capable of love. And love will always find a way."

****

"You're being released. It seems the fellow who identified you as the delivery man in the steamcab heist has gone missing. We've searched half the city and can't come up with him. So no lineup, and we can't hold you. The powers that be have decided they can't prosecute without his testimony in court, and there's no other evidence." Brendan Fagan, who had come to the cells in person to deliver the news, narrowed his gaze on Reynold. "You wouldn't be knowing anything about his disappearance, would you?"

Not unless prayer worked a hell of a lot better than Reynold expected. Aloud he said, "How could I? I've been in here—how long?"

"Three days. Well, you're getting out now. But you're to stay on hand if we have further questions—or if the witness turns up. Right?"

"Just let me go." Before he went insane. He felt dirty, sore, desperate, and beside himself with worry about Lily. He never wanted to see another steamcab and was sorry he'd ever heard of Vern Schultz. He wanted a bath and a good night's sleep.

But not before he saw Lily.

He left the jail and loped through streets crowded at the height of the afternoon. Dodging children, peddlers with handcarts, horses, and the dreaded steamcabs, he at last reached the Haven for Disadvantaged Women, only to be met with Mrs. Gideon's regretful refusal.

"She's not here. But she's going to be very happy to see you. What happened to keep you away so long?"

Reynold ignored the question. "Not here? Where is she?"

"With some good friends, Pat and Rose Kelly. I'll give you the directions." Her frank gaze moved over him. "You might want to get cleaned up first."

"You're sure she's safe?"

"She was when Pat collected her this morning. He's…"

"I know who he is." Reynold drew a deep breath that felt like his first in days. "All right, I'll go home first and get out of these filthy clothes. I was in some trouble, but I think I've pulled clear of it now."

"I hope so." She looked stern. "Because Lily's depending on you. It's no time for you to muck about, as my husband would say."

"I understand that. Thank you for all your help."

She jotted an address on a scrap of paper taken from her pocket, and he was off again, running through the bright sunshine. He wondered what Liam thought and if he still had a job. He knew he should stop by the shop and see, but the desire to be with Lily drove him too hard.

At home, he stripped to the bare flesh and scrubbed down violently. In his scrap of mirror, he saw a stranger—wild-eyed, with a scraggly beard sprouting from his face and a gaunt, hungry look. Gazing into those crazed eyes, he asked himself a few hard questions: what did Lily see in him? What if she'd glommed onto him because he'd been the only man available? He had little enough to offer her; thick-headed and only poorly educated, he had trouble dogging his heels and might no longer possess a decent job. What if, out at liberty in the world all this time, she'd realized she could do very well without him?

Unable to look at the agony in his own eyes, he lowered his face to his hands and stood hunched over the chipped sink, wracked by pain. All he'd wanted the past three days was to see her. Now he wondered if he should.

Maybe he should do her a favor and disappear from her life.

Then again, maybe he should have the balls to tell her to her face.

He groaned and dressed slowly, his mind chasing the question all the while. Love meant sacrifice, didn't it? Would he be willing to sacrifice his happiness for hers?

Yes. But it would hurt. Damn, it might near kill him.

Still on foot and cringing at the very sight of the steamcabs that clogged the streets, he made his way to the address Mrs. Gideon had given him. He stood on the curb a full five minutes before making up his mind whether to knock.

The door was opened by a tall woman with light

brown hair and kind eyes. She gave him a swift onceover.

"Hello," he began. "I'm…"

"The missing Reynold? Oh, thank goodness. Please come in."

Reynold complied and stepped into the foyer. "I'm here to see…"

"Lily, yes. She's been beside herself with worry for you. I'm Rose Kelly, by the way."

The woman married to the automaton? Reynold stared at her.

But he had no opportunity to ask questions; Rose Kelly ushered him into a room to the left. He had a glimpse of Lily seated on a settee amid piles of books, with the automaton he recognized at Pat Kelly bent over her before Lily looked up and saw him. Books hit the floor with muted thuds as she leaped up and flew into his arms.

"Rey!"

He shut his eyes on a wave of bliss when his arms closed around her. Her now-familiar scent—that of hot metal mixed with sweet-smelling skin and hair—met his nostrils, and all his senses opened. She snuggled into him with one ear against his chest, listening to the heart that now galloped beneath his ribs, before lifting her face to his.

Bliss turned to something more as their lips met and the hot cavern of her mouth welcomed his tongue. One kiss turned to two, and he nearly forgot they had an audience.

How could he mind that? How care about anything but Lily?

A soft grinding noise recalled him to the moment.

He broke contact with Lily and set her from him with gentle hands.

"Are you all right?"

"I am." Her pale blue eyes searched his face. "But what of you? Where have you been?"

"I had a spot of trouble. Circumstances prevented me from coming to you. I'll explain when—when we're alone."

"So long as you are here now. Please meet my new friends." She tugged at his hand. "Pat and Rose Kelly. He's an automaton, and she's human. They are the ones you told me about, Rey—they are married."

"I believe we've met, Officer Kelly, in front of the Crystal Palace." Reynold extended his hand.

Kelly, who had a face like the map of Ireland, examined him frankly. "I remember. Reynold Michaels, is it? Miss Lily has been deeply concerned by your absence."

"Has she?" Reynold gazed into Lily's face again.

"Oh, yes," she affirmed. "I could not imagine what would keep you from coming to find me as you promised."

Reynold wasn't about to explain it now. Kelly was a cop, and Reynold did not consider himself far enough out of trouble to go splashing details around.

Fortunately, Lily raced on, never letting go of his hand. "Pat and Rose have been so good to me, Rey. Pat can provide all the enzyme wash I need. And they have taught me a great deal in only a few days. Look at all the books! Pat says reading can help me understand what it is to be human. He says it's like getting inside the head of a thousand men and women. Is that not a wonderful thing?"

Reynold could only echo, "Wonderful." To Kelly and Rose he said, "Thank you for taking her under your wing."

Rose smiled. "It's been our pleasure. Lily is delightful company. Mr. Reynold, I don't know where you've been these past days, but there are some things you should know. Lily's former companion, Chastity, who is back in Dr. Landry's hands, has been under repair. Pat's been able to learn through the grapevine that Dr. Landry's well on her way to a successful restart."

"It begins with drying her out," Kelly said somberly. "I know, firsthand, units such as Chastity can withstand a drenching. I myself once went over Niagara Falls with only minimal damage. When I was dried out and my boiler was restarted, I retained all my memories."

"You're saying Chastity will recall the part I played in getting her and Lily away."

"I regret to say so."

"Will this Dr. Landry be able to get the information out of her if she doesn't want to tell?"

"I keep saying to Pat," Lily put in, "Chastity will never betray us."

"Not if she can help it," Pat amended.

"What I think Pat means is she may have no choice."

Pat nodded. "Dr. Landry created Chastity's artificial intelligence and may well have full access to it. Unfortunately, that puts us—and Mrs. Gideon—in a bind. Having Lily in our company will be considered possession of stolen property. I am sorry, my dear, but under the law you have an owner. I do not see how to get past that."

Oh, hell, Reynold thought. Out of the frying pan and into the fire.

Chapter Thirty-One

"Hold me Rey, please—closer. I want to feel your heart beat right through me. When I do, it feels as if I have a heart of my own."

"I don't think we can get much closer than this," Reynold replied truthfully.

Lily considered it. Maybe he was right; he'd just finished emptying his seed inside her, and they remained joined, his body covering hers. She had her arms wrapped around him so she could absorb not only each heartbeat but his every breath. She wished she could remain like this forever, would ask nothing more.

She had insisted on accompanying him back to his room straight from the Kellys', even though he said it wasn't safe. Chastity knew the location of this place. At that moment she'd been willing to trade her safety to be with him. They'd tumbled onto the bed, where they now lay, and the shabby room became a mansion.

"Lily, we need to talk."

"Yes, Rey."

He withdrew from her gently and rested on his elbows to look at her. She loved the way he touched her naked body with his hands and his gaze, adored being unclothed beneath him. But trouble now filled his eyes.

"Are you going to tell me where you were?"

"Yes. In jail."

She tipped her head on the pillow, searching out

references. Reynold had loosened her hair, and it lay tangled around them. He had kissed it just before he entered her.

"Jail is an institution where criminals are held. You mentioned it before. But you are not a criminal."

"Lily, I've done some things I'm not proud of, in order to be with you. I can't tell you exactly what, because then it's information the authorities might get out of you. And I can't talk about it in front of Patrick Kelly because he's a cop. But I was hauled in for theft. So if I'm found in possession of you, well, it's like Kelly says. You'll be considered property, and I won't have a chance."

"You're saying I could prove dangerous to you."

"Yes, very."

She did not want to be a danger to him. And how could she be property when she had the ability to desire, and follow those desires? Humans had the right to choose; she did not. It always came back to her not being human.

"Rey, this is difficult for me to understand."

"It's hard for me to understand, too."

"I love you. Do I not have the right to be with you?"

"I'm afraid not. And that means—well, my first concern has to be keeping you safe."

"And you. It will not be safe for you to be found with me."

"I don't give a hang about that. What worries me is the chance of you getting returned to Dr. Landry—forced back into that old life once she rebuilds the Palace. A slave again."

Lily said nothing. She felt him draw a breath, a

deep one. His hand cradled her cheek.

"Listen to me, Lily."

"I always listen to you, Rey."

"Good. Because I did a lot of thinking while I was in jail, an awful lot. I'm glad you met the Kellys and they can help you with all your needs. Maybe it's a good thing Kelly's a cop—he may be able to keep tabs on what's going on with Dr. Landry. Between him and Topaz Gideon, you'll be taken care of."

"You will take care of me."

"No, Lily. No."

"But I want to be with you."

"You said you'd listen."

"Yes, Rey."

"I'm no good for you, Lily. I realized that, inside. What do I have to offer you? Sasha's right about me: I'm a loser, a laugh. I've nothing to brag about but a job pushing corpses around the city, if I still have that. A shabby room and no money. Sure, I was a stop-gap measure for you, and I've loved every minute we spent together. But it has to be over now."

"Over?" For an instant Lily's intelligence, incapable of processing the word, stuttered. She froze where she lay beneath him.

"Look," he hurried on, "I can't do anything to help you. I can only harm you. Stay with Mrs. Gideon and pretend to be human. Let the Kellys assist you and get you free of Dr. Landry. Become all you wish to be."

"I wish to be your wife."

"Lily—darling—that's impossible."

"It is not. Rose is Pat's wife, and they are like us."

"Not impossible for that reason but because of who I am."

"But I love you."

"You only think you love me because I'm the first man you latched onto. You had no—no information to tell you what a lousy choice you made."

"Lousy?"

"Bad. Mistaken."

"You're the one who is mistaken, Rey."

"Lily, no. There are thousands of better men out there, if you want to be with a human."

"I want to be with you." Again her intelligence faltered and kicked back in with a force that hurt. "Perhaps it is you who do not want to be with me because of what I am."

She should have expected this. In jail, as he said, he'd had time to think. Now that the effects of Miss X's adventures had worn off, he saw he wanted to be with a real woman, one who could give him warmth, children—something more than steel cloaked in flesh.

"No, it's not that," he said, but the words came slowly, too slowly to convince her. "I should never have taken a chance and brought you here. And I don't think we should see each other again."

What had he said? For an instant, Lily refused to assimilate the words; her intelligence whited out. It felt as if her shutoff switch had been tripped, even though she'd expected to experience only darkness in that event. Then she found herself still in the bed, Rey's body still half covering hers, gazing up into the face she loved more than anything else in the world.

He did not want her. Her very reason for existing, gone. Her impetus for reading and learning and caring—gone. Her reason for moving through her days…

She might just as well be a machine.

She began to tremble, her body juddering violently, limbs quivering, water splashing in her thorax. Her eyes rolled and the bed rattled with the force of her convulsion.

With no further warning, the fire in her boiler winked out.

****

"Lily? Lily—Lily!"

Reynold first whispered and then shouted the words at the figure that lay beneath him. Her arms, so recently clenched tightly around his torso, had fallen away, limp. Her pale eyes gazed at the spotty ceiling. Worst of all, her mouth fell open, emitting a few tufts of dark-colored steam. More trickled from her ears and out from the corners of her eyes.

By God, what had he done?

Panic gripped him, thick, black, and smothering in its intensity, so for a moment he couldn't breathe.

"Lily—Lily!"

He seized her chin and turned her head; it flopped on the pillow. Her eyes, now turned to his, held nothing. Gone. All her innocence, all her silly humor, all her love.

Just—gone.

A cry tore through him, half strangled wail, half grunt of pain. He slid from the bed and stood staring.

What to do? How to bring her back again? He gathered her into his arms, realized they were both naked, and set her down. He rolled her onto her side and, with shaky fingers, sought the flap that concealed her shutoff switch, failing to locate it. He sucked in a breath and forced himself to try once more.

It wasn't there. And she was dead.

Dead. And he might as well go away somewhere and off himself too. For he realized in that instant he couldn't live without her—well, didn't want to, though he supposed he could go on breathing, his heart might keep beating.

His heart.

She'd told him over and over again that it beat for both of them. But he'd gone and withdrawn it from her, and only look what had happened.

She'd died underneath him.

Oh, God, oh, God, oh, God.

His fingers at last found the concealed flap on the opposite side of her body and peeled it open. More steam came from it in a little whoosh. He found the button inside. Pushed it.

Nothing.

"Lily," he choked. "Come on. Come back to me. Please!"

Push, push, push.

No response. Lily lay looking like a dead woman, apart from the flap open at her side and the faint haze of steam.

"What have I done?"

Stupid. He'd always been hopelessly stupid, and good intentions counted for nothing. Sasha was right about him. They were all right about him.

He lowered his head to Lily's breast, fighting the blackness that swamped him. Stupid he might be, but he couldn't just let her lie here. He had to do something.

Only one person might know how to help her—one he could go to, anyway.

He dressed himself with shaking hands and shoved Lily into her clothing as best he could. Then, with her caught high in his arms, up against his heart, he went out into the night.

****

Rose Kelly answered Reynold's frantic pounding on the door and let him in, a look of horror on her face.

"What's happened?"

"I need your husband."

"He's not here—working. His shift started shortly after you left. He won't be home till seven."

"Can you reach him?"

"Maybe. Here, set her down. Tell me what happened."

"I killed her."

"What?"

Reynold laid Lily carefully on the Kellys' bed and stood back, trembling. "I told her we shouldn't see each other anymore. She just—shut down. I found her button—her *button...*"

He froze on the word. Rose Kelly pushed him down onto the edge of the bed. "Here, sit before you fall. Take deep breaths."

"She has a switch. Oh, God."

A curious expression crossed Rose Kelly's face, sympathy mixed with cool understanding.

"Listen to me, Reynold. I don't know what made you tell Lily you don't want to see her again, but I can imagine what it did to her. She adores you from your socks to the top of your head."

"I know. I don't deserve her adoration."

"She's a hybrid automaton. It doesn't matter what you deserve. It only matters that she decides. I may be

233

one of the few people in the world who understands your position. I stand where you stand."

Reynold blinked at her, knowing it for truth. "You married him."

"I did, and I thank my stars for it every day. Do you suppose I'm any more worthy of Pat than you are of Lily? I'm not. When I met him, I hated myself. Hated. I wanted only to die. He brought me back from that. He stands guard over me every day and shelters me with his love. Yes, love." Her brown eyes turned fierce. "I'll go up against anyone, any day, who says steamies don't have feelings, or that they can't love. Because I know different. I live his love hour by hour and moment by moment."

Reynold's throat closed. Somehow he forced the words through. "I'm not good enough."

"You think I am? I tell you again, it doesn't matter. She needs you. And sometimes we have to put others ahead of ourselves."

Reynold's eyes moved to the form on the bed. "But she's…gone. There was only a breath of steam."

"Pat may know how to get her restarted. We'll have to wait and hope."

A sound at the door interrupted her, the turn of a key in the lock. "There's Pat now. I wonder why he's home so soon?"

Pat Kelly came in, dressed in his uniform, looking barrel-chested and taller than ever. He took in the scene with superhuman speed, nodded at Reynold, and looked at Lily laid like a corpse on the bed.

"Ah, this is convenient. I thought I'd need to chase you down."

"Why?"

"The news is all over the city—Candace Landry has revived Chastity, who has given a description of the man that spirited her away. There is a citywide search on for the fellow who stole both her and Lily." Pat quirked one red eyebrow. "As I understand it, that is you."

Chapter Thirty-Two

"What do you mean to do?" Reynold eyed Pat Kelly with misgiving. A police officer, member of an elite squad no less, and on duty. What could he do?

Pat Kelly took off his hat, laid it carefully on the arm of his chair and strode to the bed.

Reynold sprang to his feet as if hauled up by ropes. "I won't let you take her."

Kelly gave him a look from bright green eyes. "If you intend to engage me physically, I assure you, you will not prevail. I have the strength of at least four men."

"It doesn't matter. You'll have to pound me into pulp before I'll let you take her back to Dr. Landry and her old life."

Kelly tipped his head before looking at his wife. "He loves her."

"It seems so, Husband."

"Mister Reynold, I have no intention of turning her over to Dr. Landry."

"You don't? But you're a policeman. You have orders."

"And I bend them when I think I should—for moral considerations. What has happened to her?"

"She…she shut down."

"Do you know why?"

"I'm not sure. I told her I didn't think we should

see each other anymore. She started shaking real bad, and went into this…this state you see."

Kelly bent a hard green stare on him.

"Easy, Pat." Rose laid her hand on the sleeve of his uniform. "He meant it for the best. He didn't feel himself a worthy recipient of quite so much love."

Kelly swiveled his head to look at her, and she took a step closer to him. For a moment Reynold thought she meant to push her way into his arms, but she merely gazed at him. Suddenly, tenderness filled the room.

"Remember," Rose said softly, "we talked about this. It is not easy being responsible for another person's happiness. It was not easy for me."

"I understand," Pat said. He looked at Reynold again. "I also understand how it felt for her, having your presence withdrawn. It stunted her operations. She has…ceased."

"Can you restart her? And how long will she be all right like that?"

"Indefinitely. We can keep her tissues nourished with the enzyme formula. And I may be able to restart her. I do not know for sure."

"Try. Please. I'll do anything you ask, anything at all. You can turn me in to the authorities if you like. So long as Lily's back."

"I do not like. And I do not believe it would be a good idea to restart Miss Lily now."

"Why not?"

"It will be easier to hide her in her current condition."

"Hide her?" Reynold swallowed convulsively. "But you're a cop."

"Above all, I am her friend."

"But where can we hide her? Not at Mrs. Gideon's."

"No. Too many eyes there. If Dr. Landry has indeed extracted the information from Chastity and word gets around the city that one of Landry's Ladies is missing, along with a description of Miss Lily, one of the girls there is sure to put the pieces together."

"Oh. Then, where?"

Pat looked at the bed. "She looks like a corpse, does she not?"

"Yeah," Reynold agreed unhappily.

"And did Miss Lily not tell me you work transporting corpses around the city? What could be more likely?"

"You mean…"

"I suggest you go get whatever conveyance you commonly use in your business. There has been a death at this address. You have been called to collect the corpse."

"I… Yes, I guess I could do that." Through the dark streets, with everybody looking for her… He shuddered inwardly.

"But where can I take her that they won't look?"

"It would be natural for you to convey a corpse you have collected back to the coffin shop where you work. Is that not where you usually take them?"

"Yes, mostly. We fit them for coffins before either taking them to the cemetery or to their families."

"Then I suggest you hide her in one."

"A coffin?"

"Yes, just until the situation stabilizes. Meanwhile, I shall call upon Miss Topaz and my fellow members of the Irish Squad to institute a movement for change. It is time we put an end to Dr. Landry's practices and established rights for those such as we."

"Do you think you can?"

"I do. My good friend James Kilter is fighting for the rights of animals, and Miss Topaz for disadvantaged women. We are no different."

"Well, that's a battle I'll fight at your side. But I still don't think I'm good enough for her."

"Mr. Reynold." Pat leaned forward. "It's simply not up to you to decide if you are or you are not."

****

The empty cart rattled alarmingly over the brick streets as Reynold trundled his way back to Pat Kelly's house. He humped it up onto the sidewalk, hoping to progress more quietly, to little effect.

Halfway along, on a corner, he ran into a policeman on patrol. The fellow strode along purposefully, swinging his stick. Reynold could almost feel it make contact with his skull.

The officer slowed as he approached and eyed Reynold up and down.

"Hey, there—what are you doing out at this hour?"

All the breath promptly fled Reynold's body. If Chastity had already spoken to Dr. Landry, the police could have his description. They might be able to figure out where he worked. This cop, appearing so casual, might already be onto him.

"Just out on a job, sir," he choked out, sounding as humble as he could manage.

"What sort of job? What do you have there?"

"Nothing, sir. It's empty."

The officer eyed him up and down, and Reynold felt grateful for the darkness, the fact that the night was overcast, and they were between street lamps.

"Funny time to be pushing an empty cart around, isn't it? The middle of the night."

"I work all hours, sir. I'm from McMahon's, picking up a corpse."

The officer backed off a step. "You got a corpse in there?"

"No, not yet. I'm just on my way. I told you, it's still empty."

The officer twitched aside the leather sheet with which Reynold routinely covered the corpses, moving as if he expected to see a giant spider. The boards of the cart bottom came into view.

"Well—what's the address where you're bound?"

Reynold gave the number on Bryant Street.

"Pat Kelly's place?"

"Yes, sir."

"Must be all right then. Who died there? Nothing wrong with his wife, is there?"

"No, sir. It was a…a visitor he was helping, as I understand."

The officer grunted. "Well, be quick about it."

"Just as quick as I can, sir."

Reynold rumbled off, sweating. When he looked back, the officer had moved on.

He reached the Kellys' in a state of agitation to find Pat had returned to work. He begged a blanket from Rose, not liking to lay Lily on the boards where so many corpses had rested, and placed her there with tender care.

"Hide her well," Rose cautioned. "Pat said to warn you if Dr. Landry does have your description, the authorities may look for you at the coffin shop."

"Yes, I thought of that."

"Good luck."

He crept through the streets like a ghoul, keeping to the shadows and making his journey all the longer by avoiding the main thoroughfares. By the time he reached the rear of McMahon's, he wanted to fall down. But he parked the cart in its usual spot before lifting Lily in his arms and carrying her inside.

Good thing he knew the place so well. He dared not light any lamps, and almost no illumination trickled in from outside.

He stood with Lily clutched to his chest, trying to determine what best to do with her. None of the coffins in the showroom would serve. Several of those in the storeroom were, as he knew, spoken for. That left a huge mahogany job and a couple pine coffins knocked up for emergencies.

He'd much rather place his treasure in the fancy model, yet this definitely qualified as an emergency, and since there were two pine coffins, he had one to spare.

He carried Lily into the storeroom, which smelled of raw lumber.

"Forgive me," he whispered as he laid her down long enough to open the coffin that lay along the back wall.

Liam McMahon refused to make a substandard coffin. Even this model had a soft lining and pillow. As he tenderly placed Lily there, Reynold told himself she didn't need to be comfortable and wouldn't know where she was.

"I'm sorry," he told her and pressed his mouth to hers. "Sorry I ever said what I said. If we get you going again, I hope you'll understand what I meant. I love you, Lily."

He closed her eyes very gently, placed the lid on the coffin, and stacked the second pine model on top of it, telling himself again she wouldn't mind—couldn't mind. Then he staggered outside and stood taking deep breaths until convinced he could keep the contents of his stomach down.

****

"You look like hell. Where did you spend the night, under a whore?"

Reynold turned a glare of some intensity on Sasha.

"I hate to say it," Liam spoke mildly, "but he's right. You sure you're feeling all right, lad?"

All three of Reynold's fellow workers looked at him with varying expressions, Sasha's full of sly enjoyment, Pete's curious, and Liam's sympathetic.

"I'm not feeling great. Think I ate something bad."

Sasha sniped, "He likely caught something from one of those doxies he's been poking—or in jail."

Reynold flushed. He'd explained his absence and made his excuses—and abject apologies—to Liam as soon as he came in, worried as to whether he still had a job. If Liam turned him off, what would he do about Lily lying back there in the storeroom?

But Liam had been understanding, saying, "It happens to the best of us from time to time."

"Nothing was proved against me," he snarled at Sasha now. "The matter's been dropped."

"The police should know you are too stupid to pull off any kind of criminal activity. Dumb as a stump."

"I'm not too dumb to smash your face in," Reynold retorted, suddenly aware he wanted nothing—almost nothing—so much.

"Go ahead, fool!"

"There'll be none of that here in my establishment! Rey, if you're up to it, go and fetch the corpse waiting at Mr. Hennessy's boarding house on Swan Street. It's a charity case, mind. Man has no family. He'll have to go in the pine coffin."

Reynold froze. "Are you sure?"

Liam flashed him a look. "Sure I'm sure. I'm not after putting him in that big, grand model, am I?"

All right, Reynold told himself. They still had one pine coffin to spare. He could manage this.

But leaving Lily there in the back with the three men in the building taxed him to the limit. Feeling the effects of his trying night in full, he once more rolled out his cart and made his way to the address in question with as much speed as he could muster. Once there, he found his charge in a squalid room that smelled of vomit, sprawled in his own filth. He made a mental note never to lodge there and hurried the corpse back to McMahon's.

To his horror, he found Pete in the storeroom, only partially hampered by his still-damaged hand, and the top pine coffin standing open.

"What are you doing?" he gasped.

"Thought I'd get the coffin ready for you. Want a hand cleaning him up?"

Reynold eyed the second coffin; barely an inch of pine protected Lily from Pete's gaze. Best to get the boy out of there.

"Yeah, all right," he told Pete. "He's a right mess."

"Come on, buddy. I won't let you suffer on your own."

Chapter Thirty-Three

"You are up to something, aren't you? I can smell it on you."

Reynold started and spun to see Sasha leaning in the open doorway of the storeroom with his arms crossed and the familiar, avid look on his face.

He pumped out a breath. Thinking himself alone, he'd been about to lift the coffin lid for a peek at Lily— a close call.

"I would almost think you were guilty of stealing those steamcabs, if I did not know better."

"I thought you said I was too dumb to be a criminal." Reynold turned his back square on Lily's coffin and faced Sasha fully.

"That is how I know better. But you are looking sneaky, Rey. And I know you wanted money to go see your little dove."

Jesus, Sasha was getting way too close. Reynold considered smashing him in the face just for the sheer pleasure of it, weighing the odds of it landing him back in jail. He couldn't afford that now.

"I wonder how many men have had her since you. Maybe I will go there after the place reopens and see if I can poke her—I mean, it—myself."

"They're going to reopen?"

"*Da.* I hear that woman who runs the place announced it. They have already started rebuilding."

Reynold, swamped by consternation, said nothing.

"So tell me how it feels, Rey, banging a machine. Can you tell?"

"No."

"*Nyet*, I suppose they could not charge so much if you can tell. And I hear they will do anything, those machines. Just think how many men she had in her mouth before you kissed her."

"Shut up."

"What did you say to me?"

"I told you to shut the hell up." Reynold stepped toward him. "Don't you remember what happened last time you flapped those ugly lips of yours? Do you really want to keep prodding at me?"

"I do not fear you. I am twice the man you will ever be," Sasha sneered. "You could only satisfy a whore—or a machine." He grinned. "Like that piece of steel trash you paid so much for."

"Shut up!" Rey hollered. His hands fisted without his permission and, focused as an enraged bull, he waded in.

He caught several satisfying images of his fists crashing into Sasha's face and the blood flowing before Liam and Pete pulled him off the other man. By then, he'd smashed Sasha off every surface in the room, lastly the lid of Lily's coffin, which bounced with the impact and slid an inch or two awry.

That paralyzed him even before Liam seized hold with powerful hands and dragged him off his target.

"All right, lad. Enough."

"He had it coming—again!" Other than being out of breath, Reynold felt unharmed. But, damn it, his hands hurt.

He peered down at Sasha, who at last lay silent, his face a welter of blood and his blue eyes open.

"Is he dead?"

"I don't think so. Pete, check him out."

Pete hunkered down while Liam hauled Reynold still farther away. Sasha, as Reynold saw, lay mere inches from Lily's coffin.

"He had it coming," he repeated.

"No question. I only hope you haven't killed him—'twould be bad for my business and land you right back in a cell."

"Still breathing," Pete reported. "He's probably too ornery to die."

Sasha groaned and began to swear. Sitting up, he spat blood, accompanied by several teeth, and focused on Reynold with difficulty.

"I'll have you for battery," he bellowed. "Liam, call the police."

"Ah, don't be such a nancy," Liam told him. "Sure, do you want to involve the police in a squabble between friends?"

"He's no friend of mine. And I want to see him back behind bars where he belongs."

"Is that why you provoked him?" Liam asked. "You've tormented him ever since you came to work here and been twice as brutal lately."

"I did not ask him to attack me."

"I think you did," Pete said surprisingly.

Sasha struggled to his feet, bleeding from several orifices. "That is not what I will tell the police."

"It's what I'll tell them," Liam said evenly, "along with the fact that you threw the first punch."

"I did not!"

"You threw enough verbal punches at him to warrant twelve thrashings. You have to admit, Sasha, you got what you asked for."

"I will never admit that."

"Well, if you want to keep working here, you'll keep this between just us. Pete, make sure he gets home all right and help him clean up. Sasha, I'll see you tomorrow morning."

The two went out, Sasha still swearing.

"Why didn't you dismiss him?" Reynold asked bitterly.

"Did you never see the man join a molding? Better sit down. You all right?"

"I'm not sure." Reynold looked at his hands...shaking.

Liam pushed him onto a stool and grinned. "That's just the aftershocks of the rage. Believe me, lad, I've been there."

"I think I broke my hand."

"Nah—you'll be fine. Just rest there a moment. You made a right mess of my storeroom, though, didn't you?" Leaving Reynold where he was, Liam began moving about the room, righting stools and an overturned tool cabinet, working his way ever closer to Lily's resting place. Reynold wanted to say something, but his throat had closed.

He croaked wordlessly as Liam reached out to straighten the lid that sat askew. His hand bumped it and it slid aside instead, revealing Lily's motionless form.

"Jesus, Mary, and Joseph!" Liam ejaculated. He backed off, staring, and took a look at Reynold. "Is that what I think it is?"

"She. She's not an it, she's a she." Reynold groaned.

"One of those expensive steam units that belong to Dr. Landry?"

"She doesn't belong to anyone. She's her own person."

"That's where you're wrong, lad." Liam contemplated the situation unhappily. "You stole her? And you're hiding her here—on my premises?"

"I didn't steal her. I helped her escape. It's a completely different thing."

"Not in the eyes of the law it isn't. Holy hell!" He peered more closely at Lily. "She looks dead."

"Not dead. She's shut down. She got upset because I said we shouldn't be together. She loves me—" Reynold stopped speaking when his throat closed again.

Liam backed off another step. "Loves you?"

"We love each other. But I'm not good enough for her, so…"

"She's a machine."

"She's not, though, Liam. She's so much more. And she was a slave at the Crystal Palace. Pat Kelly says…"

"Pat Kelly knows about this? About her? That she's here?"

Reynold nodded vigorously. "It was his idea I should bring her here."

"Jesus, Mary, and…"

"Liam, Liam, you won't turn her in?"

"Well, I don't know, lad. You know me—I have more than the usual amount of sympathy for the dead. Not that she's dead, exactly. Or alive. I need to think about this." Very carefully, Liam replaced the lid on the coffin. "You say Pat knows?"

"He's been helping us, helping her. Liam, do you consider Pat Kelly alive?"

"Well now, there's a question." Liam rubbed his chin. "One I've never been able to answer, to tell you the truth. He's a machine, sure, but he's alive. And I owe my life to the fact that even more than a machine, he's an Irishman."

"He has an ordinary life, and a wife—and a spirit, so Mrs. Gideon says. Lily's no different. She's funny and warm and—and innocent despite the things she's been forced to do. I'd sacrifice my life to protect her. I can't let her get sent back to the Crystal Palace to be a slave. Liam, she minds the things the clients make her do. What choice did I have but to help her get away?"

"And fall in love with her?"

"That happened before I knew it."

"Will wonders never cease? All right, lad. For the sake of love—and because Pat Kelly's on your side—I'll keep silent. You're just lucky Sasha didn't get a glimpse of her. The jig would have been up."

"I know."

"But you can't keep her here, mind."

"Where else? I need to keep her hidden till the heat dies down, so Pat Kelly can get her restarted."

"Does he know how?"

"I hope so."

Liam shook his head. "I need to talk to Pat Kelly—now. Ask him over here. I'll guard your wee friend till you get back—no one will harm her, so I promise."

"I'll try to find him, but he could be anywhere. I may have to search all over the city."

"You'd better get a move on, then, hadn't you?"

Chapter Thirty-Four

"All hell's broke loose," Pat Kelly told Liam as Reynold led him in through the back door of the coffin shop, "and no mistake."

In the end, Reynold had found Kelly at, of all places, the Crystal Palace, right down the street. Accompanied by a number of uniformed officers, he'd been standing out front giving orders, facing off against a large group of bystanders.

Now he made the grinding noise that denoted his version of laughter. "A riot, and it's all my doing."

"Riot?" Liam's eyebrows shot aloft. "Over what?"

"It would seem a radical idea is afoot—that automatons should have rights."

"You don't say."

"Ah, Mr. McMahon, I do, I do—and the Crystal Palace seems to be the epicenter, so to speak, of this wild idea. Dr. Landry and her surviving automatons are barricaded in the portion of the building that is still standing. Protestors are aligned outside. There is to be what I believe in the old west is called a showdown."

"To what end? Do you truly think automatons will win rights for themselves?"

"I do. It may take a while, but I am sure it will come. Already I have won the right to marry. It seems the rest must follow in time."

"Is Chastity there—in the building?" Reynold

touched Pat's arm. "Is she operating? Do you think she's really identified me?"

"Well, now, friend, that is an interesting question. Word from inside is that Chastity, restored and restarted, has indeed told Dr. Landry all about the man who helped her and Lily to escape. She gave an excellent description of the fellow, which Dr. Landry has shared with the police. About fifty years of age he was—a former client of some means who, with an eye to using the two of them privately, hired a steamcab to get them away. The police are now actively searching for this man—seventeen stone, bald, and with a black moustache."

Reynold's mouth fell open. "She…lied? Chastity lied?"

"Created a story, apparently, yes. A woman of some talents. I confess I look forward to meeting her."

"So I'm off the hook?"

Kelly's green eyes met his. "At the moment, yes, it would appear so."

Reynold flushed with relief.

"Not so quick," Liam put in. "You're still in possession of stolen property—on my premises." He pointed at the coffin. All three men stared at it.

"Ah—yes," Reynold admitted. "Officer Kelly, what can I do with her? I can't leave her here."

"No, he cannot," Liam rejoined.

"I do have a suggestion." Kelly pulled a bottle from his uniform jacket. "Here is a measure of the enzyme formula she requires. Treat her well—everywhere—nail down that lid, and take her off for burial."

"What?"

"It is the safest option."

"You're asking me to bury the woman I love?"

"Only temporarily. If this matter ends the way I foresee, we'll be able to disinter her and hopefully restart her once she's free."

"Free?"

"So I hope, friend."

"But I can't just cart her off to the graveyard. They won't be expecting her. There'll be no place."

"There will, though." Liam snapped his fingers. "Go get old Bernie. Pete and I shifted his coffin out back."

"Bernie?"

"The poor fellow from the boarding house. They're expecting him at Potter's Field and will have a grave all opened up."

"But…"

"We'll roll your doll up in canvas and then lay him on top of her. He's a skinny enough corpse—they should both fit."

"Genius," Kelly declared.

"I have my moments."

"I can't put the woman I love in the ground with a corpse!"

"She'll never know," Kelly assured him. "Will not remember a thing. So long as we get her up again before the gentleman on top decays too extensively, all should be well."

"Why can't we put Lily on top?"

"Just in case the sextons at Potter's Field decide to peek inside."

"Why would they? It'll be nailed down."

"They have a reputation for pryin' out the nails and

lifting the lids to see if there's anything worth stealing," said Liam. "Didn't you know that?"

It seemed to Reynold he didn't know a lot of things.

"You stay, mind, till the coffin goes in the ground, and mark the grave well. We don't want to go digging up the wrong one later, do we?"

Reynold shuddered. "No."

"Right, then." Liam rubbed his hands together. "Let's have Bernie's coffin back in here and get the deal done."

****

Reynold loitered miserably in the shadow of the fence that surrounded Potter's Field, hoping the gloom of approaching night would conceal him from any curious eyes. Back at Liam's, he'd treated Lily well with the formula Pat brought—Liam and Pat had left him alone for that part—and kissed her goodbye. He'd rolled her lovingly in a canvas and laid her tenderly in the bottom of the pine box, beneath the lining.

Liam had helped him place old Bernie on top.

"Now get him there quick, so they plant him before nightfall."

He'd done his best, trundling his load through streets thronged with policemen and pedestrians. No one paid much attention to him—they were all looking up Niagara Street, where a huge crowd now swarmed around the Crystal Palace. Pat had told the truth; something was definitely happening there.

When Reynold arrived at Potter's Field, he found the two gravediggers in their shed, drinking tea out of cans. They knew him by sight from past deliveries and put aside their tea so they could point him toward the newly opened grave. They followed with their rolling, workmen's gait.

"We can take it from here, chief."

"Maybe I'll just stay and…er…pay my respects."

They stared at him in surprise. "You knew this fella, did you?" asked the one without any teeth.

"No but he's a charity case—no family. Seems a shame for a man to go in the ground all alone."

"Ain't alone," said the other man, who reeked so strongly of booze it made Reynold wonder just what had been in those cans besides tea. "We's here."

They chuckled and manhandled the coffin into the grave so roughly Reynold feared it might come apart. But even Liam's least expensive model was made too strongly for that.

Still, what if Lily, on the bottom of the box, were damaged? What if her boiler ruptured or some more delicate part suffered beneath Bernie's weight, slight as it was?

"Careful," he begged.

The sextons laughed. "He won't feel nothin'. There, he's in. You run along now while we fill in the grave."

"Yeah—it'll be dark soon. You don't want to be here after dark. Some of 'em get up and walk around, you know."

So against his better instincts, Reynold withdrew to the fence, where he watched until the last spadeful of earth went on. Then, in near darkness, he crept back and stood over Lily's grave.

"I'll come back for you, I promise. Just as soon as I can."

He stood there till it got too dark to see and then

stumped off back to the coffin shop, wheeling his empty cart.

****

"A mad scene, isn't it?" The man standing beside Reynold—a stranger—spoke to him excitedly. "They called the police to quell the riot, and they joined it instead."

Reynold narrowed his eyes. He'd walked up Niagara from the coffin shop to view the scene as, it appeared, had half the other residents of the city. Hard to keep away. It looked like some garish stage set, all steam lamps and flaring torches, people as far as the eye could see. Amidst it all, the Crystal Palace—half burnt—stood like a castle under siege, surrounded on all sides by steam mechanicals of every description, from the most basic, well-battered models to the members of the Irish Squad. They formed a metal-and-flesh chain around the building and shouted their demands.

Free the Ladies.

No more slavery.

No more oppression.

Rights for us all!

"It's outrageous," said another man standing nearby. "Those are machines. How dare they make demands?"

"They're thinking, feeling beings," said a woman on Reynold's other side in a voice he recognized. He turned his head to see Topaz Gideon standing not far away with a fair-haired man at her side.

Topaz, catching Reynold's eye, nodded at him. "Good to see you again. I trust our mutual friend is in good company."

Reynold's stomach turned over. He could barely stand to think about Lily. "Not really. But safe for now, I hope. Have you come to put a stop to things here?"

She grinned an assassin's smile. "On the contrary, my husband and I have come to join in. I've brought all my girls to speak up on behalf of their spiritual sisters. If anyone understands the plight of the woman forced into prostitution, it is they. Isn't that so, Rom?"

She turned to her husband and kissed him on the lips—hard—before gesturing to Reynold. "Come on!"

They surged forward, but Reynold stayed where he was. He'd learned that lesson and didn't want to risk coming to the attention of the authorities.

A great cheer went up when the reinforcements joined the crowd at the front of the building.

A figure climbed onto the stairs of the Crystal Palace and raised his arms. When he called out, Reynold recognized him as Pat Kelly.

"We demand justice both for ourselves and for those trapped inside this building. We are thinking, reasoning beings and deserve fair treatment. We will no longer be used, held, and forced to labor against our will. This country was founded on fairness for all, and we are part of the all!"

Wild cheers arose along with a faint cloud of steam. A detail of Buffalo Police arrived and abandoned their wagon when they couldn't force it through the crowd. Reynold wondered how the police would handle a confrontation with…the police.

"Cease and desist!" cried one of the newly-arrived officers. "This is an illegal assembly. Arrests will be made."

No one moved from around the building or among

the crowd.

Pat Kelly called out, "Hello, Bob. I didn't know you were on duty tonight."

After a moment's consternation, the officer replied, "I wasn't! Got called in special 'cause of this."

"Sorry about that, friend. But there is such a thing as right of assembly. You'll have to go home."

"Right of assembly's for humans, ain't it?"

"I think it pertains to all citizens. And, since we are native to this place, we claim the right of citizenship."

"Well, but—"

A small metal steamie at the edge of the crowd started a chant: "Free our sisters! Justice for all! Free our sisters!"

The gathered units took it up in a variety of voices—wheezing, grating, clicking, bellowing—a cacophony arose into the Buffalo night sky and echoed like thunder.

A chill ran down Reynold's spine.

"Stop!"

At first the woman's command was lost in the chant from the crowd. But she repeated it and stamped her foot. One by one the steamies realized the front door of the Crystal Palace had opened.

Candace Landry stood there, backlit by bright radiance.

The chant died to a murmur before trailing off altogether.

"You will not have my units!" Dr. Landry shouted. "They are my life's work, and I will die before I allow you to take them."

Chapter Thirty-Five

"Candace, you have to give them up. You can't continue to exploit intelligent, feeling beings."

To Reynold's surprise, Topaz Gideon rather than Pat Kelly mounted the steps to face Dr. Landry. Topaz's husband, poised for action, stood a few steps below her but didn't interfere.

"This is madness," Dr. Landry exclaimed, waving her hands at the gathered crowd of combined steamies and humans. "My Ladies are machines; they have no feelings! And you"—she focused on Topaz—"were in favor of these units being built and used for their assigned purpose."

"I was wrong, Candace, and I'm not afraid to admit it. You made them too well, too close to human. It's not right to use them against their will."

"I shall never surrender them. They are the crowning jewels of my life's work. And they are my possessions. Now, Officer…" She gazed past Topaz to the newly-arrived squad. "I want all these machines cleared from my property at once."

"How do you suggest we do that, ma'am? There are too many of them. And I suspect Officer Kelly's correct in saying there's no law prohibiting steamies from having the right to assemble…"

"They are machines, you fool. They have no rights!"

An angry murmur started among the gathered steam units and spread like a contagion. The girdle of steel around the Crystal Palace seemed to contract.

Overhead, a light appeared, splitting the dark sky. For a terrible moment Reynold thought God had parted the heavens. Then he heard the thump of engines and realized the police had put their airship aloft.

The dark blue blimp came over the roof, and the gondola, manned by police officers, appeared. One of them raised a bull horn.

"Disperse! Disperse, or we will employ water cannon."

Pat Kelly bellowed up at the gondola, "Will you fire on your own citizens?"

"We will get this scene under control! Take yourself away out of this, Pat."

"I can't, Chuck. It's too important. The imprisoned automatons are our sisters. Would you back down if your sisters were being forced into prostitution?"

"For pity's sake!" Dr. Landry cried. "I will not say this again. They are machines. They don't care whether they're scrubbing floors or taking care of a client's needs. They're my creations and my property. And before I give them up I'll destroy them. Do you hear me? I'll march back in there and shut them all down permanently!"

The crowd went silent, so quiet the drone of the airship's engines seemed deafening. Reynold understood by now that to a steamie—any steamie—*shut down* was the ultimate threat, and his breath stilled in his chest.

At that moment, he wanted to confront the figure that was Dr. Landry, argue with her, reason and persuade and convince. He knew to his soul that these beings, to varying degrees, had feelings. The finer the creation, the finer the discernment, but they all *felt* and *minded* and were capable of loyalty and love.

But Dr. Landry had become a wild and desperate figure, determined to be right. She stood stiff and defiant before the doorway of the Golden Palace, spotlighted by the powerful ray from the airship.

The moment drew out impossibly and suddenly snapped. Rey distinctly felt it happen, like the breaking of a guy line under unbearable tension. From the open, well-lit doorway behind Dr. Landry, figures emerged.

They looked like a bevy of lovely ladies, well-dressed, with shining hair and perfect skin. Reynold caught a glimpse of Chastity's dark head among them just before they surged forward to surround Dr. Landry. For an instant it looked as if they meant to support her, to embrace her. Not until he heard the first blows land, audible below the throb of the airship's engines, did he realize their intent. By then it was too late—the small mob of automatons had engulfed her, closed in tight, and taken her down.

People in the outer circle of onlookers screamed, but the hundreds of watching steamies remained uncannily silent. Topaz Gideon, closest to Dr. Landry, moved forward as if to leap to her defense, but her husband caught her back and wrapped her in his arms.

The human police mobilized and rushed the steps. The automatons there, including members of the Irish Squad, moved to block their way. The officers on the airship shouted orders and dragged water cannon into place, but as swiftly as they moved it became obvious any intervention would be too late.

It did not take long for twenty well-constructed steam units, however well-clad, to beat a single human to death. Steel lay beneath those delicate hands and arms, strength in the narrow fingers.

"Jesus Christ!" exclaimed the man beside Reynold, who'd gone white. As one, the human onlookers stepped back even while the encircling automatons continued to observe the scene in rapt silence.

"Do something, Pat," shouted the officer Kelly had addressed as Bob. "You're a policeman, by God!"

Kelly climbed the rest of the steps and looked at the bloody pile of clothing that had been Candace Landry. He bent down and touched her with solicitous hands even as the automatons outside the doorstep, most with bloodied arms and clothing, formed a chain, hand in hand.

Pat Kelly turned to face the crowd. "Dr. Landry is dead."

The buzz started among the automatons, which had been so silent, and the humans took yet another step back. The newly-arrived police officers bustled their way in, steam cannons drawn, forcing a path through humans and steam units alike. They stood at the base of the stairs, staring up at the gory scene.

"Pat?" Bob called.

Kelly took his place with the Ladies, who stood hand in hand. "With their owner dead," he called out, "I declare these steam units free beings. Come along, lads, and assist them."

Assist, or arrest? Reynold pushed forward, wondering if he might have to intervene.

"Arrest them," bellowed the officer from the airship. And indeed, members of the Irish Squad climbed the stairs, moving past Rom and Topaz Gideon and past Pat to approach Landry's Ladies. Each of the hybrid police officers took one of Landry's Ladies by the hand.

Officer Bob now stood at the base of the steps, looking up at Pat Kelly.

"Have your men lead them back that way—we have the paddy wagons parked as close as we could get."

"Sorry, friend," Kelly replied. "We are not arresting them."

"What?"

"Until the law is made equal for human and automaton alike, they are not subject to it."

"You mean to let them walk away? They just killed a woman in front of a thousand witnesses!"

"In the event they are at some point declared subject to the law, they may establish the fact that they acted in self-defense. She intended to *shut them down*."

Officer Bob, craning his neck, appealed for help to his fellow officers in the gondola, who now leaned so low over the rail they appeared to be in danger of falling out.

"Clear the area," ordered the officer in the gondola. "Disperse! Return to your homes, or there will be arrests."

The members of the Irish Squad had now paired with Landry's Ladies and led them one by one away into the darkness. The rest of the automatons began to move, shifting like a flock of birds with one mind, and the humans farther back got out of their way with alacrity. Officer Bob and his squad raced up the stairs and gathered around Dr. Landry. The airship, engines droning, went higher aloft and withdrew over the roofs of the city.

Done. Was it done?

A member of the Irish Squad escorted the final Lady from the doorstep away into the night. Humans continued to drift off. Reynold turned around and encountered Liam, just behind him, blue eyes wide and reflecting the torchlight.

"Liam? What just happened?"

"Not sure, old son."

"Why weren't they arrested?"

Liam's lips curled. "What's the point? Everyone here just heard their victim declare they have no rights. Hard to prosecute in that case, isn't it? I tell you, Rey, Pat Kelly is one smart son of a bitch."

Reynold paused and looked over his shoulder again. The police regulars had gathered up Candace Landry's remains and placed them on a stretcher.

"Whatever just happened," he told Liam, "I think it's shaken this city to its roots. People were never afraid of steamies before. Now I suspect they are."

"I don't doubt you're right." Liam threw his arm around Reynold's shoulders and drew him away. "Most steamies, though, are instructed not to kill."

"That's the thing, Liam—those ladies were too. Somehow they overcame that prohibition."

"Self-protection is a strong instinct, Rey—maybe the strongest there is."

"Besides love."

"Right, lad—besides love."

Chapter Thirty-Six

"Do not so much as look at me—do you hear? And do not come near me. Or you just may find you meet up with a hard wooden plank in the dark."

Reynold turned a deaf ear to Sasha's angry words. The man had showed up for work that morning looking like a veteran of a foreign war. But Reynold had no time to waste on Belsky and instead continued to pace the workroom like a caged tiger, waiting for the arrival of Pat Kelly.

Pete spoke up from the workbench where he awkwardly sanded trim work with his left hand. "Sasha, I'd be careful how I spoke to him, if I were you. He's friends with any number of steamies, and these days you can never tell what a steamie will do."

"Balderdash," Liam pronounced soundly. "They're not dangerous, by and large."

Sasha, one eye swollen shut and the other turned black and purple, with cuts and bruises all over his face, spoke again in a croak. "Not dangerous? They killed a woman last night, so I hear."

No one in the room said anything.

"What I do not understand," Sasha went on, "is why they were not taken into custody and shut down. They are machines."

"They're not subject to human laws...yet," Liam said calmly. "Change will have to come, I reckon."

"There are far more steam units than humans in this city," Sasha went on in a half-rant. "What if they become too full of themselves and riot? One of those mechanical whores could maul her john and ruin him for life."

Especially given the way they were treated, Reynold thought.

Liam drawled, his Irish brogue becoming bright, "I'm thinking it wasn't too clever, then, using them as prostitutes. Good thing all that's over, eh? I heard this morning the Crystal Palace is to be torn down."

"Good," Reynold barked. Site of too much misery—and, incidentally, his meeting with Lily. Where the hell was Pat Kelly? If he had to wait much longer, he'd explode.

"Change usually comes slow in this city." Liam rested his gaze on Reynold. "But I'm thinking that in this case it will have to come fast."

Sasha shook a bruised fist at Reynold. "Well, keep away from me—and keep your damn steel friends away, too, if you know what is good for you."

"Speak of the devil," Liam said half under his breath as Pat Kelly strode in. "Here's one of them now. Hello, Pat. What's the word?"

Pat Kelly, looking much the same as ever and dressed immaculately in full uniform, tipped his head.

"The word is *interesting*. Things have become quite interesting."

Liam grinned. Sasha backed off a step and pointed a finger at Reynold.

"Officer, I hope you have come to arrest that man. He attacked me."

Kelly gave Sasha the onceover. "Is there any

evidence, *sor*?"

"Fool of an Irishman—look at me! I am the evidence."

"You look quite well to me, *sor*. Are there any witnesses to this alleged attack?"

Liam and Pete looked at each other and shook their heads. "No, Officer."

"Then I am afraid I cannot make an arrest. Liam, if I might borrow your employee for a time, I would be most grateful."

Liam waved a big hand. "By all means, Pat. We're all at sixes and sevens here today anyhow; not sure we'll get much work done."

Kelly nodded gravely. "The whole city is at sixes and sevens. As I am assured through my reading, enlightenment can be a painful process—like a butterfly emerging from a chrysalis."

Sasha uttered what could only be a curse word in his native tongue.

Kelly shot a look at Reynold, who virtually danced with impatience. "Come along, friend."

They went out into blinding sunshine and heat that already gathered thick and heavy above the bricks of the street. The day would be a scorcher.

Reynold barely waited to be out of earshot before words burst from him. "What's going on? I thought you'd never come."

"Many things are going on. The Crystal Palace—or what remains of it—will be torn down as soon as this afternoon."

"Good riddance. What about you? Are you going to get in trouble for what happened last night?"

"Trouble?"

"I'm amazed to see you weren't disciplined, at the very least."

"That is what my wife said. She was pleased to see me when I got home."

"I'll bet."

"We had a most touching reunion."

That made Reynold blow out a breath and damp down his impatience. More softly he said, "I'm glad."

Kelly shot him another look. "I like you, Reynold Michaels. You have a rare ability to look upon individuals as *individuals*. You are like a shining star in this world."

"Me?"

"Yes. You will be one of the ones to lead this city toward the enlightenment I mentioned."

"Well, thank you. But—I still don't understand why you and the others didn't get in trouble."

"I, in fact, did nothing illegal. There are no laws on the books concerning the assembly of steam-powered automatons."

"No? But what about the Ladies? They—they beat Dr. Landry to death. Why haven't they been arrested?"

"As described by Dr. Landry herself, they are machines. One does not arrest a boiler that explodes and kills a man. Dr. Landry's creations apparently went awry last night. It seems she did not build them as faultless as she supposed."

"So you're saying they went haywire?"

"In a sense."

"What will happen to them? Are they free now— independent like you and the other members of the Irish Squad?"

"The circumstances are somewhat similar. There

was much debate after my creators were taken into custody. Many wanted us destroyed. Officer Brendan Fagan argued hard that we could be put to beneficial use. In the end, we were deemed to be autonomous beings and removed from the ownership of the men who constructed us. The Ladies' situation is slightly different. Their owner is now dead. As yet, no one has any known claim on them."

"What will they do?"

"Many of them have decided to marry."

"What!"

They paused on a corner, waiting for traffic to clear so they might cross. Kelly gave Reynold yet another look, this one very bright.

"It seems my fellow members of the Irish Squad have decided to take wives. The Ladies like the idea. They need places to belong."

Reynold remembered the hybrid steamies leading the ladies away down the stairs last night. His head reeled at the implications.

"Will they be allowed to marry?"

"I fail to see why not. My wife and I have been trailblazers, so I am assured. Is that not a grand word?"

"Er, yes. So you mean to tell me they'll all marry?"

"No. Some will make other choices. The important thing is that they get to choose. And we will help all of them."

"We?"

"It is that about which I wanted to speak with you today. I hoped I could count you in."

Reynold's step faltered. "But I thought we were going to revive Lily."

"We are. May I ask you a personal question?"

"Yeah, go ahead."

"Do you mean to marry Miss Lily?"

Reynold thought about it. The last words he'd spoken to Lily had upset her so much she'd shut down. He wasn't sure if he could fix that. Grimly he said, "If she'll have me. And if you can get her restarted. It's not as if we can fall back on Dr. Landry now, is it?"

"Alas, no."

"Do you think you'll be able to revive her?"

"To be honest, I am not certain. I will have some assistance in the attempt."

"Where are we going now?"

"To Potter's Field. I trust you remember the correct grave."

"Yes, but I didn't bring my cart."

"I have a steam wagon waiting. I thought it best to be as circumspect as possible about this."

Reynold, impossibly anxious, started to ache. He wanted so badly to hold Lily in his arms he could barely contain the desire. But Pat was right—if a miracle occurred and Kelly succeeded in awakening her, Reynold knew it must be her choice whether or not to be with him.

She had other options, and she'd explored so few of them so far. How dared he hope she'd pick him?

Either way, he wanted to get her out of that grave and away from poor Bernie's corpse.

"Let's hurry," he told Kelly.

"Patience, friend. I would have arrived earlier, but I had to obtain the order of exhumation."

"So this is all legal, right?"

Kelly's only answer was a soft, grinding sound.

****

At the entrance to Potter's Field, they met with a small troop of men dressed in rough trousers and shirts, armed with shovels. Reynold realized they must be off-duty members of the Irish Squad.

They nodded at him and Pat.

"Lead the way," Kelly told Reynold.

Reynold already sweated freely. "Where are the sextons?"

"In their shed. My friends here persuaded them to keep away for a while."

One of the others in the group made the now familiar grinding sound. "Amazing what a fifth of whiskey will accomplish." Like Pat Kelly, he had an Irish accent.

Reynold's mind reeled.

"Here. I think it's this one."

The troop stopped, and Kelly raised an eyebrow. "You think? It would be best to be sure."

"It was nearly dark, and all the rows look the same. But yes—this is it. Newly dug. And I recognize that marker there."

"All right, lads. Have at it."

"Be careful," Reynold adjured.

The crew set to, working in unison with the smooth power of…well, machines. Reynold grew more and more tightly strung as the job progressed. When the first spade scraped wood, he nearly jumped out of his skin. One of the automatons looked at him. "Here." He handed over his spade.

The sun now beat down mercilessly. Reynold eyed the familiar lid of Liam's pine coffin and went to work with tender care, his heart nearly pounding out of his chest.

He brushed away the last of the dirt with his bare hands while lying on his belly over the grave. When he rose, the automatons lifted the coffin up and set it on the ground beside the heap of dirt.

"Careful," he said again, even though they moved gently. One of them handed him a crowbar, and he pried up the lid, fearing the worst.

A strong smell of decay preceded his first glimpse of Bernie. He gagged and turned his head; no one else reacted. He realized they could smell nothing.

"All right, lads. Lift him out—easy now."

They placed old Bernie on the ground behind the coffin lid. Reynold flung himself back to his knees and lifted the lining to reveal the roll of canvas, only slightly stained.

"There now," said Kelly. "They were not in there very long."

Reynold lifted Lily from the coffin tenderly and, laying her across his knees, began to unroll the canvas.

"Better not, friend." Pat Kelly placed a hand on his arm. "Not here. Let's take her home."

"Home?"

"My place. As I say, I have assistance waiting."

Reynold nodded and rose with Lily in his arms. He stood while the impromptu crew placed Bernie back in his coffin and lowered it back into the grave.

"Come along," Pat Kelly told him. "The lads will take care of things here."

"Yes, all right." Reynold spun to face the crew, Lily clutched tight to his chest. "Thank you—all of you."

"There now," Pat Kelly crooned to his men. "Did I not tell you he was special?"

Chapter Thirty-Seven

"Is she all right?" Reynold gasped the question, his ragged breathing loud in the room.

Two heads—one dark and one red—leaned in to take a closer look at Lily. The owner of neither one breathed at all.

Reynold had found Chastity waiting at the Kellys' house when he carried Lily in. No longer clad in her finery, the automaton wore simple clothing like an ordinary woman of the city, and her hair hung in a single braid down her back.

She'd helped Reynold unwrap Lily from the canvas with care and place her on the Kellys' settee. He couldn't help remembering those same gentle hands had helped beat a woman to death last night.

Now she brushed a wisp of hair from Lily's forehead and made no reply.

Kelly said, "A bit of deterioration there at the corner of her mouth and on her brow. There will be more elsewhere, but nothing the enzyme wash cannot heal." He fixed Reynold with a green stare. "Would you like to bathe her or try to restart her first?"

"Restart her, please." Reynold's voice sounded harsh. "Do you think it will work?"

"Miss Chastity and I have discussed it. Neither of us has sufficient knowledge to be certain."

"The only ones who could restart her for sure

would be Dr. Landry or perhaps Nadia, but Nadia was badly injured in the fire—the one I caused. I am sorry, Reynold. I should have thought about the knowledge being lost last night before Dr. Landry's life was taken. But I did not know, then, that Lily lay in this state. And I do not think I could have held back my sisters for any reason."

"No." Reynold thought again of the steel arms rising and falling, rising and falling. "They were defending their own lives."

"We must refill her boiler, make sure she's stocked with coal, and try to ignite the vital spark—not that for her fire, you understand, but that other which makes her *Lily*."

Reynold turned half-seeing eyes on Chastity. "You were restarted, right? After you went in the river."

"Yes, but Dr. Landry achieved that, and I do not remember. Pat was also restarted once, after he went over Niagara Falls."

"That was different," Pat contributed. "Though my boiler went out, my artificial intelligence continued to function throughout. Miss Lily's has clearly ceased."

"You're saying she really is…dead?" Reynold choked.

"Friend, there is no 'dead,' as such, for us. Where, Miss Chastity, to begin?"

"With her shutoff switch, I expect."

"I tried that," Reynold told them. "Right away after she shut down."

"Then let us try it again."

Moving gently, the two automatons rolled Lily over and removed enough clothing to reveal the concealed flap beneath her left arm. Reynold backed off a few steps while they worked in tandem, hardly able to believe what he watched. The woman he loved held coal and water, had a steel hopper in her belly and fire where her heart should be. Seeing the plain truth of that didn't make him love her any less. Because he loved her essence—the innocence with which she looked at him, the loyalty that burned just like that fire at her core; the funny things she said and the way her spirit embraced him whole, making of him something he'd never been.

Needed, valued, worthwhile.

He couldn't go on without her. He couldn't.

The two automatons consulted together in soft words not meant for his ears. When they had Lily's fire ignited, they sat her up, Kelly supporting her from behind while Chastity applied herself to the flap over the vital button.

One push. Reynold's harsh breathing stopped as he caught himself tight; the silence became complete.

Nothing. Lily stared with pale blue eyes which Chastity had carefully opened, fixed enough to be made of glass.

He groaned. "Just what does that switch do?"

Kelly answered, "Unfortunately, neither of us knows. One of our first tasks will be to dismantle one of the units destroyed in the fire to see if we can find out."

"I suspect it sends an electrical pulse to the artificial intelligence," Chastity said. "But Lily's circuit may be broken—shorted out."

"Could—could you rewire her?"

"If we had the exact knowledge, perhaps. Or a blueprint. As I say, we do not have access to the information."

"One of my creators is still alive," Kelly offered, "but unfortunately clinically insane."

"Let us try again." Chastity fixed Reynold with her dark gaze. "I suggest you should pray, if you know how."

Pray? He'd get down on his knees, if he had to. Because he didn't care if she was flesh, half-flesh, or machine. He needed Lily's company, her presence in his days, in his life, far more fundamental than any classification of human or otherwise.

Chastity pushed the button once more. Lily, seated on the settee and slumped against Pat's shoulder, didn't move, didn't stir. She looked quite dead, the deteriorated patches on her cheek and forehead stark.

Reynold gasped and fell to his knees, seized her hands. He stared into her empty eyes. "Lily? Lily, please!"

He squeezed her hands more tightly. "Try again please, Chastity. One more time."

****

Lily.

She knew that voice. It hummed through her receptors and seemed to vibrate along her steel frame, more warming than the fire in her thorax. Love lay in that voice, and belonging. Her very identity.

Rey.

His heart beat for her even as her nonexistent, virtual heart beat for him. She could almost feel it, almost…

Reach, reach, reach.

Her intelligence ticked over like a semi-seized engine, grinding at first, protesting at the extreme effort, and then working more easily. Her opened eyes began to see. The darkness cleared, and she beheld…

A pair of brown eyes that encompassed her world. Right now they brimmed with human emotions she identified as anguish and hope. And another that trembled on the edge of her understanding.

Love.

"Rey."

"Oh, my God, Lily—oh, my God, oh, my God!"

He lowered his head and pressed it to their joined hands. Through that conduit she felt everything he was and everything she meant to him.

Her fire flared more brightly, and she squeezed his hands in return.

"There now," said Pat Kelly who, unaccountably, stood at Rey's side. "It is as the writers state: third time is the charm."

Rey began to laugh. Lily couldn't tell if he'd ever cease.

Chapter Thirty-Eight

"Now, lie still," Rey instructed Lily. "Pat and Chastity both say I'm to treat you everywhere. We need to undo any tissue damage. You were in the coffin a while."

Lily lay back obediently. They had returned to Rey's room following her resurrection—exactly where she wished to be—and he'd placed her on the bed before undressing her with tender care.

He had not allowed her to walk when they left Pat Kelly's, insisting on carrying her and hiring a horse-drawn cab. She hadn't protested then, either, because with her head pressed against his chest she could feel his heartbeat.

He'd poured a measure of enzyme wash into a basin, found a cloth, and now treated her assiduously. She concentrated on enjoying it.

"I do not remember a coffin."

"That's because you were…turned off. Lily, we need to talk about that. Why you shut down, I mean."

She consulted her artificial intelligence and found the resource. "Yes. Not now, please."

"But…"

"I would just like to enjoy you tending me."

"Do you enjoy it when I touch you?"

"Yes." *Oh, yes.*

"Lily, when you shut down…"

277

She stared into his eyes. "Not now, Rey. Please."

"Ah, all right."

She closed her eyes as he slid the cloth up her arm and across one breast. Her sensors tingled. But something niggled at her. "Why was I in a coffin?"

"We needed to hide you so you wouldn't be taken back to the Crystal Palace."

"But won't Dr. Landry still be looking for me?"

"No, Lily." He hesitated. "She's dead. You no longer have an owner. You and the other surviving Ladies are free."

Lily opened her eyes. "Dr. Landry, dead? What happened to her?"

Rey pressed his lips together before he replied, "Maybe we shouldn't talk about that either, not yet. I want to make sure you're well, first."

"Rey, how did she die?"

"There was a riot at the Crystal Palace. She threatened to shut all the Ladies down and…they beat her to death."

"We are unable to kill."

"Darling, that can't be true. I saw it happen."

"You saw?"

"Me and a bunch of other people, and about a thousand steamies."

"And I missed all this because I was in a coffin?"

"It seemed the safest place."

"Where was the coffin?"

"In the ground."

"There is much for me to assimilate."

"Does that mean think about? Yeah."

"Was Chastity one of those who killed our creator?"

"She was, actually, yes."

"Will she be punished?"

"There's still some debate about that, but it seems not. The law doesn't quite apply to hybrids—well, to any automatons, really, not yet. Plus, it was kind of self-defense. It's a gray area."

"Gray?"

"Not black and white—murky."

He dipped the cloth again, slid it across her other breast.

"How long was I in the coffin?"

"I guess it seemed longer than it was. Just part of a day and a night. But some of your tissues are showing damage. I'll have to examine you closely—everywhere."

Their eyes met. A new feeling flooded through Lily. Only she wasn't supposed to be able to experience feelings.

"Lily." He put the cloth in the basin and caught both her hands. "Tell me why you shut yourself down."

"I did not. It just…I just shut down."

"Why?"

"You said you did not want me anymore."

"I never said that."

"You said it would be better if we did not see one another, if the Kellys and Mrs. Gideon looked after me instead of you." She consulted her intelligence. The memory remained—bright and hot enough to sear her again. "We were right here in this bed."

"Yes, I remember. I didn't want you to shut down, Lily. It scared the living hell out of me."

"Why did you say we should not be together? I do not want to exist if I cannot exist with you."

He squeezed her hands harder. Just as it had when he'd called her back from oblivion, his touch gave her a reason to be.

"I understand that now. I'm sorry if what I said seemed cruel. I just didn't think you saw the truth about me."

"The truth?"

"I'm not very smart, Lily, or very successful. People like Sasha Belsky sneer at me."

"I do not like Sasha Belsky, and I do not care for his opinion."

"Neither do I, now."

"Then why does he matter? Why do any of them matter? This is about you and me."

"It is."

"You may not feel important. But you are the most important person in the world to me."

"I see that now. Lily, promise you'll never shut yourself down like that again."

"I did not shut myself down, Rey. I believe I overloaded at the thought of not being with you. Promise me you will never reject me again."

"I promise, Lily. I couldn't stand it."

"Then we will stay together." The flood of emotion came again.

"We will—for better or worse. I don't know what will happen in the future…"

"I am not concerned about that now."

"You're not? But—"

"Not now." She lay for a moment enjoying all the things going on inside her, the way she hummed when he touched her, the new references in her intelligence.

"Rey, I need but one thing."

"What is it?"

"For you to kiss me."

He complied, bestowing one, two, three sweet kisses, tender, grateful, and claiming.

She raised her hand and pressed it to his chest so she could feel his speeding heart.

"Rey, something has just occurred to me. Perhaps I cannot offer you enough."

"Don't start all that again."

"But I have no heart and so cannot give it to you. Even my kisses are not real."

"Lily, you're the most real person I've ever known. Now, you lie there and let me finish my work, all right?"

Lily stretched luxuriously and smiled.

Chapter Thirty-Nine

"Are you sure you wish to marry him?"

Lily asked the question of Chastity as she adjusted the angle of her friend's hat and lowered the half-veil. Today's mass wedding at the park on Delaware Avenue, north of the city, had been arranged by Patrick Kelly, who had very definite ideas about weddings. He'd insisted all the former Ladies and members of the Irish Squad who had paired up should be joined at the same time.

Lily had been startled to realize Chastity numbered among them.

"I am sure," Chastity averred. Her dark eyes looked...content.

Should that be so surprising?

Referring to the many books she'd read in the three weeks since Dr. Landry's death, Lily said, "You barely know him."

"But he took my hand that night, that terrible, terrible night when...when our creator threatened to kill us all. And it felt safe. I like the way I feel when I am with him."

"Terence, you mean."

"Terence Greely. He insists I call him Terry. I think he is very handsome. Blue eyes and wavy, blond hair. His donor was an Irishman. I find it endearing that he uses the accent."

"Yes." Lily did not consider Terence as handsome as Reynold but did not say so.

"He has his own house and is—I believe it is called 'a good catch.' "

"A good catch, yes," affirmed Lily, who was currently reading Jane Austen.

"I believe we will be happy together. And I never again need worry about being used against my wishes."

"True." Pat Kelly had mentioned that the male automatons lacked the appendage necessary for penetration. Though, as Pat had once also explained, he was able to keep his wife satisfied.

As for Lily, she lived for the times Reynold joined with her physically. At those moments, she truly felt alive. Again, she did not say so.

"There, Sister, you are all ready."

"Do I look beautiful?"

"Very much so."

"But not as I did at the Crystal Palace?"

"Not at all." The gown Chastity had chosen for today was primrose yellow, with a high lace collar and long sleeves, quite—well, chaste. "That color suits you."

"I never again wish to feel the way I did at the Crystal Palace. I never again want a stranger's hands on me."

"All that is behind us now."

"Yes. I will have a home and a husband, like a real woman. Only one thing troubles me."

"What is that, Sister?"

"Real women have children, do they not?"

"Some do," admitted Lily, recalling the conversation at the Haven.

"Most do," Chastity corrected. "Often many children. Possibly Terence, not being human, will not mind."

But what about Rey, if he remained with her, Lily? Would he mind the absence of children? That question had already appeared in Lily's intelligence, surfacing repeatedly like a bit of trash in a rainy gutter.

"What of you?" asked Chastity, very nearly echoing Lily's thoughts.

"I cannot bear children."

"I know that. What about you and Reynold? Will you wed?"

"He has not asked me."

"Do you know why?"

"I do not."

"I half expected you would be part of today's ceremony. But you will attend, will you not? You are my best friend. I wish for you to be there."

"I will attend, and Rey, too. He is working but says he will call for me in time."

"Thank you for helping me prepare, Lily. We have been through so much together. And there is so much still ahead. Terence says there may be protests at the park today. The city is still astir over what happened to Dr. Landry. People say we are dangerous, that we should not be allowed to marry."

"Pat and Rose Kelly are married."

"That is different; they are like you and Reynold— one automaton and one human. Humans have rights."

Lily hoped nothing happened to spoil the beauty of today's event. The way she saw it, Landry's Ladies and the men of the Irish Squad had suffered enough and deserved whatever measure of happiness they achieved.

"It is a blot on my joy," Chastity said, "what happened to Dr. Landry. I acted in defiance of the first instructions instilled in me. Do you think that makes me bad, Lily?"

"No, Sister. I do not think it makes you bad."

Chastity seized both Lily's hands. "What if the city passes a law that all automatons should be shut off? Terence and I would both die."

"That will never happen. Who, then, would do all the humans' work for them? Clean their houses? Serve their meals?"

"What if they legislate to shut down the hybrids such as us?"

The thought daunted Lily and made her tremble. Separation from Rey for any cause would be unbearable.

"Then we will fight. And I believe the rest of the automatons will stand with us the way Rey told me they did the night…well, the night we were freed."

Chastity nodded. Lily drew her close and hugged her tight. "I wish you every happiness. Thank you for being my friend."

Releasing Chastity, she asked, "What time is Terence calling for you?"

"At two. The ceremony is set for three. Pat Kelly has arranged for horse-drawn carriages to collect us. It will be quite the spectacle when we arrive and gather beside Hoyt Lake."

"I must go home and prepare. I shall see you at the ceremony."

****

Lily found a mysterious white box propped against the outside of Rey's door when she arrived home from the rooming house where the former Landry's Ladies had taken up temporary residence. She carried it into the room and set it on the table carefully.

Reynold had not yet arrived. He'd told her last night while she lay in his arms that he had a body to collect early this morning—a young child from an orphanage—and several errands to run.

The package must be for him, she decided. Yet when she read the tag affixed to the top of the box, she saw it said *Lily Landry*.

That was her. Should she open it?

She debated the question as she moved around straightening the room. She did not suffer from curiosity as such—except she did. The unopened box was like an unopened book. She needed to find out what was inside.

Perhaps, though, she should wait for Rey to arrive. One of her biggest challenges operating in the human world had proved to be sequencing. She had difficulty with *when* things should happen, and humans seemed to keep strict rules about it. From her reading, she'd learned they operated largely on emotion and felt certain things should happen at certain times.

But the large white box drew her, and at last she crossed to the table, severed the string, and lifted the lid.

Brown paper and a little square card with printing on it. The printing, rather uneven, was difficult to decipher, but at last she discerned it read, *For you to wear today*.

Odd. The note, unsigned, might be from anyone. She unfolded the brown paper and saw...

A hat. Small, and with a tiny, ruffled veil attached,

it was ice-blue in color and matched exactly the pile of fluffy fabric that lay beneath.

Not a pile of fabric; a gown.

Lily lifted it in her hands and shook it out. Lace cascaded down, and the softness set all her sensors alight.

"Do you like it?"

So distracted had she been she had missed hearing Rey come in. He shut the door behind him and stood looking tentative.

"It is the most beautiful dress."

"Good. Then you'll wear it?"

"Today?"

He smiled. "Today. You'll be the loveliest woman there."

"I am not certain about that, Rey. The former Landry's Ladies are very beautiful."

"They are."

"And I have just finished helping Chastity prepare for her wedding. She looks most beautiful."

"She couldn't be prettier than you."

Rey stepped farther into the room. Lily noticed, belatedly, that he did not wear the same clothing he had when he left early this morning. Instead, from somewhere he'd obtained a crisp white shirt and a black suit that fit his large body like a glove.

"Where did you get those clothes, Rey?"

"From Pat Kelly. He's been helping me...well, with quite a few things."

"You are all ready for the ceremony."

"I think I am."

Stepping up to her, he took her hand in his, engaged her eyes, and dropped to one knee.

"What are you doing?" Lily's intelligence—speeding through all she'd read—caught up. "Is this a marriage proposal?"

"It is." Reynold's skin turned ruddy red. "I've practiced, so please don't interrupt."

"Very well."

"Lily, I never dreamed of meeting anyone like you. The first time I saw you getting off that tram—well, you were like a star high up in the heavens. How could somebody like me ever hope to touch a star? But then I met you, and you were better than beautiful—funny and…and adorable, and willing to love me. *Me*." Reynold's eyes went wide with wonder. "I can't imagine trying to live without you now. The best thing I can imagine is for you to become my wife. Will you?"

Lily went still. For an instant—as it had before—her intelligence stuttered and threatened to fail.

"Lily? Are you all right?"

"I am still operational, Rey."

"Oh, thank God—for an instant there I thought you'd shut down on me again."

"I—I am all right. You wish for me to marry you?"

"Marry me, yes. Today."

"Today?"

"As part of the ceremony at Hoyt Lake. Pat's arranged it. You need only say yes. I have a ring." Using his free hand, he dug in his pocket, from which he produced a plain gold band. It sat like a jewel on his rough palm.

"That is what human women wear."

"You will be my wife, just like a human woman."

Lily sank to her knees also; the ice-blue gown came with her. She released it to fall in a puff between them and laid both her palms against Reynold's face, the better to gaze into his eyes.

"Rey—my love—I fear my answer must be *no*."

Chapter Forty

"No? You're refusing me?" In all the scenarios that had danced through Reynold's head, this one had been conspicuously absent. He'd imagined she would accept quickly, gladly—that maybe they'd have time to make love before the ceremony, and he'd have to get out of this monkey suit into which Pat and Rose had wedged him. He'd worship her there on his bed and then help clothe her beautiful body in the gown he'd chosen, so pretty it was almost—*almost*—worthy of her.

But she'd said no. Ah, God!

She still had his face cradled between her hands and leaned close enough to kiss him. He often had trouble guessing what went on behind her pale-blue eyes; now he had no chance.

"I thought you loved me." He sounded like a lost child even to his own ears—one of those back at the orphanage maybe, from whence he'd collected a second little corpse this morning.

"I do love you, as well as an automaton can love. But I am an automaton. And that is why I must refuse."

"Lily…"

"No, please, Rey. Listen. I've learned a lot through my reading."

"That's *reading*. Stories. Not real life."

"It shows me what it is to be human. It shows me I am not human in many ways that matter."

"All that matters is I love you. I had a taste of what it would be like without you when you shut down. I never want to live through that again."

"Chastity said something to me, Rey, something that fit together with the things I've read. You deserve to marry a real woman."

"How do you know what I deserve? Or what I want? Lily, I don't care about all that."

"You might one day. You may take a look at me and all at once see the things I lack. I could not bear that."

"I want to be with you. It's as simple as that."

"You want to be with me now. And I am willing to stay with you—for now. I will stay with you, live with you. But marriage, the way I understand it, is forever."

"Is it because I'll age and you won't? I talked to Rose about that. Neither of them minds. Nor do I."

"Not that."

"Then what? Tell me one good reason why you won't marry me."

"Children."

"Eh?"

"I will never be able to give you children. And they are important to humans."

"They are, yes. But I tell you, I don't…"

She caressed his cheeks. "Not now, maybe. But if the day came that you did mind, and you began to look at me with regret, what would I do then?"

"Lily." He sat flat on the floor and gathered her into his arms. He could feel the heat from her boiler, her foreignness. He could also feel the familiar comfort of holding her close. He tucked her head beneath his chin and held tight.

"If you'll consent to marry me," he said, seeking desperately for words—the right words, "ours will not be an ordinary union, no. We'll be pioneers like Rose and Pat—like all the others getting married today. Why should our family be ordinary, then? That doesn't mean we can't have one."

"No?"

"No. Lily, in this city there are children longing for someone to love them—aching for it the way I ached for you even before I met you."

"As I ached for you when all those other men pawed me?"

"Yes. Yes. I guess it doesn't require a heart for someone to long for love. Or maybe—maybe love doesn't come from the heart after all. Maybe it's part of the spirit. Anyway, I'd like nothing better than to get some of those little ones out of the dark, cold places they've been sent to live. Give 'em a home. A family."

"Us?"

"Us, if you'll marry me."

"Would these human children be able to love me, Rey?"

"I defy anyone not to love you." He tipped her face up and kissed her, long, slow, and gentle.

When the kiss ended, she placed her palm against his chest, over his heart.

"So what do you say, Lily? Will you become my wife?"

"Today? At the park?"

"Today."

"Best to hurry and get me into that gown."

****

The procession of horse-drawn conveyances

wound its way slowly through the city—carriages, wagons, buggies, all decorated with flowers and driven mostly by human grooms. It paused frequently to pick up couples who at first glance appeared human also. When the last of them had been collected, the colorful snake turned up Delaware Avenue and wended its way to the park.

There, beside Hoyt Lake, the stage had been set. Splashes of color lay everywhere—mountains of flowers, and tables shaded by multi-colored umbrellas. When the brides disembarked—a mobile rainbow—it only became more beautiful.

The day couldn't be more perfect for a wedding. Fluffy white clouds dotted a sky of azure, and a light breeze fluttered skirts and veils alike against the emerald grass.

Around the perimeter of the park, a chain of blue had formed. The Buffalo Police had come out in force and formed a barrier against the human protestors who thronged farther out. Some hurled stones and insults. Several were promptly arrested. No one who gathered there beside the lake paid them any attention. Protests were expected. But within the ring of blue, as invited guests, was every steamie that had been able to get away from its assigned duties, a wall of silver.

Reynold stood in the bright sunshine, not far from the edge of the lake, with Lily's fingers clasped tight in his, and Chastity and Terence to one side of him. The gathered couples formed a semicircle. Opposite them stood the human justice who, with impressive open-mindedness, had agreed to join them all in marriage.

Reynold turned his head and looked at Lily. The clever little hat hugged her head—which barely reached his ear—and the ruffled veil danced in the breeze. The gown fit her perfectly, and he could only marvel at her beauty.

This, he knew, would be one of those moments he'd remember forever, like that when he'd watched her get off the tram for the first time.

He might be surrounded here by circle upon circle of individuals, but at this instant he was the luckiest man alive.

The justice began reading out the lines, and dozens of voices repeated them dutifully. When it came to the last part, Reynold lifted Lily's hand and pressed it against his heart.

"Yours," he whispered, and she lifted her face to him. "Yours forever."

"You may kiss your bride!"

Joyfully, Reynold obeyed.

And the air of the park resounded with steel kisses.

A word about the author...

Born in Buffalo and raised on the Niagara Frontier, Laura Strickland has been an avid reader and writer since childhood. She believes the spunky, tenacious, undefeatable ethnic mix that is Buffalo spells the perfect setting for a little Steampunk, so she created her own Victorian world there. She knows the people of Buffalo are stronger, tougher, and smarter than those who haven't survived the muggy summers and the blizzard blasts found on the shores of the mighty Niagara. Tough enough to survive a squad of automatons? Well, just maybe.

Thank you for purchasing
this publication of The Wild Rose Press, Inc.

If you enjoyed the story, we would appreciate your
letting others know by leaving a review.

For other wonderful stories,
please visit our on-line bookstore at
www.thewildrosepress.com.

For questions or more information
contact us at
info@thewildrosepress.com.

The Wild Rose Press, Inc.
www.thewildrosepress.com

Stay current with The Wild Rose Press, Inc.

Like us on Facebook

https://www.facebook.com/TheWildRosePress

And Follow us on Twitter
https://twitter.com/WildRosePress